PASSAGEWAYS

*Edited by Camille T. Dungy and
Daniel Hahn*

TWO LINES   WORLD WRITING IN TRANSLATION

© 2012 by Two Lines Press
The TWO LINES: World Writing in Translation series
Two Lines Press, 582 Market Street, Suite 700,
San Francisco, CA 94104

Series Editor: CJ Evans
Design by Ragina Johnson
Cover: detail of a mural (untitled, 2007) by Scott Hove

ISBN: 978-1-931883-21-4

Published in the United States by Two Lines Press, a program of the Center for the Art
of Translation. TWO LINES® and the Center for the Art of Translation® are registered
trademarks of the Center for the Art of Translation.

Distributed by The University of Washington Press
Printed in Canada by Friesens Corporation
Indexed in the MLA International Bibliography

ART WORKS.
arts.gov

amazon.com

This project is supported in part by an award from the National Endowment for the Arts
and a grant from Amazon.com.

Najin Marie Aidt

Rachel Morgenstern - Clar

Erica Mena

Contents

Brazil

Editors' Notes

There's a habit we have, those of us who work in the translation world, that's somewhat perverse, I think. Perverse, and perhaps unhelpful, too. We talk about literature in translation as though it were a category of thing—there's literature that's translated, and literature that isn't, and these two categories are discrete and somehow meaningful. But the reading experience belies this entirely, of course. There's no reason one translated work should have anything in common with another—it's not their translated-ness that defines them, that gives them value, that makes them pleasurable for a reader to consume. Reading submissions for this edition in the TWO LINES: World Writing in Translation series, I've been struck more than anything by the range of pieces that we've been offered. They are rarely stylistically comparable, or thematically congruent, or even contemporary with one another. So what did we find? An excerpt from a French novel, a series of micro-stories from the Netherlands, and they appear in these pages alongside works from Denmark, Italy, Slovakia, and Spain (both Spanish and Catalan), and a special section of pieces (among themselves ranging widely) from contemporary Brazil. All these are, of course, translated literature. Translated literature is not, then, a small, contained category—it's merely what happens when you strip away from All Of Literature those bits of noisily insistent prose emerging from a tiny handful of countries—translated literature is Everything Else. It is massive, and as various as literature has the capacity to be.

Translation itself is about access. It allows us passage to all these multifarious things—indeed, any true diversity, any true pluralism, demands it. It is thanks to translation, then, that the pieces in this collection span continents; they cover grand themes and domestic moments, they are lyrical and crisp, weighty and solid and nimble and light, they are also dark, rich, breathless, unsettling, witty, tender and odd. Some are sharp, high-impact; some burn very, very slowly, and you won't see how reading them is transforming you till it's too late.

Now, my opening premise was perhaps not entirely true; literature in English translation does often share one common feature. The bottleneck that makes it so hard to get literary fiction translated into English for publication has (to mix the metaphor) one silver lining. The quality of the thing. The bar (to muddle it still further) is set very high, meaning that on the whole it's pretty hard for the mediocre to squeeze its translated way into our markets. And in this constricted, refined part of the book trade, the few literary translators able to make a career as literary translators to the Anglophone world will have to be among the finest writers we have. A translator is required to be an all-seeing, deeply-feeling reader, and a supreme writer. Among the translators in this volume are Margaret Jull Costa, Alison Entrekin, Lydia Davis—just about as good as any translators you'll find in the language, and just about as good as any other writers, too.

The story goes that when Gregory Rabassa was translating García Márquez's *One Hundred Years of Solitude*, he was asked whether his Spanish was really good enough to undertake such a dazzling piece of work. "That's the wrong question," Rabassa is said to have replied. "The question you should be asking is, is my English good enough?" Like Ginger Rogers dancing backwards in heels, Lydia Davis has written A.L. Snijders, but in a whole other language. In the Brazilian folio, Margaret Jull Costa and Alison Entrekin have used English, too, to create a Brazilian fictional world properly designed to be told in Portuguese. As you read on, you'll see by just how much their English, yes, is good enough. And then some.

Maybe that's the other thing the great translated literature has in common, then: the presence of not just one, but two great writers required to bring it to life. Both with those remarkable skills, and both with the good fortune to have found one another, their perfect match. Maybe that's why the very best of it seems so rare, and so special, and such a discovery.

DANIEL HAHN

Oh, dear Ms. Dickinson, do you know how often I think of you? Now, for instance, when I am called to write this note about why I chose the poems I chose for *Passageways*. I am reading the poems again, after more than a month without seeing them, and what can I say about them except that, page after page, the top of my head is blown off. I can tell you that with each poem I feel the little jump in my heart that only happens when I read something necessary and perfectly sad. I am sighing like a schoolgirl, because these poems are teaching me what language can do and because I am made young in the presence of the ancient cult of poetry. Yes, the top of my head is blown off, and with each page I turn it happens again.

This was such a wonderful commission, selecting these poems. It was the kind of work I was eager to do. The tour of world literature alone made it worth the effort. We have poets from Vietnam, Puerto Rico, Brazil, France, Russia, Israel, Italy, and Romania, to name but a few. Sometimes the poets or translators were writers whose reputations preceded them, more often they were new to me. This might be my own deficiency as a reader of world literature, rather than any strike against the reach of the poets, but the good luck is that with each of the poets I selected I wanted to learn more about the writer whose vision I'd been introduced to. Each of these translations is a new object, and I've been expanded by having experienced them. "…it's the foreign that / makes and transforms you," says Forrest Gander's translation of Benito del Pliego's "El camaleón," and the poems I chose, at once foreign and familiar, transformed me.

What I encountered in these poems: love, death, dreams, hunger, the longing for home, again and again the same questions (what shall we do with ourselves after, during, caught up in some war, in whom shall faith reside, in what shall faith reside, what faith?). The poems are often comprised of lists, one idea piling upon another, and they are as likely to draw on evidence well beyond the scope of the poet (the ancient myths, the intricacies of the weather) as to stay in the interior space of the poet's house, the poet's garden, the poet's mind. The lists state one thing and then another and then another, until I finally understand. They are regimented and precise, not particularly florid, as if the poems don't have time for fanciness and frills. Many of these poems are direct to the point of near blandness, but in the way that a concrete floor shellacked with gold glitter is straight-forward and potentially bland. The translators' selections of plain speech allowed for the sparkle of detail, the turns that changed my reaction to every-thing I'd thought I'd understood. But a number of the poems danced away from the rational, challenging my sense of the practical order of things. "There are," as Alexis Levitin's translation of Rosa Alice Branco's poem declares, "pugilistic verses. Every punch they let fly, / it's as if our backs were turned." There are dreams on these pages, and I've chosen them for you because they've taken the top of my head right off.

CAMILLE T. DUNGY

PASSAGEWAYS

Blackcurrant

Naja Marie Aidt
Translated by Denise Newman
Danish (Denmark)

Since her debut in 1991, Naja Marie Aidt has published nine collections of poetry, three short story collections, several children's books, a
screenplay for a feature film, song lyrics, and several plays. "Blackcurrant" is from Aidt's third collection of short stories, *Bavian* (Baboon),
which won the prestigious Nordic Prize in 2008. She currently lives
in Brooklyn and is at work on her first novel.

Aidt was born and lived in a remote village in Greenland until the
age of seven. Although her stories are mainly set in Denmark, they
brim with an intensity I associate with that vast frozen landscape. Her
stories are tough and uncompromising; she puts her characters under
great psychological strain in order to reveal what's lurking beneath
the veneer of civility. Always brutally, almost unexpectedly honest,
Aidt's portrayals of characters touch on a universal existential core; it's
not surprising that *Bavian* has been translated into eight languages.

What makes Aidt's prose challenging to translate is also what
makes it so pleasurable to read. She has a poet's sensitivity to language and her stories are as economical, rhythmic, and image-rich
as her poems. I appreciate how the spare surface of Aidt's writing is
achieved with the utmost precision and control of all the elements.
In "Blackcurrant" the particular challenge had more to do with what's
unsaid between the two main characters. Although Helle doesn't

speak, her presence and the effect she has on the narrator is clear. It's actually her physical presence that creates the emotional tenor of the story, and so I had to find the right tone for the descriptions of her gestures and movements, which, as we discover, foreshadow the revelations at the end of the story.

Original text: Naja Marie Aidt, "Solbær" from *Bavian*. Copenhagen: Gyldendal, 2006.

Solbær

Så længe der var bær på busken, blev vi ved med at plukke. Det havde vi aftalt. Helle sagde ikke noget, og så var også jeg tavs. Solen bagte. Man kunne se køerne på marken bag haven. Vi sad på jorden inde midt i buskadset. Det var midt på dagen, og jeg var bange for at få flåt. Vores hænder var blå, og vi havde allerede fyldt en hel spand. Der var nok til mange glas syltetøj, og jeg tænkte på, hvor rart det ville blive at stå i køkkenet, i den søde duft fra solbærsyltetøjet, mens vi skiftedes til at skumme. Så ville vi snakke. Der var så meget, vi ikke havde fået talt om. Jeg tænkte på, hvordan jeg skulle tilberede den kylling, vi havde købt hos købmanden. Jeg tænkte på, om Helle ikke snart blev træt af at plukke bær, så vi kunne komme ind og få kaffe. Men hun blev ikke træt. Hun tørrede sveden af panden med bagsiden af hånden, kneb øjnene sammen og så op mod solen, men så fortsatte hun. Jeg kiggede på den tatovering, hun har på overarmen. En falmet rose. Det er længe siden, hun fik den lavet. Jeg var med hende den nat, vi var fulde, og hun hylede af smerte hver gang tatovøren satte nålen i hendes hud. Men bagefter drak vi en øl med ham, Helle tørrede tårene væk og gav ham et kys midt på munden. Jeg kan huske, at jeg tænkte, at det slet ikke lignede hende, hverken at gøre noget så vildt som at få en tatovering eller at kysse en mand midt på munden, bare sådan. Men vi var jo fulde. Det var vi tit dengang....

Blackcurrant

As long as there were berries on the bushes, we'd continue to pick them. That's what we agreed on. Helle didn't say a word, and so I was silent too. The sun baked. You could see the cows in the field beyond the garden. We sat on the ground in the middle of the shrubbery; it was the middle of the day and I was afraid of getting a tick. Our hands were blue, and we had already filled an entire pail. There were enough for many jars of jam, and I thought about how wonderful it would be to stand in the kitchen, in the sweet scent from the blackcurrant jam, taking turns skimming it. We'd talk then. There was so much we hadn't had the chance to talk about. I wondered how I should prepare that chicken we bought at the grocery store. I wondered if Helle would soon be tired of picking berries and we could go in and have coffee. But she wasn't getting tired. She dried the sweat off her forehead with the back of her hand, squinted her eyes toward the sun, but then she continued. I looked at the tattoo on her upper arm. A faded rose. She got it a long time ago. I was with her that night, we were drunk, and she yelled out in pain each time the tattooist pricked her skin with the needle. But afterwards we had a beer with him; Helle dried her tears and gave him a kiss right on the mouth. I remember thinking that it didn't seem like her at all, either to do something as wild as getting a tattoo, or to kiss a man right on the mouth like that. But of course we were drunk. We were often drunk back then. Afterwards, we bought some fresh morning buns and cycled out to the beach, and sat there watching the sun rise, and I tore off all my clothes and ran into the water and pretended I was drowning, but Helle was already walking away, and I yelled after her, but she didn't stop, and I saw her stagger up over the dunes and disappear. Then I cried. I sat and cried and shivered and got sand in my eyes and under my dress. But of course I was drunk. I don't remember how I got home, and a few days went by before Helle called, but we never spoke about it, why she left without saying good-bye.

Helle pulls the pail toward her and crawls over to the other side of the bush. I make an attempt to pull a handful of berries off the stem to get around picking them one by one, but they just smear in my hand and I lose most of them. I'm thirsty. I can hear the neighbor driving the tractor back around the barn. He's probably going in for lunch now. There's a sheep that bleats somewhere. I pick at a scab on my knee and look over at Helle's dark head. Her hair is matted. "I'm thirsty," I say. But Helle doesn't answer. A bit later I get up; my legs hurt from having squatted so long, and one of my hands is asleep. It is really boiling hot. Red spots dance in front of my eyes, and for a moment I'm so dizzy that I think I might faint. I turn to look at Helle, but she's still bending over the bush; I can see her hands working fast and steady, the berries nearly flying through the air as she tosses them into the pail.

Once I loved a man passionately. It was a couple of years after Helle got tattooed; he was red-haired and had close-set eyes. He was so gifted that when he spoke, I thought I was the luckiest person in the world; his words were like colorful pieces of gum wrappers floating inside my head, and my heart lifted up, and I was so light, and I looked at him and I could almost feel my pupils enlarging so I could suck him and his whole brilliantly colored language right in. I begin thinking about this as I walk through the house. And as I drink water from the faucet in the kitchen, I think about him, about his soft fingertips running over my face. Although his fingers never ran over my face; I don't know if he even loved me; anyway we never got that far. I open the refrigerator and look at the chicken. It's big and pale; I have no idea what to do with it. I wonder what became of that man. But we have onions and tomatoes so I can just as well throw the whole thing in the oven. I sit down on a stool, and at the same moment I hear Helle come in through the door to the garden. She puts down the pail on the kitchen counter and goes into the bathroom. It sounds like she's splashing water on her face. "Helle?" I shout. She doesn't answer. She turns off the water, it's quiet. I start removing leaves and small twigs from the berries, while listening to figure out what she's doing. But I only hear the neighbor on the road driving by on the tractor, or it could be his son because the neighbor usually rests after lunch. And suddenly I too am overwhelmed by fatigue. On the way into my room I very carefully open the door to Helle's room. She's lying on the bed, staring up at the ceiling. I see her chest rising and falling, but otherwise she looks like she's dead.

I get in under my blanket. I think about the man's eyes; the light that shone from them. I see the faded rose on Helle's arm clearly in my mind. And then I must have fallen asleep.

The next thing I remember, Helle is standing in the doorway. She has the chicken in her arms. When I look her in the eyes, she turns on her heels and walks away. She looks confused. For a moment, I think it's a dream. But when I stumble into the kitchen, she's standing at the window looking at the neighbor's son. He's walking down the dirt road pulling a black sheep with him.

Then Helle takes some onions out and begins to peel them. "Are you hungry?" I ask. She takes a knife out of the drawer and cuts the onions in quarters. Then I rinse the tomatoes and turn on the radio. Heavy rock is playing, but I leave it on. I try to slice the tomatoes so that all the slices are the same size. Helle lights the oven and places the chicken in front of me on the counter. But I pretend that I don't get the hint and instead put some water on for coffee. She's sat down on the stool. I turn up the radio and hand her a cup of coffee when it's ready. I look into her blue eyes, and keep looking until she looks down. I reach out and carefully touch the rose on her arm. "What's the matter, Helle?" I ask.

We never cooked that chicken. I sauté the tomatoes and onions in the pan, and we eat rye bread with them. Helle has a tremendous appetite. She gets up several times during the meal and opens the refrigerator. She takes out cheese and sausages. She stuffs herself. After this she opens the box of chocolates I got from my grand-mother and eats half of it. I just sit watching her eat. The neighbor drives the tractor out, and now I can see clearly that it's him. I get up and go over to the window, and he waves at me when he drives by. We've always had good relations: he and his wife are both friendly and helpful. Then Helle washes the dishes and goes back to her room. I start rinsing the blackcurrants. I boil them and measure the sugar. I turn off the radio and enjoy the sounds from the garden flowing in through the open window; the birds chirp and a soft breeze whispers in the large elm. Dusk creeps over the garden and rises like a blue shadow. I scald the glasses and pour in the jam. I lick my sticky fingers. And think about another man I have known. He was dark and short and stocky and had gentle eyes. His skin was so soft that I was surprised each time I touched him. We clung to each other. He made me laugh at things that weren't even funny. I made him long for me wildly, just by walking to the store for cigarettes. I remember every inch of his body. Every little hair that grew on his toes. And when I close the door to the garden behind me and gather Helle's green jacket around me, I think about his voice. About what he said to me when he left. We don't have words for everything. It was just that there was someone somewhere else. The gravel crunched under my wooden clogs. I turn left at the road and see that there's a light on in the stable. But the neighbor must have gone to sleep long ago. A sheep bleats loudly. I can't stop myself from opening the door a little and peeking in. The few cows in there look as if they're sick. There's a sharp scent of manure and ammonia. And there, in the narrow path between the stalls, I see the neighbor's son on his knees. He's holding on tightly to the black sheep's fur. And he pushes his groin hard into the animal's backside. The sheep bays loudly. He lifts his head backwards. And as he rattles out a cry like a howl, I see that he has braces on his teeth. Train tracks. I hold onto the doorframe with both hands and shove myself out backwards.

At home, Helle has probably already fallen asleep. I sit down in the kitchen and eat jam with a spoon. It's still warm. Helle could've said something before. That she's pregnant and will not have the child. As if I could read her mind. The jam looks almost black now.

The next morning the chicken is still lying on the kitchen counter. It's beginning to smell. I pick it up and carry it all the way across the garden and up to the road. There I let it drop down into the garbage container. Then I wave to the neighbor and his sweet wife, who are just now backing out of their driveway.

They are probably going out shopping.

Two Poems

Benito del Pliego
Translated by Forrest Gander
Spanish (Spain)

Benito del Pliego has published many books in Spain and Latin America, most recently *Fábula* (2012) and *Muesca* (2010). He has translated Isel Rivero's English poetry and, in collaboration with Andrés Fisher, edited José Viñals' anthology *Caballo en el umbral.*

The poems included here are part of a long abecedarian, one of the two sequences composing del Pliego's book *Fábula* (Fable). These poems might be considered, as the author offers, "a hybrid between Aesop and the I Ching, a post-avant-garde take on neoclassical Spanish." Del Pliego, who has written extensively about Spanish exiled writers in the Americas, has found himself one of them. Born in Madrid in 1970, he now lives and works in the United States. These poems, with their references to friends and fellow poets, evolved as del Pliego dealt with feelings of exile and poetic isolation in the rural landscapes of Georgia and North Carolina.

With their gnomic adages—"Those who see only what others look for don't know how to see what they find"—their vernacular quotations, their paradoxes and puns, the poems seem as though they might have been written anywhere. They don't delineate any particular geography apart from the poet's own mind: his memory of friends, incidents, sentences, and literary allusions. As such, the poems form a kind of traveling world, a poetic companionship, a mode of thinking.

They also take on a horoscopic quality. I can imagine a calendar with a page given to each poem's title: "The Ass," "The Bucket," "The Chameleon," etc.

The major challenge of translating an abecedarian involves the titles. What works as A, B, C in Spanish—Araña, Burro, Caballo— doesn't carry into English—Spider, Burro, Horse. So I juggled the sequence in order to preserve the abecedarian form.

Original text: Benito del Pliego, "El camaleón" and "El dado" from *Fábula*. Badajoz: Aristas Martinez Ediciones, 2012.

El camaleón:

— «Ni el ser ni el parecer te pertenecen: lo ajeno es lo que te hace y te transforma.

Si miras a fondo, despreocupado del color de los ojos con que miras, lo que ves te libera.

La verdadera pasión, la pasión del instante, adelanta la disolución final, que es camuflaje perpetuo.»

The Chameleon:

—"Neither being nor seeming concern you: it's the foreign that makes and transforms you.

If you glance back, incognizant of the color of the eyes through which you look, what you see frees you.

The real passion, the passion of the moment, brings on the final dissolution, which is continuous camouflage."

El dado:

(Joan Brossa)

—«Apuesto que le preocupa el destino y que el sabio no
adivina la tirada —quizás el poeta.

Tiene razón quien dice: "El resto del poema es el futuro,
que existe fuera de vuestra percepción."

Aunque podría decir "En el destino, no en el dado de oro."
Con eso basta. A cada jugador su turno.»

The Die:

(Joan Brossa)

—"'I imagine you're worried about your fate and worried the sage can't read the dice'—supposes the poet.

It makes sense, what's been said: 'All that's left of the poem is the future, which lies outside our perception.'

Although you might say "In destiny, not in a golden die."

Enough then. Each player in turn."

Two Poems

Arseny Tarkovsky
Translated by Philip Metres and Dmitry Psurtsev
Russian (Russia)

Arseny Tarkovsky (1907–1989) spent most of his life as a well-known translator of Turkmen, Georgian, Armenian, Arabic, and other languages. During the Second World War, he worked as a war correspondent until he was wounded in a German attack, which cost him his leg. His first book of poems had been accepted for publication in 1946, but in the wake of Zhdanov's attack on Anna Akhmatova and Mikhail Zoschenko—in which Zhdanov, a proponent of socialist realism, banned writers deemed too individualistic or bourgeois—the book was never released. Tarkovsky's first published volume, *Before the Snow*, was published in 1962, at the age of 55, to the acclaim of Akhmatova, who called his work "both contemporary and eternal."

In a time when official Russian poetry was anything but independent, Tarkovsky's verse maintained its resolute allegiance to a poetic sound and vision that hearkened back to the masters of Russian poetry. Akhmatova said of Tarkovsky, "of all contemporary poets Tarkovsky alone is completely his own self, completely independent. He possesses the most important feature of a poet which I'd call the birthright." In his spiritual and poetic independence, he outlasted the dross of totalitarianism. Vividly musical, rich in Biblical and folk echoes, Tarkovsky's poems exude a poignant gratitude for living on earth, and a childlike wonder in nature, even though they are often set in the backdrop of terrible heartbreak of one of the most miserable centuries in Russian history.

The most difficult aspect of translating Russian poetry is carrying across the richness of its music—the diversity of meters, rhythms, and rhyme; Tarkovky's poetry is, in the end, a poetry that lives through its music. In "The Book of Grass," for example, Tarkovsky employs a tight couplet rhyme and a folk song, the imagery moves the poem from the "walled city above a river" to, in our translation, "nuzzling in the native womb." From defensive walls, in other words, to pantheistic union with earth. As a way to the sound of the poem, we've adopted an irregular series of linking off-rhymes and full rhymes— "river," "water," "star," "shore," "war," then "rampart," "shot," and "fate," then "coast" and "grass," and finally "home" and "womb." By contrast, we adhered more intensively to the alternating rhyme scheme (though with slant rhymes) in the bittersweet "You evening light, you dove…," one of Tarkovsky's classics. One poetic choice was to translate the "pigeon-colored" to "dove- / Colored," for reasons of sound and association.

Original text: Arseny Tarkovsky, "Kniga Travyi" and "Vechernii, sizokryilyi…" from *Sud'ba Moya Sgorela Mezhdu.* Moscow: Eksmo, 2009.

Книга травы

О нет, я не город с кремлем над рекой,
Я разве что герб городской.

Не герб городской, а звезда над щитком
На этом гербе городском.

Не гостья небесная в черни воды,
Я разве что имя звезды.

Не голос, не платье на том берегу,
Я только светиться могу.

Не луч световой у тебя за спиной,
Я — дом, разоренный войной.

Не дом на высоком валу крепостном,
Я — память о доме твоем.

Не друг твой, судьбою ниспосланный друг,
Я — выстрела дальнего звук.

The Book of Grass

I'm not a walled city above a river,
I'm the city's coat of arms.

Not the city's coat of arms, a star above the shield
On the city's coat of arms.

Not that heavenly visitor in a blackness of water,
I'm the name of the star.

Not a voice, not a dress on that far shore,
I can only shine.

Not a ray of light beyond your vision,
I'm a house in ruins from the war.

Not a house on the high rampart,
I'm the memory of your home.

O not your friend, but one who's sent by fate,
I'm the sound of a distant shot.

В приморскую степь я тебя уведу,
На влажную землю паду,

И стану я книгой младенческих трав,
К родимому лону припав.

I lead you to the steppe along the coast,
And I lie down on the humid earth.

I become the book of newborn grass
And I nuzzle into the native womb.

«Вечерний, сизокрылый...»

Вечерний, сизокрылый,
Благословенный свет!
Я словно из могилы
Смотрю тебе вослед.

Благодарю за каждый
Глоток воды живой,
В часы последней жажды
Подаренный тобой.

За каждое движенье
Твоих прохладных рук,
За то, что утешенья
Не нахожу вокруг.

За то, что ты надежды
Уводишь, уходя,
И ткань твоей одежды
Из ветра и дождя.

"You evening light, you dove… "

You evening light, you dove-
Colored and blessed light,
As though from the grave
I trail you with my eyes,

Thanking you for each taste
Of fabled elixir
In the hours of final thirst
That you deliver.

For your cool hands,
And the way they flutter
For how I cannot find
Consolation anywhere.

For your taking all hope
When you leave again,
For the stitch of your clothes
Made of wind and rain.

Ulysses

Benjamin Fondane
Translated by Nathaniel Rudavsky-Brody
French (France)

Though born and raised in Romania, poet and critic Benjamin Fondane spent the last two decades of his life in Paris and is known as much for his French writing as for work in his native language.

Born in 1898 in the old Jewish community of Iași, where his father was a storekeeper and his mother came from a well-known intellectual family, Fondane studied law but did not pass the bar, as his professor routinely failed Jewish students. He published poems, translations (from German and French), and criticism in the journals that flourished between the wars in his hometown and Bucharest, where he moved in 1919. In the capital, he was always at the center of a flurry of avant-garde artistic activity, yet in 1923 he moved to Paris like so many other Romanian artists and intellectuals, drawn to the city whose literature and culture was its own second language. Eugene Ionesco was his friend, Constantin Brancusi a witness at his wedding, and in later years the young Emil Cioran would visit him for encouragement. He devoted seven years to learning French well enough to write in the language, while working at an insurance company and as an assistant director and screenwriter for Paramount Pictures. Bit by bit he earned an audience, especially for his criticism; Jean Cocteau called his book on Rimbaud "the only book which could have been written" about the poet. And he met the philosopher

Lev Shestov, of whom he was to become both a close friend and only disciple. In French, he published the long poems *Ulysse* (1932) and *Titanic* (1937), but the many poems he wrote during the occupation of Paris—including *The Sorrows of Ghosts* and the collection *In the Time of the Poem*—were only published posthumously.

The three extended poems: *The Sorrows of Ghosts*, *Ulysses,* and *Titanic,* were all inspired by two journeys Fondane made to Argentina, once invited by Victoria Ocampo to give a series of lectures, and once to direct a film that was unfortunately never released. All three poems take as their central image the Atlantic passage. *Ulysses* identifies its Homeric title character with the storied Wandering Jew, and draws on the mass emigrations that brought many of Fondane's fellow Romanian Jews to America. Its tone and ideas anticipate the late masterpiece *The Sorrows of Ghosts,* written in occupied Paris in the shadow of the camps, whose ghosts, waiting on the quay to embark, then crossing the ocean in giant steamers, are fleeing a world falling to pieces. Their estrangement—from that lost world that was never theirs in the first place, from their own past (both the immigrants' and Fondane's, who was never sure how to confront his own Jewish heritage), and, as seekers of a hard truth like Shestov, from the crowds around them who accepted the world as they saw it—is ten years distant from the still-young poet. The voice, however, is the same, as are the concerns and the uniquely warm and sympathetic way of seeing a wide and unfriendly world.

Original text: Benjamin Fondane, "Ulysse" from *Le mal des fantômes.*
Paris: Paris-Méditerranée & L'Ether Vague, 1996.

Ulysse

à Armand Pascal, dans la mort…

Et c'est l'heure, ô Poète,
de décliner ton nom,
ta naissance et ta race
        SAINT-JOHN PERSE, *EXIL*

No retreat, no retreat
They must conquer or die
who have no retreat
        MR. GAY

J'etais un grand poète né pour chanter la Joie
– mais je sanglote dans ma cabine,
des bouquets d'eau de mer se fanent dans les vases
l'automne de mon cœur mène au Père-Lachaise,
l'éternité est là, œil calme du temps mort
est-ce arriver vraiment que d'arriver au port?
Armand ta cendre pèse si lourd dans ma valise.

Voici ta vie immense qui fait sauter les ponts.
Tu sais nager, je sais, mais que le fleuve est long!
Nous étions écrasés par cette lumière inhumaine.

Ulysses

for Armand Pascal, in death...

Et c'est l'heure, ô Poète,
de décliner ton nom,
ta naissance et ta race

No retreat, no retreat
They must conquer or die
who have no retreat

I was a great poet, born to sing Joy
—but I sob in my cabin
bouquets of seawater wilt in the vase
the autumn of my heart leads to Père-Lachaise
eternity is there, calm eye of a dead time
is this the last call, coming at last to port?
Armand, your ashes are so heavy in my suitcase.

Here is your vast life, bridges blown to the sky.
You know how to swim, I know, but the river is long.
We were crushed by this inhuman light.

BENJAMIN FONDANE | NATHANIEL RUDAVSKY-BRODY   27

Pourquoi chanter à tue-tête? Gorge pleine
qui ne demande qu'à chanter?
Si le château était hanté?
si les dieux s'amusaient à nous prendre pour cible?
Tu es entré vivant aux mains du dieu terrible
et jusque dans la mort tu es resté vivant…
… Que le flot ne veut-il m'emporter?

                                        Océan
ta vague furieuse fouette le vieil automne!

À l'hôpital cette blancheur d'angoisse, jaune.
Que de bateaux ici chassés par les typhons,
blessés dans leur ferraille tendre
ont coulé par le fond!
Des visiteurs parfois y entrent en scaphandres
qui gardent en esprit la corde qui les lie
au monde extérieur. Ils pensent à ce monde
tout le temps qu'ils sont là, penchés sur quelque lit,
et les mourants y pensent aussi et des bulles d'air montent
à la surface. Mais que font donc les vivants?
qu'attendent-ils pour mettre en marche les poulies?
Le film, le film est-il tellement captivant
que projette la mort sur l'écran de la vie?
Oh que ta voix est lasse
laisse-moi près de ta voix
splendide, tu jouais avec le ciel d'en face
je veux dormir près de tes mains
le grand rideau tombait avant la fin et cependant
la vie applaudissait de se sentir émue
dans les cris d'autobus, les accidents, les bris,
elle applaudissait à tout rompre
– pourquoi ne pas venir saluer le public?
Une aube d'au-delà sur ton visage tremble…

Why sing at the top of our voices? Wide throat
that only asks to sing?
What if the castle was haunted?
What if the gods passed time taking shots at us?
Alive you entered the hands of the terrible god
and into death remained alive...
...And the river's waters will not bear me off?

                                        Ocean

your furious waves lash the old autumn.

At the hospital the white of anguish, yellow.
Here, so many boats chased by some typhoon
their tender scrap iron battered
sunk to the bottom.
Visitors in diving suits sometimes come in
who hold in their hearts the cord that ties them
to the world outside. They think of that world
the whole time they are here, bent over a bed
and the dying think of it too and bubbles rise
to the surface. But then what do the living do,
what are they waiting for to start the pulleys?
Is it so captivating, the film
that death projects on life's screen?
Oh your voice is weak
let me stay near your voice
splendid, you played with the facing sky
I want to sleep near your hands
the great curtain fell before the end and yet
life applauded deeply moved
in the cries of buses, accidents, broken glass
it clapped as hard as it could
—why not come out and greet the public?
A dawn of hereafter trembles in your face...

Ami, ami nous étions venus de loin, ensemble,
unis comme les branches des ciseaux
pépins d'un même fruit
le même rêve à partager, le même pain
la même soif plus grande que le monde.
Nous avions de quoi conquérir plus qu'un monde:
Nous aura-t-on trompés, rusés?
Sisyphe, vieux Sisyphe que tu es donc usé!
Céderas-tu? Consentirais-je
au seul droit de la force?
Ce n'était rien, un piège.
Il ne faut pas cedar. Pas d'issue, pas d'issue!
Ils doivent périr ou vaincre ceux qui n'ont point d'issue!

Quelle barque jamais, au royaume des cieux,
aborda sans péril, par calme plat? Tes yeux
se sont peut-être ouverts ailleurs. Mais le tempête
ce soir t'a rejeté sur nos bords. Salut, mouette!
Entends-tu l'océan pendant que tu es là?
Tu es au moins aussi vivant que moi,
tu es mon rire et ma mémoire
je suis enceint de ta mort
je te porte plus haut que mon buste,
je hais la mort, je hais la vie.
J'ai si grand pitié des hommes
je me hais et je m'aime
pardonne-moi d'être vivant, d'écrire des poèmes,
je suis encore là mais je parle aux fantômes!
Est-il réponse ou non aux questions de l'homme
quelque part? Et le dieu existe-t-il, le Dieu
d'Isaïe, qui essuiera toute larme des yeux
et qui vaincra la mort –
quand les premières choses seront évanouies?

My friend, my friend, we came together from far
united like a pair of scissor blades,
seeds of the same fruit,
sharing the same dream, the same bread
the same thirst wider than the world.
We had what it took to conquer more than one world:
could we have been deceived, taken in?
Sisyphus, old Sisyphus, you are worn out.
Will you give in? Would I concede
to the rule of force?
It was nothing, a trap.
We must not give in. No retreat, no retreat!
They must die or conquer, who have no retreat.

What ship will ever, in the kingdom of the heavens,
make land without danger, the sea flat and calm? Your eyes
have opened elsewhere, perhaps. But the storm
this evening threw you up on our shore. Greetings, gull!
Do you hear the ocean while you are there?
You are at least as alive is I,
you are my laughter, my memory,
I am pregnant with your death
I carry you higher than my chest
I hate death, I hate life.
I feel such pity for men
I hate myself and love myself
forgive me for being alive, for writing poems
I am still here but I speak to ghosts.
Is there an answer somewhere to the questions
of men? And does god exist, the God
of Isaiah who will overcome death,
when the first things have passed?

✤

Cette nuit une lampe oubliée, allumée,
vacilla tout à coup en moi comme un oiseau
l'aile meurtrie et déplumée…
Était-ce bien le *même* monde?
était-ce un monde renversé?
… Elle était là encore la Terre, elle était ferme,
et pourtant j'entendais ses craquements futurs
– il ne faut pas s'y attarder
– il ne faut pas lui faire confiance,
quelque chose aura lieu. Quelque chose, mais Quoi?
Les événements couraient les uns après les autres
ils se suivaient au galop,
leur chevelure était fuyante
– à quoi bon regarder en avant, en arrière?
ce fleuve allait, bien sûr, m'emporter dans ses eaux
la vie allait, bien sûr, me traverser de part en part
– je vous salue, ô richesses!
que ferais-je à présent de tous ces rubans de lumière,
de ces choses qui naissant de l'eau, du crépuscule,
j'errais aveugle dans le pas perdu des gares
je demandais aux trains le but de mon voyage
pourquoi voulais-je aller si loin, quitter mon lit,
nourrir ma fièvre de banquises?
Juif, naturellement, tu étais juif, Ulysse,
tu avais beau presser l'orange, l'univers,
le sommeil était là, assis, les yeux ouverts,
l'espace était immangeable,
le sang mordait au vide et se sentait poreux
un gros poisson touchait au monde, de sa queue
– son cri était long et sordide…

✤

Last night a forgotten lamp
flared up in me, sudden like a bird
with a battered and plucked wing…
Was it really the same world?
Was it a world inverted?
…The Earth was still there, still solid
and yet I heard the sound of its future breaking
—you must not linger there
—you must not trust it,
something will happen. Something, but what?
Events came running one after the other
following each other at a gallop
their hair thrown back
—what good is it to look ahead or back?
This river was always going to bear me off
and life was always going to go right through me
—I hail you, riches!
what would I do now with these ribbons of light?
with all these things born of water, of twilight,
I wandered blindly in the lost halls of stations
I asked the trains what was the point of my journey
why did I want to go so far, leave my bed
and stoke my fervor for seas of ice?
A Jew, naturally you were a Jew, Ulysses,
it did you little good to squeeze the orange, the universe,
for sleep was there, seated, its eyes open
space could not be eaten
your blood took the void's bait, felt porous
a huge fish touched the world with its tail
—and gave a long sordid cry…

… la fin du monde et moi, ici, sur le balcon?
J'appelais au secours, d'une voix d'exception
mais à quoi bon me plaindre, geindre?
Un bonheur inconnu me léchait les reins,
je criais d'être libre, heureux, mais l'épouvante
me jetait un soleil cruel, à peine mûr,
il pourrissait au contact de mes mains
– qu'en ferais-je?

Seul! J'étais seul au monde avec moi-même,
feuille morte pareille à une feuille morte.

…The end of the world, and me, here on the balcony?
I called for help in an urgent voice
but what's the use of moaning or complaining?
An unknown pleasure licked the small of my back
I cried to be free and happy, but fear
threw me a cruel sun, barely ripe,
that rotted when it touched my hands
—what could I do with it?

Alone, I was alone in the world with myself
dead leaf like any dead leaf.

On Rain's Street

Constantin Abăluță
Translated by Victor Pambuccian
Romanian (Romania)

Born in 1938 in Bucharest, Constantin Abăluță studied architecture, graduating in 1961. His first volume of poetry was published in 1964, and in 1969 he stopped practicing architecture to devote his time entirely to writing poetry, prose, literary criticism, theater; translating, and to drawing (he designed the covers of all of his books, numbering forty volumes, and drew all the illustrations). Several of his poetry books have been translated into French, one volume has been translated into Dutch, and another one into English. The recipient of several Romanian and international prizes, he is the Vice-President of the Romanian PEN Club.

His is an unusual poetry, most often centered on the world of objects and that of small creatures. Several of his volumes of poetry are of surrealist inspiration. His prose and theater have Eugène Ionesco's theater of the absurd, the fervent South American imagination, and Swift's pamphlets as their starting point.

Rain has figured quite prominently in Romanian poetry, its main chronicler being George Bacovia (1881–1957), in whose poetry it almost became a state of mind. In Abăluță's poems it acquires an entirely different quality, becoming the background for a world of objects that leads to associations and fuses with the inner life of the narrating subject.

Original text: Constantin Abăluță "Pe strada ploii" from *Drumul furnicilor*. Bucharest: Casa de pariuri literare, 2011.

Pe strada ploii

Pe strada ploii aşa e dintotdeauna
gardul dărăpănat al parcului e plin de melci
când şi când rafale de vânt le sparg cu zgomot cochiliile
câte-un bătrân tresare pe o bancă
şi-şi astupă urechile cu ziare.
E aşa de lung gardul că mergând pe lângă el îl uiţi
cu totul şi cu totul, aşa cum ai uitat casa
în care-ai locuit jumătate de secol.
Ai uitat camera de la răsărit, ai uitat camera de la apus
ai uitat glasvandul dintre ele şi umbrele
care se perindau, instalatorul chior
băiatul cu butelii, vecina cu un borcan cu ţânţari
femeia de la mansardă cu intrigile ei naive
ca nişte flori de câmp. Ai uitat totul
şi acum cobori pe strada ploii
prin vânt prin pocnetele înfundate
ale cochiliilor de melci

On Rain's Street

Everything's forever the same on rain's street
the park's dilapidated fence is full of snails
now and then gusts of wind break their shells with a cracking sound
some old man gets startled awake on a bench
and covers his ears with newspapers.
The fence is so long that walking its length you completely
forget about it the way you forgot the house
in which you lived for half a century.
You forgot the room on its east side, the one on the west side
you forgot the glass partition between them and the shadows
that were moving around, the one-eyed plumber
the boy with the propane tanks, the neighbor with her mosquito jar,
the woman in the garret with her simple-minded intrigues
like some flowers on the plains. You forgot everything
and now you get off on rain's street
through the wind through the clogged sound of
snail shells snapping

Twenty-One Days of a Neurasthenic

Octave Mirbeau
Translated by Justin Vicari
French (France)

Frequently associated with anarchism and erotic literature, Octave Mirbeau, born in 1901, was also a master satirist in the tradition of Jonathan Swift. In *Twenty-One Days of a Neurasthenic*, Mirbeau creates a fictional sanatorium which doubles as Dante's Inferno, and then consigns his various political, literary, and social enemies to its winding circles. Mirbeau had more than a glancing acquaintance with the machine politics of late 19th century France, astonishingly similar to the machine politics of recent U.S. history. Financial corruption ran rampant among elected representatives, insider trading was as rigged as a shell game, and French multinational corporations ate up the interests of the working-class and the poor for breakfast.

Because satire depends so much on the humor of timely references, a decision was made to open up the novel, in places, so that unwieldy footnotes would not be required to absorb the pungency of Mirbeau's deliciously twisted jokes. I was indebted to the meticulously annotated French edition published by the Société d'Octave Mirbeau. In particular, Dreyfus is a sort of phantom character in the novel, obsessing a number of the book's ultra-conservative figureheads. The narrator, much like Mirbeau himself, tries to defend the falsely accused soldier on a number of occasions, only to be met with flagrantly anti-Semitic backlash.

Mirbeau's book involves so much human wickedness, in fact, that its few tender passages are often centered around a love for animals. Indeed, people are more bestial than their zoological counterparts in *Twenty-One Days of a Neurasthenic*. A case in point is the passage excerpted here, in which the narrator adopts and domesticates a small hedgehog, whose press into the human family has untoward results. Mirbeau carries out his sketch of the grunting, guzzling critter in full faux-tragic tone, but the irony is not without tears, for Mirbeau was a kind of scientific poet: he saw lyricism within the clinical, the way a surgeon might see beauty in a scalpel..

Original text: Octave Mirbeau, *Les 21 jours d'un neurasthénique*.
Paris: Éditions du Boucher, 2003.

Les 21 jours d'un neurasthénique

Un jour que j'étais descendu à la cave — Dieu sait pourquoi, par exemple —, je trouvai, au fond d'une vieille boîte d'épicerie, sous une couche épaisse de petit foin, dit d'emballage, je trouvai... quoi?... un hérisson. Roulé en boule, il dormait de ce profond, de cet effrayant sommeil hivernal, dont les savants ne nous ont point encore expliqué la morphologie — est-ce ainsi qu'il faut dire? La présence, dans une boîte d'épicerie, de cet animal, ne m'étonna pas autrement. Le hérisson est un quadrupède calculateur et fort « débrouillard ». Au lieu de chercher, pour l'hiver, un peu confortable abri sous un dangereux et aléatoire tas de feuilles ou dans le trou d'un vieil arbre mort, celui-ci avait jugé qu'il serait plus au chaud et plus tranquille dans une cave. Notez, en outre, que, par un raffinement de confortable, il avait choisi, pour l'hivernage, cette boîte d'épicerie, parce qu'elle était placée contre le mur, à un endroit précis où passe le tuyau du calorifère. Je reconnus bien là un des trucs familiers aux hérissons, qui ne sont pas assez stupides pour se laisser mourir de froid, comme de vulgaires purotins. L'animal, réveillé par moi progressivement, au moyen de passes savantes, ne parut pas non plus s'étonner outre mesure de la présence, dans la cave, d'un homme qui l'examinait indiscrètement, penché sur sa boîte. Il se déroula lentement, s'allongea peu à peu, avec des mouvements prudents, se dressa sur ses pattes basses, et s'étira comme fait...

Twenty-One Days of a Neurasthenic

One day, I went down to the cellar (searching for God knows what), and discovered... down in the bottom of an ancient mason jar from the grocery store, under a thick bed of fine straw leftover from the packing... I discovered... what...? A hedgehog. Curled in a ball, he was asleep in there, deep in a terrible, comatose hibernation whose morphology our learned scholars have never been able to explain to us—can it even *be* explained? This animal's presence in a mason jar did not surprise me one bit. The hedgehog is a shrewd, highly resourceful quadruped. Instead of seeking out a winter sanctuary closer to hand, under a risky, unsecured drift of leaves or in the hollow of some dead ancient tree trunk, this one had decided he'd be safer in a basement—not to mention warmer, for, as a further guarantee of creature comfort, he had chosen to hibernate inside this mason jar precisely because it sat against the wall right below the current from a heating duct. In this I noted one of the well-documented traits of hedgehogs, who are not stupid enough to let themselves freeze to death like vulgar rats.

As I gradually awakened him with cautious caresses, the animal did not seem unduly startled at the presence of a man in the cellar, leaning over the jar and staring at him. He uncoiled slowly and cautiously, then he stood up on his hind paws and stretched himself like a cat, scratching the ground with his claws. An extraordinary thing: when I picked him up and held him in my hand, not only did he not roll into a ball, he did not stick out a single one of his quills and he never once pricked me with the barbed-wire pleats around his little cranium. On the contrary, by the way in which he grunted and chattered his jaw—by the way, too, in which his tiny snout wriggled—I observed that he was conveying joy, trust, and… appetite. Poor little bastard! He was pale and, as it were, wilted, like a salad sitting out for too long in some musty corner. His jet-black eyes kindled with a strange luster I recognized from the eyes of anemics; indeed, his eyelids, slightly damp with sweat, revealed to my trained etiologist's eye an advanced case of anemia.

I carried him up to the kitchen, and he immediately astonished us all by his friendliness and the ease with which he made himself at home. Like a starving man, he sniffed at the *pommes frites* simmering on the stove, and his nostrils inhaled, with delicious desperation, the aromas of sauces wafting through the air.

I poured him some milk right away, and he drank it down. After that, I tempted him with a morsel of meat, and he hurled himself upon it voraciously, as soon as he smelled it, like a tiger on its prey. With his two front paws crossed over the meat as a sign of absolute ownership, he tore it to shreds with the corner of his growling mouth, and his black pinpoint eyes sparkled in fierce flashes. Thin red fibers dangled from his jaw, and his snout dripped with sauce. In a matter of seconds, the meat was all gone. It was the same story with the potatoes; a bunch of grapes, too, disappeared the instant it was offered. He slurped a bowl of coffee in big resounding gulps… Afterwards, sated, he dropped onto his serving dish and fell asleep.

By the following day, the hedgehog was as tame as a puppy. I made a very warm bed for him in my room, and whenever I came in he leapt up, overjoyed, and ran straight to me, contented only when I picked him up. Then, as I stroked his back (his quills were so deeply retracted that they were as soft as the fur of a kitten) he spoke in brief, low cries, which soon settled into a continuous, sleepy drone, like a purr.

Yes, it is important for naturalists to know this: hedgehogs purr.

Since he gave me so much pleasure, and since I was falling in love with him, I gave him the honor of allowing him to sit at my table. They set his dish next to mine, and he ate every bite; it was amusing to see him huff in peevish annoyance when he watched them taking away a plate from which he had not been allowed to sample anything. I've never met an animal less finicky in his eating habits: meats, vegetables, pickles, desserts, fruit, he ate everything. But his favorite was rabbit. He could always smell it cooking; on those days he went mad, and could not get enough. On three occasions, he suffered severe attacks of indigestion from eating too much rabbit, and he might have died, the frail thing, if I had not acted quickly to administer potent laxatives.

It was a stroke of bad luck that I, out of human weakness, perhaps out of perversity, got him used to alcohol. After drinking liquor, he stubbornly refused to drink anything else. Like a connoisseur, he took his daily glass of the finest champagne. There were no bad side effects, no problems, no signs of inebriation. A hard drinker, he held his booze like an old sea captain. He became addicted to absinthe, too, and it seemed to do him good. Now and then I caught him staring off into space, as if preoccupied, with something like faint glimmers of lust in his eyes. Certain he would find his way back home, I turned him loose in the woods on warm, lovely nights to seek the companionship of female hedgehogs, and in the morning, right at the crack of dawn, there he was by the door, waiting to be let in. He slept like the dead the whole next day, recovering from his nocturnal orgies.

One morning, I found him stretched out on his bed. He did not leap up when I approached. I called to him. He did not move. I picked him up; he was cold. Nonetheless, his body still palpitated… Oh, his tiny eye, and that look he gave me, with all the strength he could muster! I will never forget it… that almost human look, filled with astonishment, pain, tenderness, and so many profound mysteries I longed to understand…. He took one more breath… a kind of faint rattle, like the gurgle of a bottle being drained… then two shudders, a spasm, a cry, another spasm… then he was dead.

I couldn't stop sobbing….

I stared at him in my hand, uncomprehending. There was no sign of a wound anywhere on his body, crumpled, now, like a rag; no visible symptom of disease revealed itself. The night before, he had not gone to the woods, and that evening he had richly, heartily savored his glass of fine champagne. What could have killed him? Why this sudden turn?

I sent the cadaver to Triceps for an autopsy. And here is the brief letter I received, three days later:

Dear friend,

Total alcoholic inebriation. Cause of death: dropsy. An unprecedented case among hedgehogs.

Yours,

ALEXIS TRICEPS, M.D.

Description of a Flash of Cobalt Blue

Jorge Esquinca
Translated by Dan Bellm
Spanish (Mexico)

Poet and translator Jorge Esquinca (Mexico City, 1957) has received the Aguascalientes Prize, Mexico's top poetry award, as well as a national Poetry Translation Prize. His nine books of poetry include *Región* (collected poems, 1982–2002) and, most recently, *Descripción de un brillo azul cobalto* (Description of a Flash of Cobalt Blue), which won Spain's Jaime Sabines Spanish-American Poetry Prize. Esquinca has translated books by Pierre Reverdy, Henri Michaux, Adonis, H.D., and W. S. Merwin, among others, and has published a book of essays and a book for children. He lives in Guadalajara.

Description of a Flash of Cobalt Blue is an extended elegy in 24 linked sections for the poet's father, also a writer. The French Romantic poet Gérard de Nerval and German poet Rainer Maria Rilke's book of poems in French, *Les Roses*, both recur in Esquinca's poem as favorites of his father's. Presented here are translations of two of the final sections of the book: a vision or waking dream that combines the father's deathbed with memories of him in a barbershop in old Guadalajara, and at the end of the book, a scene in which the father and Nerval together cross the river of the dead, here transposed to the ancient Mexican city of Chiapa de Corzo.

A significant challenge of translating this work is to render, in a continuous thread, the way the poem combines and alternates such a multitude of voices and places. The father dying in a hospital bed appears, transfigured, alongside Gérard de Nerval, whom we meet on the last day of his life. The Mexican countryside leads suddenly to a bridge over the Seine. A child saint who has the miraculous power of levitation reveals that this river is also the Nile, which by the end of the poem has wound its way back across the backyard of a Mexican country house. A wounded horseman from a classic Mexican ballad who is also the Lone Ranger of a 1960s childhood crosses the hallucinatory lowlands of Jalisco. A family drives to the sea in a cobalt blue Vauxhall while the children in the back seat are transformed into the swans of Hans Christian Andersen's story. *Description of A Flash of Cobalt Blue* has a remarkable way of remaining a deeply personal work even as it dissolves distances of time, place, and character, presenting wakefulness and sleep, life and death, as two sides of one coin.

Original text: Jorge Esquinca, from *Descripción de un brillo azul cobalto.*
Madrid, Buenos Aires, & Valencia: Editorial Pre-textos, 2008;
Mexico City: Ediciones Era, 2010.

(22)

Al salir de casa
la mañana huele
a loción de afeitar

con trote de niño
que cruza
invisibles fronteras

pasajes   vivas
urdimbres   presencias
simultáneas   abiertas

hasta el quicio reluciente
de la peluquería   una
garza un nudo de rizo

un salvavidas flotante
azul blanco rojo
en la espiral junto al rótulo

(22)

The morning smells of
aftershave
as I leave the house

at a child's trot
crossing
invisible borders

passageways   living souls
a warp and weft of synchronous
open   presences

until I reach the bright doorway
of the barbershop   like a heron
to a reef-knot of curls

a floating life preserver
the red white and blue
of the spiral next to the sign

donde se lee   LA MARINA
los espejos límpidos   altos
sillones de cuero escarlata

parecidos a viejas manzanas
cabellos delgadísimos   todo
suspendido en el aire

como en esas fotografías
de la lluvia   "léanme
Las rosas"   dijo sin voz

la saliva sabe a espuma
de afeitar brillan las tijeras
las navajas ingrávidas   sólo

se oye el murmullo de los abanicos
allá arriba   en el techo hueco
como un cielo de mar

ceñido en una sábana hasta
el cuello aguarda mi padre
reclinando en el sillón giratorio

parece dormir ha perdido
mucho peso "demasiado"
pienso al mirarme mirándolo

en los espejos   tampoco soy
el mismo llevo una barba
zapatos negros

that reads   LA MARINA
the crystal-clear mirrors   the raised
seats of scarlet leather

that have the look of old apples
slenderest hairs   all
suspended midair

like in those photographs
of rain   "read me
The Roses"   he said without a voice

saliva tasting of shaving foam
the scissors the weightless
razors   glisten   not a sound

but the sighing of the fans
overhead   on a ceiling empty
as the sky over the sea

wrapped tight in a sheet up to
his neck my father waits
reclined in the swivel chair

he seems to be asleep   he has lost
a lot of weight   "too much" I think
as I see myself looking at him

in the mirrors   nor am I
who I was   I wear a beard now
black shoes

camisa blanca   *navego*
hacia el origen   dijo sin voz
mi padre   entendí entonces

que estaba muriéndose   voy
hasta él entre espejos
que multiplican nuestras dos

soledades   humedezco
un paño en el agua caliente
comienzo a deslizarlo suave

por su rostro arrasado   el vapor
lo envuelve esa sensación
de soles disueltos ese

momentáneo bienestar que intento
extender cuanto más   somos
una figura que se borra

como el vapor en la atmósfera
de un hospital donde mi padre
abre los ojos para que yo vea

la muerte habitarlo súbita
violenta eficaz insondable
la muerte que vuelve

a ocupar un espacio suyo
desde siempre   así
como lo digo   en un santiamén

a white shirt   *I'm sailing back*
to the beginning   my father said
without a voice   so then I understood

that he was dying   I move
toward him between mirrors
that multiply our

solitudes   I wet
a cloth in hot water
I begin to pass it gently

over his ravaged face
the steam enfolds him that sensation
of dissolving sun that

momentary well-being
I try to prolong   we are
a shape disappearing

like vapor in the air
of a hospital where my father
opens his eyes so that I can see

death inhabit him   sudden
violent efficient unfathomed
death that comes back

to occupy a space that has always
been its own   as swift
as saying the word *amen*

al salir de la peluquería
el aire claro huele
a lavanda   cómo

explico la sonrisa
que asomó al hundirse
en su último rostro

I step out of the barbershop
the bright air smells
of lavender   and how

can I explain the smile
that appeared even as it sank
into his very last face

(24)

Anochece en Chiapa de Corzo
una nube densa se posa
en el sombrero de mi padre

mientras baja hacia el río
silbando aquella tonada
indescifrable   lleva un ocote

encendido que apenas
le permite guiar sus pasos
entre las ceibas

del terraplén
rodeado de sombras
camina resuelto

hace frío   guarece su mano
libre bajo la levita   junto
al corazón que no podemos oír

(24)

Nightfall in Chiapa de Corzo
a dense cloud settles
on my father's hat

as he goes down to the river
whistling that indecipherable
tune   he carries a lit

pine branch that barely
helps him find his way
among the *ceiba* trees

on the embankment
he walks resolutely
surrounded by shadows

it's cold   he protects his
free hand beneath his coat   next
to the heart that we can't hear

en el muelle de tablas está
la barca   en ella hay otro
que espera taciturno

bajo su sombrero   sube
mi padre con el ocote
humeante   apenas puede

ver al otro pasajero   se sienta
en el espacio libre en la popa
dice "buenas noches señor"

luego de un suspiro el otro alza
una mano "bonsoir monsieur"
bajo el cielo constelado

advierten los ojos amarillos
del barquero que los interroga
sin palabras   ambos extienden

sus monedas   al alejarse
de la orilla se escucha
el rumor de las aguas

el sonido de los remos
las voces forasteras
una canción egipcia

the boat is there at the wooden
dock   someone shaded by
a hat is waiting in it

silently   my father
gets in with his smoking
pine-torch   he can hardly

see the other passenger   sits down
in the vacant spot at the stern
says "*buenas noches señor*"

the other sighs and lifts
a hand "*bonsoir monsieur*"
beneath the starry sky

they notice the boatman's
yellow eyes wordlessly
questioning   they hand over

their coins   and as they push off
from the bank the murmur
of the waters can be heard

the sound of the oars
the voices of strangers
an Egyptian song

Y=1285/x

Marco Candida
Translated by Elizabeth Harris
Italian (Italy)

Marco Candida, from Tortona, in the Piedmont region of Italy, has published five novels since 2007. He is widely respected in Italian literary circles for his stylistically innovative, metafictional work. Candida's first novel, *La mania per l'alfabeto* (Alphabet Mania), is structured as a series of post-it notes in which the reader steadily sees the main character lose all attachment to reality in his obsession for writing; Candida's second novel, *Il diario dei sogni* (Dream Diary), follows a structure based on a log/commentary of the protagonist's steadily more hallucinatory, paranoid dreams about his former girlfriend.

Candida has commented that, with his more recent work, he is steadily coming closer to the reader: "I've done a bit of restyling in my writing: instead of writing such long sentences that the reader can hardly breath, I've begun to use a style that's more readable, that will make the reader less cross-eyed, even as I continue to pursue the thematic concerns closest to my heart."

Candida's story, "Y=1285/x," from his forthcoming collection, *Bamboccioni Voodoo*, reflects this tendency in his writing. Here we find a far more limpid prose than is seen in Candida's earlier work. The challenges in translating Candida remain the same, however: his prose is extremely musical, whether he writes in convoluted, longer sentences or with this quieter, briefer phrasing. While translating this strange and touching story, I found myself steadily paring back, reconsidering every word choice, every punctuation mark, as I worked to maintain Candida's clear style. This is one of my favorite stories that I've translated of Candida: the voice here is sincere and quiet; I was reminded of Kafka, who manages to make the fantastic seem so utterly commonplace; also like Kafka, while Candida's story has a fantastic premise, its concerns are humane, and ultimately, tragic.

Original text: Marco Candida, "Y=1285/x" from *Bamboccioni Voodoo*. Rome: Historica Edizioni (forthcoming).

Y=1285/x

La nonna è ritornata. Ora siede di la' nel suo salotto davanti alla televisione. Non sta guardando i telegiornali. Invece guarda una puntata di *La ruota della fortuna* con Mike Bongiorno. Per quel che ne so Mike Bongiorno non è tornato come la nonna, perciò deve trattarsi solo di una puntata registrata. La nonna è tornata da una settimana. Ci hanno telefonato dal cimitero e ci hanno detto di venirla a prendere. Noi all'inizio abbiamo pensato a uno scherzo. Erano le quattro del pomeriggio. Una settimana fa era il 26 settembre. C'era un bel solino. La temperatura era gradevole. Quando mia madre ha preso la comunicazione ha prima riso e poi la faccia le è diventata rossa, qualche lacrima ha cominciato a scenderle dagli occhi. Ci sembrava a tutti e quattro di sognare. Io stavo facendo non mi ricordo cosa nella mia stanza. Forse preparavo buste con i miei curricula, come faccio sempre. Mio fratello stava di sotto, lavorava nel suo studiolo d'avvocato – lo ha ottenuto grazie a un contratto di comodato gratuito proprio dalla nonna da due annetti circa. Mio padre invece in pensione da cinque o sei anni stava davanti alla TV. Prima della telefonata mia madre doveva essere in cucina, stirava. Ripeto, dopo la telefonata ci è sembrato a tutti e quattro di essere dentro a un sogno. Per strada ricordo il profumo di un qualche fiore che mi entrava nelle narici e l'aria caldina – piuttosto insolita per la stagione....

Y=1285/x

My nonna's come back. She's there, in the living room, in front of the television. She's not watching the news. She's watching an episode of *Wheel of Fortune* hosted by Mike Bongiorno. As far as I know, Mike Bongiorno hasn't come back like my nonna, so this must be a rerun. My nonna's been back a week. They called from the cemetery and told us to pick her up. At first we thought they were joking. It was four in the afternoon. That was a week ago: September 26. A sunny day, nice weather. When my mother took the call, she started to laugh, then she turned red and started to cry. The four of us felt like we were dreaming. I was in my room doing something, I don't remember what. Probably stuffing envelopes with resumes like always. My brother was downstairs, in his tiny law office—which my nonna actually gave him in a legal contract a couple of years ago. My father, retired for five or six years now, was watching TV. Before the phone call, my mother was probably ironing in the kitchen. I repeat: after the call, the four of us felt like we were dreaming. Outside on the street, I remember the smell of flowers on the warm breeze—a little unusual for this time of year. We walked to the garage where my father parks his car—our home's very close, only five minutes away—and while we walked, we kept talking in loud voices and then growing suddenly quiet. We got in the car and I remember that while we drove (my brother was driving), we practically held our breath the whole way to the cemetery. It took around ten minutes. My brother almost ran a stop sign and came close to scraping another car, but no one complained—not even my mother who always notices these things and pipes up right away. At the cemetery gate, there were two men, and my nonna was standing between them. The men were waiting for us. They probably had to make sure we wouldn't take too long. Nonna's clothes were filthy, covered in dirt and sawdust. Her hair, too. She was holding onto one of the men. She probably couldn't see much since she didn't have her glasses. The two men looked worn out, like they'd just finished a difficult job. Their clothes were dirty, too; one of them had a torn sleeve. We stepped out of the car and my mother burst into tears, my father, too (Nonna's his mama). My mother hugged her. Nonna said, "Hello, dear." My father was crying. Soon my father's sister arrived with my uncle and cousin. Then my uncle and my father gave the two men an enormous tip for their hard work. The two men had unscrewed the front to my nonna's vault. They'd pulled out the coffin—extremely heavy—and opened it. This was no easy task, since my nonna was (understandably) moving around inside. About the time this phenomenon of "coming back" was confirmed, the cemetery started asking for volunteers to "stand watch." It's a simple job but extremely important: these volunteers walk by the graves and vaults listening for pounding and other sounds, like voices. The town has set up nonstop, round-the-clock shifts. The two men heard my nonna knocking on the tomb while they were doing some sort of maintenance. I remember they weren't wearing the usual volunteer overalls, so they had some kind of job there. So while they were receiving their tip from my father and uncle, these two men also handed them the actual bill due by mail inside the month. But never mind—I'm being nitpicky. Nonna was back. That's what mattered. She's only the fifth person in our town to come back. That's another reason we feel we've been blessed with a miracle. We've told ourselves that Nonna's lifetime of prayers must not have been in vain. Up to this point, our town of twenty-five thousand had seen the return of a twenty-two year old killed in a car accident; a man even older than my nonna; a forty-six-year-old woman who died from a tumor; and a woman of around forty who may have been better off where she was considering she no longer had legs. Nonna's picture wound up in the local paper. They interviewed her. She even appeared on the national news—though they always pay more attention when famous people return. Even today, while I'm writing this, my nonna's had some visitors. The mayor's come. Various authorities. My nonna brings them all into her living room, just like before. She offers them little snacks and bitters aperitifs and tells them what she experienced. She says she doesn't really know what to say. She opened her eyes in the tomb and realized she was alive again. She doesn't remember what happened while she was resting. But she can remember everything from before she went to sleep. My nonna uses the phrase, "went to sleep," when she talks about her passing. Doctors have visited, and they say all her vital organs are working. Her heartbeat's resumed. Blood is circulating in her veins. She has good kidney function. Everything's working. Mostly when people come calling, my nonna talks about her aches and pains, which she definitely still has. She's just like before. A bad hip. Acid reflux. She still needs glasses. She's certainly not any younger or any stronger. Actually, she came back with two big, ugly bruises (one on her right elbow, the other on her left knee), probably from when they pulled her out of the vault. Even so, she's got my father's sister to thank for not respecting her last wishes to be cremated. My mother and aunt constantly hover around her now. Just yesterday we had our midday meal all together to celebrate her return. She ate and ate. She's more fortunate than others who've returned. Her life ended at ninety-six for the simple fact that her heart stopped beating. With most people, there's a reason they go. There's a reason we leave this world, and we truly can't do a thing about it. I remember a doctor once saying: it's life that kills us—poor old death's got nothing to do with it. There haven't been cases of people coming back if they have non-functioning livers or stomachs, if their vital organs aren't pretty much intact. According to the newspapers and the doctors, coming back requires a body in fairly good shape—that the person died from too much exertion or from old age. If you're crippled or blind, deaf or mutilated, then you might come back, but not if you have a ruptured liver or ruined lungs. The people that return, or so I've heard, aren't the dead who are living; they're living, that's all. There are rumors going around that some of these people prefer human flesh, but that's just not true. Those who come back come back exactly as they were. Some might wake up with a rotted leg or arm that has to be amputated. Others have organs that don't work, and so they'll soon die again. But the people who do make it are just like before. In the United States, some of these people go around telling others they've spoken with the Almighty—like Darwington, who published a book titled *I Spoke with God*. But none of this is certain. My nonna, for instance, doesn't remember a thing. Here in Italy, no one who "went to sleep" has spoken with God or the angels. And as to the causes, we also only hear rumors. Nothing's certain. Some say the world must be coming to an end, that it's turning more slowly, or at a different angle. So the real causes are climatic, global warming, the alignment of the planets. Maybe some undiscovered bacteria's floating around out there. Basically, nothing's certain about those who've come back to life, or at least we don't know anything right now. What we do know, however, is that as of today, there are around two million of these returnees scattered across the planet and that this only started a month ago. Here at home, we're not too interested in all these cases. We just stick to dealing with the reality of the situation and what this means for us. Nonna's not one of the living dead; she is, however, an old lady. Like I said, she's ninety-six. So we've gone back to what we were doing the last few years of her life, what you always do with old people (unless you're completely irresponsible): we check on her. Luckily she stays in her little living room, watching TV and barely eating. She doesn't require constant attention. Even at the end of

Nonna's life, my father and aunt didn't have to hire a caretaker, except when none of us were available. We've been fortunate. Just like we're fortunate to have her with us again. Her sweet voice. Her gentle touch. Her words every night before going to bed: "God bless you." Her soft cheeks. Having her here is like not having her here, in a way. Like most grandmothers, my nonna was mainly a sound: the sound of the television, of slippers down the hall, of the bathroom door. Just sounds—that grew louder as she grew deaf—and now these sounds have returned, are inside right now as I write. Others have had to deal with people returning who are much more problematic. Dead prisoners. The State hasn't wanted to send them back to jail even if they didn't serve out their full sentences. Once home, though, these thugs have gone back to their criminal ways. There's a case in Argentina of a man who came back after taking his own life. The TV news and the papers reported he was screaming when they opened the coffin. In other words, he wasn't exactly happy to be back. A few days later, we heard the Argentine turned himself in for homicide. This sparked a philosophical debate about a man's right to have himself prosecuted for taking his own life. My brother, father, and I have all followed this debate, as we're interested in the rights of those who've come back to life. Earlier, I spoke of the men who pulled my nonna from her coffin (before she suffocated and died again, though the doctors have explained that those who do come back have an exceptional respiratory capacity, far beyond what's normal), and that these men handed my uncle and father a municipal bill. The State has yet to guarantee, however, that those who've returned will have their pensions even partially renewed. These people must rely entirely on their families or legal guardians. Some private employers don't hesitate to rehire a former worker who's come back to life—a bartender, cook, or waiter. But for public employees, it's a whole different story. If you want to go back to work, you either retake your public exam or find yourself another job. Italian politicians—in the rest of the world this issue seems less complicated—have been busy trying to solve this problem, but so far they haven't found a solution. And so it would seem that at least for now, those who come back to life have hardly any rights at all. That's a problem. My nonna's pension allowed her to live for years with dignity. Thanks to her husband, my nonno, my nonna had a substantial pension and could afford an apartment for almost eleven years right in the center of town. Not only that: she also never stopped giving us—my brother, cousin, and me—a weekly allowance. Now having her back without that pension might be a problem, especially for me, as I don't have a job and I don't know how I'm going to find one. I do have some savings, but the truth is I pretty much rely on my parents. My father has his pension. My mother still works. My brother tries to eke out a living with his private practice. But it will be difficult to take care of Nonna, to keep an eye on her like we used to. My brother and I have our own lives, our own aspirations: we can't be there like we were before. But as I've already explained, my nonna really doesn't require that much attention. For now, going back to her same life just means watching TV, saying the rosary at night, and going to six o'clock mass. Someone needs to take her to church, even if it's only across the street. There's my brother, but he has to work. So my mother, father, and I (we're in the apartment right upstairs) all take turns helping her. And my father's sister and her family also help out. Someone has to do her shopping. Help her change out of her clothes at night. When I think about it, there's not much else; her coming back has meant mainly this. Her life after death's no different than what it was before. And it's pretty much the same for others who've returned and might be the same for everyone. Maybe they all resume their lives and who they were. And surely having her back, a woman like her, even if it takes some effort, is better than the alternative. In our family, we like to think her prayers brought her back to life and that her prayers keep us alive, too. When she passed away, I realized there's not much you can say about death. You can suffer when someone's gone, from the empty space that's left behind. But we're just not equipped to know about death. We're alive, and all we can see is life. All we see of death is the outcome: a body moves and has a certain color, and then that body stops moving and goes white. In other words, all we can say about death is what's there. Everything we can say, can think, everything's always, only, what's there, what we can see, hear, feel, smell. Even what we imagine is what we can see. Even when we deny something, say something's missing, isn't there, we have no choice but to bring it up, to make it appear in front of us, to see it. Maybe when we think about death, this is what hurts the most. We can't think about something that's happening right before our eyes. We're not seeing something we're seeing. This makes us short-circuit. Something exists that doesn't exist. Death is the scariest monster. After my nonna died, I thought about all this. I've heard it said that when we breathe our last, our genitals release some fluid, and so we die in a state of pleasure. But I've also heard that someone has this same feeling when he dies hanging from a rope. So I've come to think that no matter how we die, death chokes us in the end. Yes, I've written what I've written up to now so I could write down these final words. Maybe what I've written isn't all that impressive, but it feels like it's all there is to say. You see, I've been doing some research, and I've found out it only takes four minutes for a cadaver to start to decay. The term here is "autolysis." I've also discovered the formula to calculate how long it takes a cadaver to decompose: $Y=1285/x$. Y is the number of days it takes to reach a skeletal or mummified state and x is the average temperature during the process of decomposition. So if the average temperature is 15° centigrade, then it will take $1286/15=85.6$ days for someone to reach a skeletal state. There are other elements, however, to the cadaver's decomposing and putrefying, various microbes that attack the cadaver: staphylococcus, candida, malassezia, bacillus, streptococcus, micrococcus, coliform, diptheroid, clostridium, serratia, klebsiella, proteus, salmonella, pseudomonas, flavobacterium, agrobacterium, amoebas, and various colored fungi, which of course include those microbes carried by flies and other insects. Seeing what I've put down here, I can only conclude that nature's made it impossible for someone to come back to life. And the truth is my nonna hasn't come back. She's not in there, watching *Wheel of Fortune*. This entire story's made up. My nonna didn't die at ninety-six; she was ninety-two. She died from intestinal trouble: a perforated intestine. Like I said, there's a reason we go, and this was the reason for her. The end came quickly. My mother told me that when nonna lay dying in her hospital bed, she asked for a sip of water, and when someone gave it to her, she said: "Thank you." This detail breaks my heart. I've thought about how much in this world is cruel, useless. Maybe I could have remembered her with a different kind of story. The story of her ghost that came to see me. But I couldn't hug a ghost, hold her close.

Hunger

Velimir Khlebnikov
Translated by Alex Cigale
Russian (Russia)

Though on first appearance somewhat uncharacteristic of Velimir Khlebnikov's work—he is primarily associated with Zaum and Russian futurism—in its brilliant simplicity, "Hunger" is representative of his frequent use of a folk-naïve style. This particular poem is charged with a pathos that eerily presages Khlebnikov's own death: weakened by a period of starvation, Khlebnikov died of infection on June 28, 1922, the year after "Hunger" was written.

The deceptively simple music of the original reveals an intricate design for the ear: "*Будет сегодня из бабочек борщ*" (budet sevodnya iz babochek borsch; "Today there will be broth out of moths.") "… *Смотрят большими глазами, / Святыми от голода*" (Smotryat bol'shimi glazami / Svyatyme ot goloda; "They stare eyes wide open, / Made saintly by hunger.") The poem's breathlessness and staggered alliteration reproduce the physical frothiness and salivation that accompany starvation.

The list of the forest's inhabitants in lines 12 through 20 represent a virtual Noah's Ark of potential sources of nourishment. As it did in Eden, the act of naming implies a mastery that produces, through the magic of attraction, if not a real then an imagined possession of the object. But in "Hunger" this naming functions as a perversion of Eden; it is not difficult to read in the pleasure Khlebnikov takes in the shapes of the vowels in the mouth his own, very real, hunger. In Russian, the sound-sense of verse that is fully accomplished is said to be written "deliciously" (*vkusno*.) I can only hope I managed to transmute some of this magic into the sounds of the English counterpart.

The poem was first published posthumously, in the anthology *Красная новь* ("The Red New": 1927, № 8, p. 181) under the title *"Почему?"* ("Why?") The present title (*"Голод"*/"Golod") is taken from a notebook variant, originally composed in Pyatigorsk, upon Khlebnikov's return, first to Baku and then to the Caucuses, from Persia, where he had spent the previous summer as an attaché of the Red Army's command on its "march on Tehran." In the context of this poem, Khlebnikov wrote, later in 1922, of the efforts of Fridtjof Nansen, one of the organizers of international aide for the victims of the Volga region famine: "A world revolution requires a world conscience."

Original text: Velimir Khlebnikov, "Golod," 1927.

Голод

Почему лоси и зайцы по лесу скачут,
Прочь удаляясь?
Люди съели кору осины,
Елей побеги зеленые...
Жены и дети бродят по лесу
И собирают березы листы
Для щей, для окрошки, борща,
Елей верхушки и серебряный мох —
Пища лесная.
Дети, разведчики леса,
Бродят по рощам,
Жарят в костре белых червей,
Зайчью капусту, гусениц жирных
Или больших пауков — они слаще орехов.
Ловят кротов, ящериц серых,
Гадов шипящих стреляют из лука,
Хлебцы пекут из лебеды.
За мотыльками от голода бегают:
Целый набрали мешок,
Будет сегодня из бабочек борщ —
Мамка сварит.

Hunger

Why do the moose and hares dart about in the forest,
Fleeing our proximity?
People have eaten up the aspen bark,
The spruce's green shoots…
Women and children wander the forest
Collecting birch leaves
For stew, soup, and tea,
The tops of firs and the silver moss—
The woods' victuals.
Children, the forest's prospectors,
Are stumbling through thickets,
Frying in the campfire white worms,
Wood sorrel, fat caterpillars,
Or large spiders—sweeter than nuts.
They capture moles, little gray lizards,
Shoot hissing critters with bows,
Bake small buns out of saltbushes.
Out of hunger chase after moths:
They have gathered an entire sack,
Today there will be broth out of moths—
Prepared by mother.

На зайца что нежно прыжками скачет по лесу,
Дети, точно во сне,
Точно на светлого мира видение,
Восхищенные, смотрят большими глазами,
Святыми от голода,
Правде не верят.
Но он убегает проворным виденьем,
Кончиком уха чернея.
Вдогонку ему стрела полетела,
Но поздно — сытный обед ускакал.
А дети стоят очарованные...
«Бабочка, глянь-ка, там пролетела...
Лови и беги! А там голубая!..»
Хмуро в лесу. Волк прибежал издалёка
На место, где в прошлом году
Он скушал ягненка.
Долго крутился юлой, всё место обнюхал,
Но ничего не осталось —
Дела муравьев, — кроме сухого копытца.
Огорченный, комковатые ребра поджал
И утек за леса.
Там тетеревов алобровых и седых глухарей,
Заснувших под снегом, будет лапой
Тяжелой давить, брызгами снега осыпан...
Лисонька, огнёвка пушистая,
Комочком на пень взобралась
И размышляла о будущем...
Разве собакою стать?
Людям на службу пойти?
Сеток растянуто много —
Ложись в любую...
Нет, дело опасное.
Съедят рыжую лиску,

At the rabbit that hops gently about the forest,
The children, as though in a dream,
Just as upon the world's bright visitation,
Enraptured, stare eyes wide open,
Made saintly by hunger,
Not believing themselves.
But it escapes in an agile vision,
The tips of its ears flashing black.
An arrow flies up after him
But too late—the sating dinner has fled.
And the children stand in enchantment!
"A butterfly, look, how it flutters there…
Run and catch it! There, a blue one!"
It's gloomy in the woods. A wolf has trotted here from afar,
To this place where last year
He had scarfed down a lamb.
Turning circles a while like a top, he nuzzles in every corner,
But there is nothing left—
Deed it to the ants—nothing but dried out hooves.
Saddened, tucking in his crumpled ribs,
He skedaddles beyond the forest.
There, the scarlet-lidded black grouse and gray capercaillie,
Who had gone to sleep under the snows, he will smother
With his heavy paw, splashed by sprays of snow…
The fluffy, fiery red fox,
Shaped like a clump, has clambered upon a stump,
Her gaze focused and fixated on the future.
What to do? Become a dog?
Go to work for people?
So many nets spread open—
may as well lay down in any of them…
No, a dangerous business.
They'll swallow up the ginger vixen,

Как съели собак!
Собаки в деревне не лают…
И стала лисица пуховыми лапками мыться,
Взвивши кверху огненный парус хвоста.
Белка сказала, ворча:
«Где же мои орехи и желуди? —
Скушали люди!»
Тихо, прозрачно, уж вечерело,
Лепетом тихим сосна целовалась
С осиной.
Может, назавтра их срубят на завтрак.

Just as they've eaten all the dogs!
There are no dogs howling in the villages...
The fox washes her muzzle with furry paws,
The fiery sail of her tail fluttering in the wind.
A squirrel roams mumbling:
"Where have my nuts and acorns gone?
People have eaten them!"
Quietly, transparently, the evening came on.
With its quiet whispering the pine was kissing
the aspen.
Tomorrow perhaps, for breakfast, they will chop them down.

Two Poems

Rainer Maria Rilke
Translated by Susanne Petermann
French (Switzerland)

The French poems of Rainer Maria Rilke (1875–1926) number nearly 400 and remain virtually unknown. They were written mostly during 1922–25, while Rilke lived in Muzot, a tiny town in a wine-growing region of French-speaking Switzerland called the *Valais*.

It was not unusual for Rilke to be writing in French. From an early age, growing up in a German-speaking household, he felt uncomfortable in the bourgeois society of his family and in the Czech culture that surrounded him in Prague. Intermittently, and most notably in 1902–03 when he worked for the sculptor Rodin, he lived in Paris.

Why Rilke wrote in French later in his life is a matter of some discussion. Did he feel he had reached the pinnacle of his powers in German? Were these merely language exercises? In my view, the lighter tone of the French poems reflects Rilke's euphoria in the wake of his long-awaited success (the *Duino Elegies* and the *Sonnets to Orpheus* had just been published). In addition, having become disillusioned with Germany and by extension, the German language after WWI, he may have been making a mildly political statement by writing in French. A third and very plausible reason, in my view, is that he fell in love with a French-speaking woman, Balladine "Merline" Klossowska, who shared his German-language background but had renounced it. The two exchanged letters in French that were published in Zurich in 1954.

Out of nine series of French poems by Rilke, the poems included here belong to *Tendres Impôts à la France*, a group of fifteen that treat a variety of colorful subjects from mythology to religion. Some even delve into unusually (for Rilke) confessional sentiments around death. In 1924 when he wrote them, Rilke was already feeling some of the acute symptoms of leukemia, which went undiagnosed until a few months before his death. The poems were found among Rilke's papers and published posthumously.

To give a brief example of my process: in "Pégase" we are presented with a vision of this white horse galloping toward us. I struggled with the volley of four adjectives in the first line, considering how to give the feeling of strength and masculinity I get from reading the French. At first their sequence seemed—dare I say it—rather arbitrary, though each pair rhymes, "ardent et blanc," and "fier et clair." After trying every possible synonym and sequence, I settled on the very same order as the original, but rhyming between the pairs instead of internally: "fiery white" and "proud bright." I was more concerned, actually, with recreating the pace of the line, its speed and percussiveness, slowing slightly in the second pair of adjectives before we rest on the final, beautiful name of "Pégase." This first line becomes a hologram for the whole poem that ends with a soft, feminine touch as we wistfully admire the curve of the horse's neck.

Original text: Rainer Maria Rilke, "Pégase" and "Tombeau" from *Sämtliche Werke, Vol. II*. Frankfurt am Main: Insel Verlag, 1927.

Pégase

Cheval ardent et blanc, fier et clair Pégase,
après ta course—ah! que ton arrêt est beau!
Sous toi, cabré soudain, le sol que tu écrases
avale l'étincelle et donne de l'eau.

La source qui jaillit sous ton sabot dompteur,
à nous, qui l'attendons, est d'un secours suprême;
sens-tu que sa douceur impose à toi-même?
Car ton cou vigoureux apprend la courbe des fleurs.

Pegasus

Fiery white horse, proud bright Pegasus,
after you gallop, oh, how I love to see you halt!
Under your sudden rearing, the trampled ground
swallows the spark and flows with water.

Relief comes to us at last from the spring
that gushes beneath your great hoof.
Are you, too, feeling its sweetness? For the flowers
are teaching your vigorous neck how to curve.

Tombeau

(dans un parc)

Dors au fond de l'allée,
tendre enfant, sous la dalle;
on fera le chant de l'été
autour de ton intervalle.

Si une blanche colombe
passait au vol là-haut,
je n'offrirais à ton tombeau
que son ombre qui tombe.

Grave

(in a park)

Sleep, child, under your stone
down at the end of the lane.
We'll stand around the emptiness
and sing a summer song.

If a snow-white dove
happens to pass overhead,
I'll offer your grave simply this:
its shadow as it falls.

Atonement

Elvira Navarro
Translated by Michael McDevitt
Spanish (Spain)

Originally written as a one-off short story, "Atonement" later went on to become the first section of Navarro's debut novella *La ciudad en invierno* (The City in Winter). In spite of what is, as yet, a fairly slight body of work (one novella and a novel), Navarro has attracted widespread praise in both Spain and abroad. She won the prestigious Jaen Novel Prize for her second novel and was singled out by *Granta* magazine in 2010 as one of the 22 Best Spanish-Language authors under the age of 35.

"Atonement" introduces us to Clara (memorably described by one Spanish critic as "the anti-Lolita"), a very young, somewhat disturbed (or at the very least disturbing) child, locked in a kind of perverse power struggle with her elderly aunt, who is looking after her one summer while the girl's parents are at work. While the story is not written in the first person, nor is any attempt necessarily made to approximate a child's language, the story is nevertheless presented from Clara's point of view, and one of the challenges (and indeed pleasures) of translating it lies in maintaining this delicate balance. Tiny details take on great significance: minute droplets of water on a foam flotation device, distant traffic approaching, movements, sounds

("Furtive glances, the ticking clock, the drawn curtains and the heavy breathing of the women slumbering on the sofa … "). Elsewhere, Navarro appears to hint at both the child's wide-eyed wonder at the world and her limited attention span, her gaze flitting from one thing to the next ("The fruit trees, the prickly pears, the specks of dust, the edge of the flower beds, an insect's flight").

In and of themselves, the events recounted are mundane, but the pervading atmosphere is at all times an oppressive, claustrophobic one, capturing the grotesque nature of the adult world from a child's eye. Clara's aunt is portrayed in a somewhat unflattering light ("'Give me a kiss,' says the aunt, fat beneath her dress, her arms stretched out like tentacles"; "the Aunt's waddling gait"), and the young girl's hatred towards her is both utterly unjustified and yet at the same time entirely believable. It is this unsettling contradiction that makes Navarro's story such a compelling one.

Original test: Elvira Navarro, "Expiación" from *La ciudad en invierno*. Barcelona: Caballo de Troya, 2007.

Expiación

El agua deja sobre la burbuja de corcho gotas muy pequeñas, de forma ovalada, que apenas resisten el vaivén imperceptible con el que la niña procura mantenerse a flote.

Está el deseo de que las gotas brillantes de sol no acaben resbalando sobre la superficie del corcho, pero es tremendamente difícil permanecer inmóvil, en primer lugar porque la burbuja se hunde un poco, y luego, una vez descartado este método, porque cualquier movimiento resulta excesivo para las gotas, que se deshacen a ambos lados dejando una estela de motitas demasiado imperceptibles para ser dignas de contemplarse.

Un estrecho cartel a la entrada del recinto advierte de que la piscina es para uso exclusivo de los habitantes de los chalets. Más allá, a la sombra de unos eucaliptos, dos mujeres están sentadas en unas hamacas. Una de ellas tiene la cabeza cubierta con una redecilla, y mira con angustia la quie tud de la niña, imaginando tal vez que el asunto estriba en descubrir las fantásticas formas sugeridas por el trazado del agua en la burbuja. En todo caso toma por concentración lo que sólo es una desesperada tentativa de suprimir el movimiento, y se siente francamente alarmada; no es posible, musita, estarse quieta sin coger frío, y además la niña no sabe nadar bien, y con la burbuja desabrochada puede ahogarse. ¿Cómo obligarla a que se abroche …

Atonement

The foam flotation device is flecked with very fine, oval-shaped drops, which struggle to withstand the imperceptible rocking motion the girl uses to attempt to stay afloat.

Though there is the desire to prevent the bright drops of sunshine from running off the surface of the float, it is extremely difficult to keep still, first because it sinks a little, and then she rules out this approach, because the slightest movement proves too much for the drops, which break apart to either side, leaving behind a trail of droplets too imperceptible to be worthy of contemplation.

A narrow sign at the entrance to the enclosure warns that the pool is for the exclusive use of residents. Beyond the entrance, in the shade of some eucalyptus trees, two women sit on deckchairs. One of them, her head ensconced in a hairnet, watches the girl's stillness anxiously, imagining perhaps that the fun is in discovering the fantastic shapes suggested by the water's traces left on the float. In any event, she takes for concentration what is little more than a desperate attempt to suppress movement, and she is frankly alarmed. *It's not possible*, she mutters, *to keep still without getting cold*, and anyway, the girl can't swim very well and could drown if she doesn't fasten the float. How to make her strap it on? Over the days, the woman has grown decidedly fearful of interrupting the girl's games and any decision on the matter presents itself as a humiliating task. The girl has taken to fleeing from her and hiding all over, forcing her to search high and low. The woman is fat, the weather is hot, and she has been aging helplessly for ten years now.

Now, aware that she has been under observation for quite some time, and with an instinct for the right moment, the girl circles the pool and takes up position in a small bend where she is out of sight and, no longer mindful of the float or the drops, waits for the waddling gait of her aunt, who, as always when caught up in such dilemmas, has consulted Estrella.

"The girl can swim, Adela," is all she gets in reply.

Adela pays her no heed. She gets up and heads over to where the swimming pool follows a haphazard curve, which is where the girl waits for her, despite not once lifting her gaze towards her. Taking care not to slip, she enters the water little by little down the ladder and swims in circles cautiously around her niece, backing off every now and then to avoid raising the girl's suspicion, wishing not only to watch over her but also to receive an invitation to take part in her game. The girl, clutching the float tightly, retreats to the other side, but her aunt follows her for a while, always stealthily and without losing hope of an invitation until, finally, resentful, she is forced to content herself with her solitary swim and keeping watch from afar.

The most hideous hour of the day draws near: the return home. Climbing the steep road, feeling the cold walls against wet fabric and toes, and the hands pulling off her bathing suit, drying her with a chafing towel and dressing her in a t-shirt and shorts to be worn until evening. These images swiftly follow in each other's wake through the girl's mind, first prompting a slight sense of unease, but then giving way to a delighted self-awareness, to which the girl succumbs, as if dead; her arm left limp across the float to avoid any effort, a pleasure comparable only to the early morning, when her limbs again make contact with the water. The midday standstill casts her small body in an unreal light. The aunt observes long and hard, now on dry land, dazed by the sun, the floating body about to make her erupt, and says to herself: she's playing dead on purpose. On purpose! She stops this train of thought and then blames herself: I'm the crazy one. She stops herself again, confused, and finally walks over to the girl and, rising over her, screams. The girl reacts swiftly, sticking her tongue out at her aunt, somewhat unsure, wavering between an accusing and a disturbed look, the embarrassment of having been caught communing with the water and the fresh pleasure of flight, concentrated in her arms and legs, which flap quickly, imitating a frog's movements. —Croak, croak!—she cries, defiant.

The ritual is the same every day of the week. Adela approaches, fat body shuddering in reaction to the horror produced by contact with a child's body that rejects her, forcing her to issue orders from the side of the swimming pool. The girl doesn't move; she falls deaf all of a sudden, or splashes around with all her might. The aunt fails to pick up on the girl's fear, always bewildered by the spectacle of disobedience stubbornly and unconsciously pushed to the limit. Adela yells, but her voice, too low in pitch, cracks under the force of the protest never quite fully realized, never with the necessary authority to be obeyed. It is precisely the woman's weakness that frightens the girl, which in turn triggers rejection, more so as there is nothing that can make the girl understand this hateful state of affairs: an aunt beside herself because of a disgusting, spoiled little brat. That power is still too great, too much to bear. Too great without words.

At last, Estrella makes her triumphant entrance, which consists of taking her place at Adela's side and shooting the girl a look that says: come now, don't make your aunt suffer. The zeal with which the girl obeys her becomes part of the game of disobedience, and the better the staging—the quicker her exit from the water and the more adoringly she looks at Estrella—the more the aunt's lip quivers, appalled by the farce. The girl casts a fleeting glance at her aunt before she sets off towards the house without waiting for them, in search perhaps of an "I hope you drown," but instead finding nothing more than the same pained, barren expression. The victory then takes on a bitter taste. Without the need for words, she is now besmirched, although she soon forgets it on the steep road home; she looks at the villas and amuses herself by coveting all those spatial dispositions, of slight and vast differences.

The residential complex is made up of some twenty seventies-style chalets, which ascend the side of the hill and all have large, parched gardens, full of rock rose and other shrubs. At Adela's home, only the flower beds that surround the house are painstakingly cared for, lush with jasmine, geraniums, pansies and begonias to the front, and to the rear with fruit trees and an extraordinary mimosa bursting with yellow flowers that gives off a very thick scent, which constitutes the signature aroma of the area. In the part facing the mountain, which can be accessed by descending steep steps, there is an enormous round stone table, with four equally enormous benches. Firewood is piled up at the back and all the thickets have been cleared away. Playing there is a bore, and the girl only goes down when she wants to see the mountain through the wire fencing, as there is nothing to come between her and the mountain beyond her aunt's house. It is the last and highest of the houses.

The most captivating image is that of the road—little more than a line in the hazy dust cloud, dissected by the sunlight glinting off the cars—which advance at great speed. At night, the sound is thrown into sharp relief, whereas when the sun is at its highest point it is just a gentle drone, even though noise is largely absent from the days. The girl sometimes keeps a very watchful eye on the passing of the cars. When one approaches, she waits with supreme impatience, because from the moment the sound is first heard until the car makes its appearance, the waiting period stretches out endlessly, and vision, strained to the farthest point on the horizon, is distorted one hundredfold by the shimmering heat. At last, the car draws near, glittering, and passes by. The sensation it leaves behind heightens until it too disappears in the distance, and everything falls quieter than before. A kind of mystery then seems to emanate from the earth and spreads out forming a landscape of small, arid red-tinged hills.

The road, the mountain, the light, the scent of jasmine and freshly watered flowerbeds, the pleasant passing of the hours, and even the muggy heat. All of this forms part of the spell cast by mute things, whose existence is fragile in comparison with that of the real world, so solid and bewildering—Adela, Estrella, neighbors who come to visit and ask her questions such as "And what do you want to be when you grow up?"—or, for example, now, staying in the kitchen while Estrella untangles her hair and the aunt prepares lunch, enveloped in atmosphere you could cut with a knife, the result of her disobedience at the pool and which means that neither woman utters a word to the other; nothing but the slow untangling, *ras, ras*, the slicing of the stuffed chicken, *tock, tock, tock*; spaced out sounds and the heavy silence outside and within them, above all outside and within, as if the aunt's movements were a sounding board. The girl closes her eyes, exhausted by so much swimming and the feeling of catastrophe and the reproaches and silence, and in this momentary darkness, says, "I'll brush my hair."

"Then go outside and let it dry off. And don't move."

The girl races outside. Once there, she sits on the stairs that lead to the entrance to the chalet, where she can hear the enraged voices in the kitchen, although she cannot make out the words. She is too afraid to move closer to the door to listen, and when she considers that her hair has been untangled, rather than prick up her ears and risk discovering something about herself, she starts making small, guttural noises. Raising her head, she finds the aunt's face framed by the window, sallow-skinned, keeping watch. Her expression is by now an all too familiar sight for the little girl and thus the one she most despises, and it is horrific to behold now for the simple reason that it is too early for such an eruption, which, on the other hand, takes place every night: her malign powers denounced by the aunt to her mother in the unchanging format: "I can't take the girl any longer,

Inés." Too early, and the day is therefore already ruined. Indeed, rather than complaints, cruel, scathing words issue forth from the old woman's lips:

"You are bad and you'll be the death of me. But mark my words; you won't leave here the same way you came."

For an instant, all that can be seen is a disembodied head, a deeply embittered, ghostly, and menacing head. The girl becomes very serious, her eyes shut as if she hadn't heard anything, wishing the head would vanish. When she opens them, the aunt will have to have gone. However, Adela stays there for several long minutes. The girl, despising her more than ever and seized by a great inner violence, resolves not to grant her the ultimate pleasure of making her presence felt, and keeps her eyes shut tight, just as when they make her stay in the living room after lunch for fear of heatstroke, although what occurs then has a different feel; it is a clinging sensation and has nothing to do with the girl herself, but rather with her surroundings. Furtive glances, the ticking clock, the drawn curtains and the heavy breathing of the women slumbering on the sofa; dead calm in which the child remains quiet, very quiet, with her eyes shut, as now, engrossed in the many-colored specks of light, until, sometimes, Estrella wakes up and, seeing her in a trance, asks her,

"What are you frightened of Clarita?"

The girl looks at her sadly. A feeling akin to helplessness descends and she knows herself to be infinitesimally small before the aunt, for whose love she feels utter revulsion.

As always when she falls into such a fretful state, the girl thinks, until finding something—an explanation, a fantasy or, quite simply, what to do—that restores her, because now, and in spite of her primal and just rebellion, that other is causing her to falter; a sort of remorse when faced with herself, immobilized. It is a terribly distressing feeling since, if she cannot come up with a solution fast, the train of events will come to a standstill with her aunt, and nothing that happens after that will touch it. She will no longer be able to play normally, to see normally, or do anything normally, until she ceases to feel it in her temples and in the pit of her stomach. Adela is conjured up in truly sinister tones, enabling the girl to give herself over to the role of victim, gritting her teeth hard and muttering: *she's an idiot, she's an idiot*, and as that certainty fails to take hold and one half of her brain is already accepting what her instinct rejects—her real, serious, and disgustingly adult responsibility—she finds herself sliding little by little towards kindness, more for herself than in any honest desire to please, only to rid herself of the clinging sensation and fall once again into the hole of just rebellion, like the pendulum on a clock. She passes quite some time like this, seated on the stairs and without coming to any decision because it is all too complicated, until, finally, just like that, she winds up being reasonable—and that word she does understand, because the grown-ups use it endlessly, something like to lovingly obey—and with great serenity she thinks, or rather feels, that her aunt is right, in part; for example when the table has been so painstakingly set and she hasn't been scolded and everything is laid out for her own pleasure. And that is just as horrific as the first scenario—to know oneself hated—because then guilt descends, and then let's say that only the woman's erratic state of mind saves her from being truly evil.

Redeemed and oblivious, because Adela has at last disappeared from the window frame and her thoughts have put her emotions in some sort of order, the girl stands up and, treading fearfully, heads towards the rear of the house, in spite of the ban on leaving the porch. To draw strength she must continue to disobey, and anyway, it feels so good to know oneself alone, out of range of the old women. She pauses next to the yellow mimosa and says, "mimosa, mimosa!"

Then adds in hushed tones, "We can't speak loudly, because those stupid women might catch on."

She falls silent, in ecstatic contemplation of the tree, an eccentric, hallucinatory yellow. It is a quarter to three in the afternoon and there is no sign of movement in the adjacent houses, or on the road. The household noises from the kitchen have also ceased and all that can be heard is the beating wings of the cicadas, and the very stillness of the air, enveloping, as if it came to rest on things and made them shine. The fruit trees, the prickly pears, the specks of dust, the edge of the flower beds, an insect's flight.

Everything takes on an unfamiliar air, and the feeling is that one could be anywhere, thanks to the mute presence of things, so strange. The girl takes stock of this vibrant state, making it vanish and returning her gaze to the tree, although with no outcome other than being overwhelmed by the heat and blurred vision. The yellow shafts of light fade away, and the game then consists of making everything fade away, until her eyes begin to hurt. She then sits down, since, despite the momentary clarity, she is unable to shake off the darkness, and for this reason and without wishing to, she sets to thinking, to thinking and imagining and remembering; "You cause me pain," Adela had told her one evening, pain, pain, pain, and with all her being she rejects this word, dark and dry as a muggy afternoon trapped inside the house.

"Your aunt and I have been talking about you, Clara," says Estrella as she takes her seat at the table. The girl concentrates, feigning seriousness.

"You are a bright girl and you must have realized that things cannot go on like this. Your behavior is utterly ungrateful and your aunt is very sensitive and she cannot allow herself such nerves."

The girl nods. She already knows what Estrella is about to say, what with her parents and the school being closed and it's all terribly upsetting. And, sure enough, Estrella says,

"And even though it'll be a problem for her to have to take you home, it'll be an even bigger problem for your parents and for you, Clara, because your school is still closed and they have nowhere to leave you."

The girl continues to look serious, although she can't help glancing at the chicken out of the corner of her eye, served meticulously on the plates, the salad to the left, the beans to the right; a presentation worthy of a restaurant, and the hunger that comes over her almost like suffering. She stops listening for a while, concentrating instead on the gestures of the two women in order to avoid looking at the chicken and thus betray her indifference, until the tone is raised and she listens once more,

"So then, do you know why you have to behave?"

The question, as unanswerable as those her aunt asks her, is addressed to her, and this takes her momentarily by surprise. She normally endures the lecture without anyone asking for her contribution. Since it is impossible to extricate herself, she ends up saying,

"Just because."

"That's not an explanation," says Estrella, falling silent once more, awaiting a more satisfactory response. The silence weighs very heavy and the woman, exasperated, takes up the thread. "First of all, you have to obey because you're just a little girl, and all little girls obey until they're grown up. Do you understand that?"

The girl replies, "yes."

"What's more," she continues, "all the more reason to obey when the person in charge is from your own family, and even more so," and here, her voice cracks, rising again in pitch to a shout, "if you are the responsibility of that person, who right now is your aunt! Do you understand?"

The girl's yes escapes in a whisper, and is almost flattened by the next question:

"And do you know why?"

The girl shakes her head.

"Well I'll tell you why! You have to respect your elders, and when they are also part of your own family, you have to love them! Do you hear me? Do you love your aunt?"

The girl nods.

"Well then, are you going to behave yourself?"

"Yes," replies the girl half-heartedly.

"Say it then. We want to hear it from you loud and clear."

"I'm going to behave myself and love my aunt very much."

"Give me a kiss," says the aunt, fat beneath her dress, her arms stretched out like tentacles, suppressing a sea of tears. "From now on, you're a good girl. Get over here and give me a kiss, and another one for Estrella."

The girl rises and barely brushes her cheek, likewise with Estrella. Satisfied, the two women launch themselves at the chicken, which they devour in no time. The girl also gulps it down as fast as she can, wishing the lunch to be over with as soon as possible. She then asks permission to spend the afternoon playing on the balcony and Adela, overwhelmed by so much reconciliation, although no less fearful, lets her leave. The girl enters her domain in a flash, and sprints to check that the road is still in place, and that the tree is still in place, and that the mountain remains still and mysterious through the wire fencing, and after this dash she has to lean against a flower bed, because her body doubles over seized by a cramp, and she ends up vomiting, and then crying in rage because Adela and Estrella have seen her from the window, and her aunt has said for all to hear:

"Just like me when I was frightened. That girl is just as sensitive as me."

The Collier's Faith
of my Mother

Tomas Lieske
Translated by Willem Groenewegen
Dutch (The Netherlands)

Tomas Lieske (1943), although only making his debut at the age of 38, is the prize-winning author of many novels and poetry collections. According to critic Rob Schouten "his core business is style, and magic, myth and the indescribable."

The poem "The Collier's Faith of my Mother" is from Lieske's 2006 volume *Hoe je geliefde te herkennen* (How to Recognize Your Lover). In 2007, this book won Lieske the VSB Poetry Prize, the most prestigious Dutch prize for a single volume. At the time, critic Piet Gerbrandy wrote about the book: "The volume, in all its baroque wittiness, is highly sacral in places. Very moving [...] a poem about the deep-felt religiosity of a Catholic mother."

This religiosity is summed up in the title phrase *kolenbranders-geloof*—a very difficult term to translate. It is Catholic in origin, literally meaning "charcoal burner's faith" defined as "perfunctory faith" (*Van Dale* Dutch-language dictionary) and "the perfection of Roman Catholic faith: 'I believe whatsoever the church teaches.'" (quote from Charles Elliott, *Delineation of Roman Catholicism*). Although I couldn't find a direct Dutch-English translation, I did manage to locate the French equivalent phrase "*foi du charbonnier*" and the German "*Köhlerglaube.*" I then sent these on to a theologian friend, who entered the phrases into various databases and came up with the 1841 book by the Rev. Charles Elliott describing it as "collier's faith," which sounds far better in both title and poem than "charcoal burner's faith," with the assonance of "collier" and "mother."

The poem affectionately describes the mother's devout belief in a homely God: "a small god / in a donkey jacket," a domestic God "to help her / in case of toddlers falling ill, of fires, of money misplaced." Sacred, yes, but of human proportions. It is therefore understandable that "all the gods [...] had the face of her husband whom she loved."

The poem could only be Lieske's. Some of his best work brings the religious, the mythical, and the historical down to size. Among the poems that I translated for the 41st Poetry International Rotterdam Festival in 2010, for example, was one about the tomb of Egyptian Queen Notmit seen from the perspective of a mummified shrewmouse.

Original text: Tomas Lieske, "Het kolenbrandersgeloof van mijn moeder" from *Hoe je geliefde te herkennen*. Amsterdam: Querido, 2006.

Het kolenbrandersgeloof
van mijn moeder

Wat zij geloofde was helder en stralend van eenvoud,
een zalig stromen van wat haar was ingeprent en waarop zij hoopte.

De vinger van God liet de zon om de aarde draaien,
de engelen vulden de hemelse concertzalen onder contract.

De zielen van de gestorvenen grepen zich vast aan schoeisel,
aan laatst gedragen kleren, aan de randen van de bedden.

Zij geloofde in een stampvolle hemel waar als bij een receptie
te veel mensen waren genodigd zonder dat er ruzie ontstond.

Goden, engelen en heiligen namen hun hiërarchieën
zonder morren in acht. Zij geloofde in een kleine god

in een bonkertje, een kort boerenjasje, in een godin
die zich aantoddikte met blauwwitte lappen,

in een reeks huisgoden, privé-heiligen die haar moesten helpen
bij de ziekte van kleuters, bij brand, bij zoekgeraakt geld

The Collier's Faith of my Mother

What she believed was clear and beamed with simplicity,
a blissful flow imprinted upon her and that she hankered after.

God's finger let the sun revolve around the earth,
the angels filled the heavenly concert halls according to contract.

The souls of the deceased held tight to shoes,
to last worn clothes, to the edges of beds.

She believed in a crowded heaven where, as at a reception,
too many people had been invited without there being a row.

Gods, angels and saints respected their hierarchies
without a fuss. She believed in a small god

in a donkey jacket, a short farmer's coat, in a goddess
who ragged herself up with blue-and-white cloth,

in a series of household gods, private saints that were to help her
in case of toddlers falling ill, of fires, of money misplaced

en haar eigen priesteressen-spreuken mompelend
schikte zij de beelden van deze penaten, de uiterlijke rommel

die het geloof in haar kop had veroorzaakt, de kolenbranders
die er stampten en die hun eindeloze litanie zongen.

Maar alle heiligen, alle goden, alle engelen hadden het gezicht
van de man die zij liefhad en zij verwierp ieder die haar

over het geloof onderrichtte en die zichzelf een belangrijke
ratel toedichtte en die niet leek op wie zij liefhad.

and mumbling her own priestess's chants
she arranged the statues of these penates, the visible jumble

that faith had caused in her head, the colliers
who tramped around inside and sang their endless litanies.

But all the saints, all the gods, all the angels had the face
of her husband whom she loved and she rejected those who

lectured her on faith and who ascribed an important rattle
to themselves and who did not resemble the one she loved.

Unter den Linden

Margarita Ríos-Farjat
Translated by Matthew Brennan
Spanish (Mexico)

Margarita Ríos-Farjat and I have the kind of poet-translator relationship that translators wish for but never dare to expect. She has always maintained that my English translations are my work. At the same time, Margarita's English is good enough that she can read my translations and advise me on my interpretations of her original meaning. While most translators have to deal with one extreme or the other—the author they're translating is dead, or the author is possessive of the work—Margarita finds a balance right in the middle. She advises me toward making the best representation of her poem in English while allowing me the freedom and permission to interpret them as I see fit.

Margarita is an attorney in Monterrey, Mexico. As a poet, she was a Fellow at the Nuevo Leon Writer's Centre, and the winner of several contests: *Literatura Universitaria, Poesia Joven de Monterrey*, and *Nacional de Ensayo Juridico* (2000). She is the author of two books of poems: *Si las horas llegaran para quedarse* (If the Hours Would Come To Stay), and *Cómo usar los ojos* (How To Use the Eyes). Her poetry has appeared in several anthologies and many magazines in Mexico, and she is a regular Op-Ed contributor to Monterrey's leading newspaper, *El Norte*. "Unter den Linden" is the first English publication of Margarita's poetry.

Margarita's poems are as versatile as they are lovely. Her language runs the spectrum from simple elegance to academic sophistication. Her subject matter ranges from the smallest human moments to poems like "Unter den Linden," which examines post-wall Berlin. The repetitive structure grounded my translation process, but there were still a few questions I had to work through. The first was the title, which is in German for both the English and Spanish versions. I had put it into English ("Under the Lindens") before deciding that preserving the German was more in line with Margarita's intention—foreign to both our languages—yet still decipherable to an English reader.

In the second line, Margarita writes, "*sobre el espejo del agua en el suelo,*" which in English is literally: "over the mirror of the water on the ground." While this image works in English, I made two alterations that I felt made the language more precise: the water mirror became a "reflecting pool" and I changed the ground to "the street." I encountered a more difficult challenge in line 18, where Margarita writes: "*sobre la vida que arroja el final de la muerte.*" Translated literally, it works out as, "over the life that throws the end of death." The problem here was that my translation wasn't matching what I knew she meant. By changing this to, "the life that shakes free of the final death," the meaning becomes more about a city recovering from war.

Original text: Margarita Ríos-Farjat, "Unter den linden" from *Cómo usar los ojos*. Mexico: Conarte, 2010.

Unter den linden

Bajo las hojas serenas del tilo
    sobre el espejo del agua en el suelo
bajo el cielo vuelto negro un día
    sobre la ceniza de todos los cielos
bajo el trazo negro de la historia
    sobre la negra penitencia histórica
bajo ecos de columna militar
    sobre la columna vertebral de la ciudad
bajo la Puerta de Brandemburgo
    sobre los libros ardiendo en la puerta del tiempo
bajo la roja estela del humo
    sobre un muro disperso en el polvo
bajo el pasado de ventanas en astillas
    sobre la ciudad saqueada
bajo memorias rasgadas en lluvias de fuego
    sobre las hojas caídas, sobre los hijos de viento
bajo las nuevas ramas de los árboles
    sobre la vida que arroja el final de la muerte
Bajo los Tilos camino sobre la historia
    sobre la cicatriz que recorre el corazón de Berlín

Unter den Linden

Under the serene leaves of the linden tree
    over the reflecting pool in the street
under the sky turned dark one day
    over the ashes of all the skies
under the dark line of history
    over the black historic penitence
under the echoes of military columns
    over the spine of the city
under the Brandenburg Gate
    over the books burning in the doorway of time
under the red trail of smoke
    over a wall scattered in the dust
under the past of splintered windows
    over the looted city
under memories torn by raining fire
    over the fallen leaves, over the sons of wind
under the new branches of the trees
    over the life that shakes free of the final death
Under the Linden Trees I walk along history
    over the scar that crosses the heart of Berlin

"My love for you is deeply animal…"

Shez
Translated by Elliott batTzedek
Hebrew (Israel)

Shez (an acronym for *shem zamani* or "temporary name") published *Dance of the Lunatic,* her first book and only poetry collection, in 1999. She has been widely reviewed in both the gay and mainstream media and received numerous awards, including the Ron Adler Prize for Poetry and a short story competition for Mediterranean women.

With its striking images and resonant language, *Dance of the Lunatic* is a midrash of incest and desire. Fragmented images of the sexual violence Shez experienced as a child inform every part of this book, as does her resistance and resilience: in the opening poem, a tree struggles with the memory of having been broken, hammered into, and urinated on by dogs, but still knows that its head is in the heavens and that its leaves are caressed by God's breath; in the closing poem, she envisions a day of redemption in which fathers who rape are finally silenced so terrorized girls can be heard.

However, Shez is also writing the story of her adult life, which includes humorous, sweet, and sensual love poems. This was the first book of completely open, unapologetically lesbian poems published in Israel, and still stands as one of only a few. Because it is a lesbian book, the expression of gendered language is a central stylistic issue. Shez places the question of the female "you" front and center in many of these poems, sometimes even adding the female you *("at")* for clarity and emphasis even when the verb form carries that information. The very cadence and sound of her work in Hebrew are defined by gender, for the sound of all the words ending with the female "you" (*at/-eikh)* is so different from writing to or about a male "you" (*ata/-kha).* The prevalence of this gendered-female grammar does not, however, mean that Shez writes with any kind of "feminine" softness. In the tradition of the definitive Israeli bisexual poet Yona Wallach, Shez's language is strong, forceful, confrontational, and explicitly sexual.

A woman writing to a woman, and a woman writing to a female-gendered God, means every choice of "you" is a social statement—and an ongoing translation challenge when working in English, with its ungendered "you." It is an issue familiar to me as a lesbian poet writing in English—if I write a love poem to a "you," how do I make that poem a lesbian poem? I want my writing to resist the silencing of lesbian lives. As a poet, I must at times value message over music. As a translator, I find myself making similar trade-offs. When working with one of Shez's poems which cannot make even plain sense if the "you" is perceived as male, I use a structure such as "Woman, you." When that information isn't absolutely necessary, as in this poem, I make the best English poem I can. Sometimes I follow the advice of Chana Block and Chana Kronfeld in their introduction to *Hovering at a Low Altitude: The Collected Poetry of Dahlia Ravikovitch* and try to choose verbs or adjectives that, to the U.S. ear, seem more "feminine" then "masculine." Generally, I am trusting that, in the context of the book as a whole, with its poems featuring breasts and cunts, the lesbian content will speak powerfully.

Original text: Shez, "ahavati elayich m'od gash'mit…" from *Rikud Ham'shuga'at.* Bnei Brak: Hakibbutz Hameuchad – Sifriat Poalim Publishing Group, 1999.

"אַהַבְתִּי אֶלָּךְ מְאֹד גַּשְׁמִית..."

אַהַבְתִּי אֶלָּךְ מְאֹד גַּשְׁמִית
אֲנִי אוֹהֶבֶת לִשְׂחוֹת בָּךְ
כְּמוֹ דָּגִיג בֶּן יוֹמוֹ
שֶׁאֵינוֹ זוֹכֵר אֶת עֲבָרוֹ
וְהוּא חֲסַר מִלִּים וְשֵׁנַּם
וְאַף פַּעַם הוּא לֹא מְתַקְתֵּק אוֹתִיּוֹת עַל מְכוֹנַת־כְּתִיבָה אוֹ
שׁוֹתֶה וִיסְקִי
אוֹ צוֹרֵחַ כְּמוֹ חַיָּה רָעָה כְּשֶׁסֶּרֶט הַכְּתִיבָה יוֹצֵא מֵהַמָּקוֹם

"My love for you is deeply animal…"

My love for you is deeply animal
I love to swim in you
like a newborn minnow
who does not remember her past
who lacks words and even teeth
and who has never, not even once, sat ticking letters on a typewriter
    or drinking whiskey
or screaming like a hellish beast as the ribbon of writing emerges
    from the room

Three Stories

A. L. Snijders
Translated by Lydia Davis
Dutch (The Netherlands)

According to Snijders's publisher, "Newspapers often introduce the writer with words like anarchist, dadaist, pig farmer, motorcycle-rider, stoic. Snijders doesn't mind."

A. L. Snijders was born in 1937 in Amsterdam. In 1971, he moved to Achterhoek, a quiet, wooded region in the east of the Netherlands where many of his animal stories are set.

In the 1980s, Snijders began writing newspaper columns, and in 2006, his first collection of what he calls "zkv's" ("*zeer korte verhalen*," or "very short stories") was published by AFdH Uitgevers. It was titled *Belangrijk is dat ik niet aan lezers denk* (The Important thing is that I don't think about the readers). Several collections followed, and in November, 2010, Snijders was awarded the Constantijn Huygens Prize, one of the three most important literary prizes in Holland, in recognition of his work as a whole and especially his zkv's. Snijders has by now written over 1500 zkv's and continues to write as many as one per week. In March, 2012, AFdH published his sixth collection.

I have translated from languages other than French, including some I really didn't know at all, such as Swedish. In each case it has been an adventure. I had not thought of translating from the Dutch until I visited Amsterdam last May. I asked a Dutch editor to recommend a writer of short-shorts, and he suggested A. L. Snijders.

Back at home, I did my best to read some of his work using the tiny, yellow, stained travel dictionary with missing pages that had made its way onto my shelf, probably brought back from a trip of my parents' to Amsterdam long ago. Since I know some German, I did not find most of the stories impossible, and some were quite accessible. I liked the modesty of the subject matter, the concreteness of the narration, the good humor, wit, and thoughtful conclusions. And for a beginner in the language, Snijders's style was just right: as he himself has confessed, he does not like long sentences. My little dictionary was somewhat useful, but soon enough internet resources took over—much faster, and especially useful for references to places in Amsterdam or to literary and political figures, which Snijders uses plentifully. I had a good time. When I had achieved a respectable version in English, I would ask one or another Dutch correspondent to read over the translation, and with his help, correcting blunders and shifting nuances, I would arrive at finished versions of these very satisfying little in-part-true moments from Snijders's life.

From my experience as a beginner in Dutch translation, then, I can conclude (not always surprisingly) that: concrete action is easier to understand; short sentences are easier; repetition of words is helpful; the more stories I read the better I can anticipate the tone or direction of the next (though they all contain surprises); cognates are helpful (Dutch *gisteren*, German *gestern* for "yesterday"; Dutch *vrouw*, German *frau* for "wife"); words foreign to both Dutch and English can provide a moment of relief (*sacerdos, sacerdos*). Whimsical jumps in logic can be momentarily baffling ("You can measure the age of the earth by the covering on his legs"); beware of false friends (*haan* is not "hen" but "rooster"); echoes of idioms are inevitably lost ("and I'm not lying" echoes a phrase very commonly tagged onto the end of a remark in Dutch conversation, my Dutch informants tell me).

Original text: A. L. Snijders, "Want zijn vrouw" from *Belangrijk is dat ik niet aan lezers denk*. Enschede: AFdH Uitgevers, 2006. "Boodschap" and "Zes woorden" from *Brandnetels & verkeersborden*. Enschede/Doetinchem: AFdH Uitgevers, 2012.

Want zijn vrouw

De haan is zo oud als een krokodil. De ouderdom van de aarde kun je afmeten aan de bekleding van zijn poten, aan de blik in zijn ogen, aan de lellen onder zign snavel, aan zijn slinkende kam. Van een jongeling in een jutezak is hij priester geworden, *sacerdos, sacerdos*. Als hij kraait, hoor je dat de dood een catastrofe is. Toch is dit maar een deel van de mythe. *Want zijn vrouw.* Zijn vrouw is een kip, net zo oud als hij. Vroeger bruin, maar nu helemaal wit (ik herhaal, en lieg niet, dat deze kip van bruin naar wit is gegaan in haar verkleurende kippenleven). Lang geleden is ze opgehouden met leggen. De natuur, zeggen de kenners, Zo is de natuur, het is natuurlijk. Maar nu is de witte kip weer gaan leggen. Eergisteren een ei, en gisteren nog een.

Because His Wife

The rooster is as old as a crocodile. You can measure the age of the earth by the covering on his legs, by the look in his eyes, by the wattles under his beak, by his shrinking comb. From a youngster in a burlap bag he has become a priest, *sacerdos*, *sacerdos*. When he crows, you can hear that death is a catastrophe. Yet this is only part of the myth. *Because his wife...* His wife is a chicken, just as old as he. Brown at one time, but now completely white (I repeat, and I'm not lying, that this chicken has gone from brown to white in her color-losing chicken-life). Long ago she stopped laying eggs. Nature, say the experts, such is nature, it's natural. But now the white chicken has started laying again. The day before yesterday one egg, and yesterday another.

Boodschap

Je ontmoet zelden christenen die hun mond houden over Jezus. Dat is logisch, want zijn boodschap is: Vertel het aan iedereen, ik ben de Weg, de Waarheid en het Leven. En niet alleen de christenen hebben deze pretentie, ook de islamieten zijn volstrekt overtuigd van hun gelijk. Als atheïst zit je goed in het verdomhoekje.

Een deel van mijn familie is vegetarisch, ik eet vlees en moet mijn bloeddorst vaak met hoon bekopen. Ik ben eraan gewend door christenen, mohammedanen en vegetariërs beschimpt te worden. Maar soms is er een gelegenheid tot wraak.

Ik rijd met mijn vegetariërs in de auto van Gorssel naar Deventer. Ik zie een kat van rechts uit het bermgras komen, gebiologeerd door een prooi aan de overkant. Ik zie dat hij plotseling zal versnellen – ik ken m'n dieren – en de weg onbeheerst zal oversteken. Ik toeter driftig en langdurig, ik wek hem uit zijn trance, ik red zijn leven. De vegetariërs hebben niets gemerkt. De christenen merken ook niet dat ik mijn naaste liefheb, om van de mohammedanen maar te zwijgen. Ikzelf zwijg erover, want ik leef zonder boodschap.

Message

You seldom meet Christians who keep their mouths shut about Jesus. That is logical, for his message is: Tell it to everyone, I am the Way, the Truth, and the Life. And Christians are not alone in having these claims, Muslims are also unfailingly convinced they are correct. As an atheist you are one of the doomed.

Part of my family is vegetarian, I eat meat and must often pay for my bloodthirstiness with heavy mockery. I have become accustomed to being taunted about this by Christians, Mohammedans, and vegetarians. But sometimes there is an opportunity for revenge.

I'm driving in the car with my vegetarians from Gorssel to Deventer. To the right, I see a cat coming out of the grass on the shoulder, mesmerized by his prey on the far side of the road. I see that he will suddenly accelerate—I know my animals—and will cross the road without any self-restraint. I honk the horn passionately for a long time, I wake him out of his trance, I save his life. The vegetarians haven't noticed anything. The Christians also don't notice that I love my neighbor, to say nothing of the Mohammedans. I myself say nothing about it, because I live without messages.

Zes woorden

In het crematorium spreekt een dochter over haar vader die in de kist ligt. Ik ken haar niet, haar vader kende ik de laatste vijfentwintig jaar van zijn leven, de halve eeuw daarvoor was hij voor mij een anoniem geschiedenisboek. Dat gebeurt steeds vaker, je ontmoet mensen met een onbekend verleden, misschien zijn ze fascist geweest of antroposoof, misschien hebben ze in de gevangenis gezeten of op het seminarie, je weet het niet, je moet voorzichtig zijn met je grapjes, je weet niet waar hun zenuwen blootliggen, je weet niet wie hun vrouwen zijn geweest en waar hun kinderen zijn gebleven.

De dochter spreekt haar vader aan, soms zegt ze pappa, soms zingt haar stem. Het is een mooie, zonnige zomermorgen, het leven is volbracht, de leeftijd is goed, het verdriet dragelijk. Ik zit bij het grote raam en kijk naar de tuin, waar een gedrongen Japanse boom staat. Ik weet weinig van de inrichting van ons land. Wie is de eigenaar van het crematorium? Een particulier die flink verdient aan het vuur? Een consortium met een brievenbus op de Kaaiman Eilanden? Of gewoon de overheid? Dat zou ik prefereren, ik vind dat alles van de overheid moet zijn, vooral de treinen en de post.

De dochter vertelt dat haar vader als achttienjarige jongen in een bootje het water opging om te schilderen en dan alles vergat. Ik denk 'Wat is het leven prachtig.' Ze vertelt dat hij tweeëneenhalf jaar voor

Six Words

In the crematorium, a daughter is talking about her father, who lies in the coffin. I don't know her, I knew him during the last twenty-five years of his life, for the half century before that he was for me an anonymous history book. That happens more and more often, you meet people with an unknown past, perhaps they were fascists or anthroposophists, perhaps they were in prison or in a seminary, you don't know, you have to be careful with your little jokes, you don't know which of their nerves is raw, you don't know who their wives were or where their children remained.

The daughter speaks to her father, sometimes she says "pappa," sometimes her voice sings. It is a beautiful, sunny summer morning, the life has come to an end, the age is good, the grief is bearable. I sit by the large window and look at the garden, where a compact Japanese tree stands. I know little about the organization of our country. Who is the owner of the crematorium? A private person who profits handsomely from the fire? A consortium with a mailbox on the Cayman Islands? Or simply the government? That is what I would prefer, I think everything should belong to the government, especially the trains and the mail.

The daughter tells us that as an eighteen-year-old boy her father went off over the water in a little boat to paint and then forgot

straf op de heide heeft gewerkt, hij wilde geen soldaat zijn. Ik denk 'Wat is de mens tot veel in staat.' Ze zegt: 'Een echte vader was je niet.' Ik denk 'Wat een prachtige zin.'

Het gebeurt soms dat de taal zo verleidelijk is dat haar oppervlakteschoonheid een hermetisch scherm over de inhoud legt. Zo wordt het dan onthouden, een latere uitleg komt er nooit meer doorheen. Zo is het met deze zes woorden die een volmaakte toon hebben, en een raadselachtigheid die alleen bij een afscheid tot volle bloei kan komen.

Ik hoor geen bitterheid in deze zes woorden, ze glijden zachtjes van een jongen die schildert in een bootje, naar een soldaat die niet wil vechten, naar een vader die van een afstand toekijkt.

everything. I think, "How splendid life is." She tells us that for two and a half years he had worked on the moors as punishment, he did not want to be a soldier. I think, "How much men are capable of." She says: "A real father you were not." I think: "What a splendid sentence."

It sometimes happens that language is so seductive that its surface beauty lays a hermetic screen over its content. Thus is the content preserved, later explanation never penetrates. And so it is with these six words, which have a perfect tone, and a mysteriousness that can come to full bloom only through a farewell.

I hear no bitterness in these six words, they glide gently from a young man who is painting in a little boat, to a soldier who does not want to fight, to a father who looks on from a distance.

the day of the guacamayas

José Eugenio Sánchez
Translated by Anna Rosen Guercio
Spanish (Mexico)

José Eugenio Sánchez is an acclaimed poet and performer, and the author of numerous poetry collections, including *Physical graffiti*, *La felicidad es una pistola caliente*, and *Galaxy limited café*, which was a finalist for the 2010 Jaime Gil de Biedma International Poetry Prize. He calls himself an "underclown," and his work eagerly engages both pop and high culture with irreverence and insight. Originally from Guadalajara, Sánchez lives and writes in Monterrey, Mexico.

While the tone of many of his poems leans toward the quotidian and comical, closer reading reveals a freewheeling experimentalism and fragmentation responsive to his position on geographical and cultural borders. Sánchez's language is intensely contemporary, aggressively playful, and inflected with slang, diction, and grammatical cadences of both northern Mexico and the United States. His embrace of this hybridity also comes through in his subject matter, as in his love for the Mexican and American cultural artifacts to which he stakes his proper claim (e.g. identifying old Hollywood westerns with the cowboy landscape of northern Mexico), or in his raucous takes on rock music, art history, drug culture, and contemporary politics.

"El día de las guacamayas" demonstrates Sánchez's delight in absurdity, but also the dark notes that give his poems shape. These are felt here in the snubbing of the actual guacamayas ("who didn't bother dressing up"), the mounting anxiety about what's going to happen now that everyone is assembled and in costume, and those "big nasty birds" that threaten the speaker. In some ways, it's a very simple poem, the central device being the poet's delight in repeating the word "guacamaya" in nearly every line. While "guacamaya" has a perfectly functional English counterpart—macaw—to translate it as such would sacrifice the sound game that motivates the poem and drain the life out of it.

Another notable challenge was posed by the line, "*carareó un discurso sobre volar sobrevolar*," with its clever collision of "sobre volar" (about flying) with "sobrevolar" (to fly over). While I couldn't replicate the morphological trick of following two words with their compound form, I found a fun alternative in the mirrored repetition of "about flying flying about." For me, the key to translating Sánchez is understanding his dark (and very silly) sense of humor, and finding ways to have the same kind of fun with English that he's so clearly had with Spanish.

Original text: José Eugenio Sánchez, "el día de las guacamayas" from *La felicidad es una pistola caliente*. Madrid: Visor Libros, 2004.

el día de las guacamayas

cordonices disfrazadas de guacamaya
avestruces disfrazadas de guacamaya
águilas disfrazadas de guacamaya
tucanes cóndores palomas mariposas disfrazadas de guacamaya
pájaros bobo de patas azules disfrazados de guacamaya
cuervos pelícanos gorriones cenzontles cardenales disfrazados de
    guacamaya
mi periquita y yo disfrazados de guacamaya
era el día de las guacamayas

las cotorritas disfrazadas de guacamaya
les daban cortón a las guacamayas que no llevaban disfraz
las urracas disfrazadas de guacamaya picoteaban cualquier grano
mazorca o calva que espulgar
los marabúes disfrazados de guacamaya rondan
las vacas disfrazadas de guacamaya no sabían qué hacer
era el día de las guacamayas

the day of the guacamayas

quails dressed up as guacamayas
ostriches dressed up as guacamayas
eagles dressed up as guacamayas
toucans condors doves butterflies dressed up as guacamayas
blue-footed boobies dressed up as guacamayas
ravens pelicans sparrows mockingbirds cardinals dressed up as
    guacamayas
my parakeet and I dressed up as guacamayas
it was the day of the guacamayas

the little parrots dressed up as guacamayas
snub the guacamayas who didn't bother dressing up
the magpies dressed up as guacamayas were pecking at every little
    grain
cob and bare spot
the storks dressed up as guacamayas circled
the cows dressed up as guacamayas didn't have a clue what to do
it was the day of the guacamayas

mi periquita es una parava de hermosura
y algunas pajarracas disfrazadas de guacamaya
nos fruncieron el pico al vernos

pero una guacamaya disfrazada de guacamaya
carareó un discurso sobre volar sobrevolar
y el plumerío festejó hasta alzar el vuelo
y admiró a la guacamaya disfrazada de guacamaya

era el día de las guacamayas

my parakeet is a flock of beauty
and some big nasty birds dressed up as guacamayas
knit their brows when we came into view

but one guacamaya dressed up as a guacamaya
clucked a speech about flying flying about
and the assemblage of feathers celebrated till it rose in flight
and admired the guacamaya dressed up as a guacamaya

it was the day of the guacamayas

When I Return

Cao Tân
Translated by Tôn Thất Quỳnh Du
Vietnamese (Vietnam)

"Mai Mốt Anh Trở Về" ("When I Return") is from a collection titled *Thơ Cao Tân* (Cao Tân's Poems), published in California in 1978 and wholeheartedly embraced by the Vietnamese diaspora. Written barely two years after the fall of South Vietnam, the poems covered the full gamut of raw emotions that sprang from the poet's traumatic experience.

The trauma of the refugee experience is palpable. Having made it to the United States while his wife was stranded behind in Vietnam, the poet's only connection to his family were the letters from home, which had to sing loud praises of the new regime in order to pass the sharp eyes of censors. In another poem he writes: "Letters from home, like a clown seriously sick / A devastated soul beneath the mask of smiles / Gaudy make-up covers layers of bitterness / Tears in eyes, yet mouthing joyous happy lines." Drinking with his compatriots would bring some solace, nurturing big dreams, but reality always comes back in the end, "The awaking man blinks at the early morning sun / What are we to do for the rest of our lives?"

I like the way "When I Return" summarizes the present refugee experience by projecting forward to an imaginary day of return: "When I go back, if anyone asks, / What did you learn while in the US of A? / Want to see my talents? Hand me a broom stick / Tell you what, I'm a top class coolie."

Overall the tone is not one of bitterness, but a gentle kind of black humor, delivered in a particular sub-register of the Vietnamese language—a blend of acceptable street slang that's sharp, tough, and irreverent. To the translator, this brings interesting choices, even at word level. A word from this sub-register, *chì*, has semantic components of bravery, toughness, and resilience; it usually goes with marines. Juxtaposing it with housework, "I wash the dishes *chì hơn* a housewife," sends subtle humor through the image of a man at the kitchen sink realizing just how tough housework is. A Vietnamese man! Going into English, on occasions such as this, often reductionism comes to the rescue. The overall net effect is a translation that is a bit milder in tone and and not so riotous in color.

Original text: Cao Tần, "Mai Mốt Anh Trở Về" from *Thơ Cao Tần.*
Stanton: Van Nghe, 1978.

Mai mốt anh trở về

Mai mốt anh về có thằng túm hỏi
Mày qua bên Mỹ học được củ gì
Muốn biết tài nhau đưa ông cây chổi
Nói mày hay ông thượng đẳng cu li.

Ông rửa bát chì hơn bà nội trợ
Ông quét nhà sạch hơn em bé ngoan
Ngày ngày phóng xe như thằng phải gió
Đêm về nằm vùi nước mắt chứa chan

Nghệ thuật nói bỗng hóa trò lao động
Thằng nào nói nhiều thằng ấy tay to
Tiếng mẹ thường chỉ dùng chửi đổng
Hay những đêm sầu tí toáy làm thơ

Ông học được Mỹ đất trời bát ngát
Nhưng tình người nhỏ hơn que tăm
Nhiều đứa hồn nhiên giống bầy trẻ nít
Còn hồn ông: già cốc cỡ nghìn năm

When I Return

When I go back, if anyone asks,
What did you learn while in the US of A?
Want to see my talents? Hand me a broom stick
Tell you what, I'm a top class coolie

I wash dishes better than a housewife
And sweep the floor cleaner than a hard-working child
Through the day I drive like a man possessed
And at night I lie in bed crying my heart out

The art of speech becomes a physical exercise
The talkative develop thick forearms
Mother tongue is reserved for vague curses
And melancholic nights toying with poetry

I've learned that America is huge and large
But human kindness is toothpick in size
Most of them innocent and child-like
But my soul is old and withered

Bài học lớn từ khi đến Mỹ
Là ngày đêm thương nước mênh mang
Thù hận bọn làm nước ông nghèo xí
Hận gấp nghìn lần khi chúng đánh ông văng

Nếu mai mốt bỗng đổi đời phen nữa
Ông anh hùng ông cứu được quê hương
Ông sẽ mở ra nghìn lò cải tạo
Lùa cả nước vào học tập yêu thương

Cuộc chiến cũ sẽ coi là tiền kiếp
Phản động gì cũng chỉ sống trăm năm
Bổ bịch hết không đứa nào là ngụy
Thắng vinh quang mà bại cũng anh hùng

The great lesson I've learned in the United States
Is that I love my country without bounds
I hate those who've made my country worse
And hate them ten-fold for kicking us off our own home

But if, one day, life changes once more
And through heroics I manage to save the nation
I would open thousands of re-education campuses
And herd the whole nation into classes learning to love

The old war, we'd consider as past
Reactionaries or not, we all have just the one life
We're all mates, nobody's a puppet
Victory is glorious, but defeat is heroic too.

Saturday

Quim Monzó
Translated by Peter Bush
Catalan (Spain)

Quim Monzó has published many books of stories in Catalan and writes regular columns in *La Vanguardia*, the Barcelona daily. His fiction has received many awards including the City of Barcelona Award, the Catalan Writers' Award and the Serra d'Or magazine's prestigious Critics' Award four times. He has translated numerous authors into Catalan, including Truman Capote, J.D. Salinger, and Ernest Hemingway. Books of his in English translation include *The Enormity of the Tragedy, Gasoline*, and *Guadalajara*.

"Saturday" is taken from Quim Monzó's latest collection of short stories, *A Thousand Morons*, which is marked by an anger that shifts from the elegiac to the bitter. Life is monotonous repetition, at best a vain performance; relationships collapse; age rots the brain as well as the flesh. His protagonists placate and contemplate the human debris with an ironic veneer perilously close to the point of explosion. It is a world of geriatric residencies where filial love frays at the edges as dementia bites in, of literary circles where young praise old as they prepare the stab in the back, of sentimental gestures of compassion withdrawn when real commitment is invoked. It is Monzó in his darkest vein describing the surreal banalities of the everyday yet with passion in his detachment.

The language of the translation of "Saturday" has to capture the obsessive actions of the protagonist, the ruthless way she settles accounts with her past whether she is snipping at photos or stuffing trousers into bags for the dumpster. When translating, say, Juan Goytisolo, metaphors and images have often to be transformed and baroque rhythms re-elaborated. Here the challenge is to maintain the constraint. Metaphor, image, even adjectives are sparely used. There is no space for letting go and the inevitable transformations in the move from Catalan to English must mirror the apparent distance between the impulses of the character and the eye of the narrator recording her massive clear out of her life in what is an unusually action-packed beginning to the weekend.

Original text: Quim Monzó, "Dissabte" from *Mil Cretins*.
Barcelona: Quaderns Crema, 2007.

Dissabte

Totes les fotos de la seva vida caben en una capsa de sabates amb les puntes doblegades. S'amunteguen sense ordre. Hi ha fotos de quan era petita barrejades amb fotos ja de gran. En seixanta anys no ha tingut mai ni un minut per agafar un àlbum i ordenar-les. I ara que per fi té temps li fa mandra i tampoc no veu quin sentit tindria ordenar-les a aquestes altures. Per tot això les fotos en blanc i negre conviuen amb les fotos en colors. I amb les sèpia: dels pares, del cosinet que va morir a tres anys amb el cap esberlat per un test d'alfàbrega que va relliscar de la finestra d'una veïna, i d'ella mateixa, ben jove i amb randes, o amb una llarga faldilla blanca, o amb una faldilla curta i una raqueta a la mà. Guarda la capsa en un armari, sota la carpeta acordió on desa les factures. La guarda a sota perquè la tapa de cartró no tanca bé i, amb la carpeta al damunt, queda almenys immobilitzada. Les fotos les mira, sempre a la taula del menjador. Col•loca la capsa a l'esquerra i en treu la tapa de cartró. Amb totes dues mans agafa un grapat de fotos i les deixa davant seu. Moltes, ni les contempla. D'una llambregada en recorda fins a l'últim detall; les ha vistes tantes vegades! Ara en busca concretament una, on ella i el marit, de bracet, miren a la càmera amb un somriure glaçat. No ha de buscar gaire, perquè, tot i que l'amuntegament podria semblar caòtic als ulls d'un estrany, el pas dels anys i l'anar mirant les fotos ...

Saturday

A lifetime's photos fit in that shoebox with their corners turned over. They're packed in without any kind of order. There are photos from when she was a child mixed up with photos of her as an adult. She's never had a minute in sixty years to organize them into an album. And now she does finally have the time she can't be bothered, and doesn't see the point in sorting them out at this particular stage in her life. Consequently black and white and color photos live cheek by jowl. Sepia ones as well: her parents, the cousin who died at the age of three when his head was cracked open by a pot of basil that dropped from a neighbor's window, and herself, as a very young child in lace or a long white skirt or a short skirt and carrying a tennis racquet. She puts the box away in a cupboard, under the accordion folder where she stashes her bills. She puts it underneath because the cardboard lid doesn't shut properly and the folder at least keeps it in place. She always looks at the photos on the dining-room table. She places the box to her left and removes the cardboard lid. She uses both hands to take a bunch of photos and set them out in front of her. There are a lot, and she doesn't exactly stare at them hard. A quick glance reminds her of the smallest detail; she has looked at them so often! She now searches for one in particular, where she and her husband, arm in arm, are staring icily at the camera. She doesn't search for long, because, although the pile might seem chaotic to the eyes of a stranger, the passing of the years and the habit of looking at the photos time and again means she always knows in which cluster of the various clusters each photo resides. She immediately finds the one she is looking for, and tears come to her eyes. His hair is greased and glinting and she is wearing a small, tulle hat and carrying a posy of jasmine. Keeping her eyes on the photo, the woman rummages in her apron pocket, takes out some scissors and, with three determined snips, cuts the photo in such a way that her husband falls to the floor and she is left by herself, missing her left arm where he had looped his right. She had hesitated for a moment, wondering whether she preferred to lose her left arm or to keep it with his clinging on, still there. She immediately places what's left of the photo on top of the heap of the other photos, stoops down and retrieves her husband off the floor and starts cutting him to shreds, with short, regular snips. Then she looks for other photos where they are together, but there aren't any. When she puts the scissors down, the minute scraps of him make a small pile that her right hand sweeps on to the palm of her left and throws in the trashcan. Then she puts the box of photos back into the cupboard and heaps up his jackets, shirts, trousers and ties. It is all destined to finish up in a large plastic sack. She bought a packet that was labeled for INDUSTRIAL USE at the supermarket. She deposits the sack in the hallway just long enough to tidy her hair and put on her coat.

It is an effort to open the dumpster and an even greater one to hoist the sack inside. When she does manage it, the dumpster top stays open. She couldn't care less. She shakes the dust off her hands and walks to the café on *carrer* Balmes where she sometimes snacks on a spicy sausage sandwich. After that, she buys croquettes at the delicatessen. She goes home, takes off her coat, puts on her apron, and clears the kitchen table and when she goes into her small sitting room to watch TV for a while, the photo at the end of the passage catches her eye, the one they had taken in that studio on carrer Manso a week before they got married, it is in a broad, varnished wooden frame, him sporting his greasy, glinting hair, and her wearing a kind of small tulle hat and holding a posy of jasmine. She immediately takes it down, goes into the dining-room, puts the frame on the table, and without bothering to look for the tool-box for the pincers for removing nails, she rips the cardboard at the back and pulls out the photo. With three snaking moves she cuts the photo in order to separate out the figure of her husband and be left by herself, without her left arm, because if she had kept her left arm, his arm, that was gripping hers, would have stayed in the picture. As a girl, she always used to cut the girlfriends she'd argued with out of her photos, and when it was a group photo—and it was very difficult to cut out one individual without spoiling the entire photo—she would score the faces and bodies of the girlfriends she'd argued with, and score them on the negatives as well, in case she ever made another copy and they made an unexpected appearance. She put the photo down on one side of the table: all by herself now in her tulle hat and with the posy her one and only arm is carrying. She contemplates for a moment the piece of the photo where he is clinging to a disconnected arm and doesn't think it strange he is roaming the world attached to an arm that doesn't belong to anyone. She heaps up the scraps of paper, and with one hand sweeps them into her other palm and throws them down the lavatory; she immediately pulls the chain, and has to do so repeatedly, because one or two pulls don't suffice to make them disappear. Back in the living room she spots some trousers and shirts on the rocking chair in the bedroom. His brown trousers, the gray ones, two white shirts and one blue, and five ties. They all end up in two plastic sacks that she takes down to the dumpster. How long will it be before one of those men comes by with a cart and a stick that he pokes inside and finds the shorts and trousers? If she were to see one, she would tell him right away. She would really like to see one soon walk down the street in one of his shirts with his initials embroidered on the left hand-side pocket. She goes to the milk bar where she sometimes snacks in the afternoon on an *ensaimada* and decaf flat white. She has a bun and flat white, buys a bottle of milk and goes home. She switches on the TV. She keeps changing channels. There's nothing interesting on. She switches it off, picks up a novel she's been halfway through for a week, looks for her bookmark and starts reading. Five minutes later she realizes, as has happened every time she has tried over the last few days, that she isn't registering a word. She puts the novel down on a coffee table, and then spots the book he was reading upside down in a corner. She opens it at his page: "As we have already seen, a calculation of the frequency with which the letters appear in the cryptogram provides invaluable clues for whoever wants to find the solution." She rips the page out, screws it into a ball and throws it on the floor. She reads the beginning of the next page—a sentence only—rips out the page, screws it into a ball and throws it on the floor. She rips the book down the middle, along the spine and, thanks to the American-style glue, tears off the pages one by one. She finishes the job off in the kitchen, above the trashcan, so the pages fall inside. Then she puts the lid on the can and, when she is about to turn around, she notices trouser leg cuffs in the heap of foul dirty clothes that has been piling up in a corner of the gallery for days. She goes over, rummages around and finds two more pairs of trousers and five shirts. As she collects them up, she sticks them in the trashcan and, as it soon fills up, she extracts the sack that is already full, takes out an empty one and sticks the shirts in that she couldn't fit in the full one. When she is done, she puts the sacks in the hall, goes to the bathroom and tidies her hair in front of the mirror.

She is carrying a sack in each hand. Before reaching the dumpster she sees a man with a cart, who is raking inside with a broom. The man is wearing a mask. When did he last have a shower? She hands him the sacks. "Here are some shirts and trousers."

Rather than just taking it, the man snatches it suspiciously. He deposits the sacks in the cart, opens one and unfolds the shirt, looking thrilled. My God! thinks the woman, next to those filthy paws even the shirts that needed washing seem clean. The man slips one over the shirt he is already wearing. The woman turns around and walks up Balmes peering into the shop windows. Then she turns left and goes home. She takes off her coat and puts on her apron. What will she do now? Tidy. Tidying up all day and it's never done. For the moment, she thinks, she has emptied the bedroom wardrobe. As she is not altogether sure, she takes another look. Right: not a handkerchief in sight. Nothing on the nightstand either. Perhaps there are some shoes in the hall cupboard? Several pairs—and a large parcel. When she tears the paper around the parcel she finds two boxes containing two unused pullovers. She shuts the boxes. She takes off her apron, puts on her coat. The elevator takes its time, because first it goes down without stopping at her floor and then comes back up to a lower floor and then goes down and up again. Finally it arrives.

She goes to the dumpster, opens it and, as best she can, because it is so full, stuffs in the boxes of pullovers. A passerby chides her for not putting the cardboard in the blue dumpster. The woman doesn't give him a glance. When she has finished, she shakes the dust off her hands, goes to the café on Balmes and drinks a tiny cup of black coffee and a glass of *anís*. Then she goes to the supermarket, buys two more packets of trash sacks, walks home, takes off her coat, slips on her apron and sits in front of the TV. She repeatedly changes channels and then, when she sees an advertisement with a son and daughter giving their parents a wedding anniversary cake, she remembers that, for their thirty-fifth anniversary, their older son gave them a present of two T-shirts imprinted with the photo of the two of them taken in that photographer's studio on carrer Manso, him with his hair glinting and greasy and her in a small tulle hat and with a posy of jasmine in one hand. Where can those T-shirts have gotten to? She looks in the wardrobe, in the T-shirt drawer, but they aren't there. She finds them mixed up with his, well, that is to say, three of his vintage undervests she drops on the floor for a moment, because what she is looking for now are the photos where they are arm in arm. She searches the other drawers. The ones for underwear, stockings, and socks; she takes a pair she adds to the two T-shirts on the floor. She searches the upper shelves, among the blankets and eiderdowns, among the jerseys and the box where she keeps wristwatches. She takes two from this box and adds them to the heap of socks and T-shirts.

She finds the T-shirts in the kitchen, in the duster drawer. She didn't remember deciding to turn them into dusters. They are cut in two. There's nothing on the back: it's all white. The photo is on the front. His hair, glinting from all that grease, is a dark patch, and her posy of flowers, a white, unrecognizable blob. She takes the scissors from the front pocket of her apron and carefully cuts out his figure from both T-shirts, and snips it into shreds above the trashcan so the bits don't fall on the floor. When there's nothing left, she returns the other bits of T-shirt to the duster drawer, gathers up the T-shirts, watches, and socks she left in the bedroom, stuffs them in the sack, takes off her apron and puts on her coat, walks to the dumpster, then wonders about stopping in the café, decides not to, and goes straight home, wondering whether she is being thorough enough.

She decides she isn't. She doesn't take her coat off, puts on her apron and again looks for the piece of photo where she figures without her left arm in the box of photos. She soon finds it. It is one of the first in the pile. She gives it one last glance, and then rips it into shreds that she gathers up in one hand and throws it into the sack of rubbish. The piece of T-shirt that she had put away in the duster drawer also ends up there in tiny bits. As does the broad, varnished wooden photo frame that was at the end of the passage. She immediately goes to the wardrobe and takes out the drawers where he always kept his socks and T-shirts. She drags them to the elevator one by one, puts them inside, except for the one keeping the elevator door open, goes back, takes off her apron, tidies her hair, takes the sack of rubbish and goes into the elevator. A neighbor shouts: "Elevator! What's up?" She stacks the drawers on the ground floor next to the entrance and starts to make trips to the dumpster. On her first she carries a drawer in one hand and the sack of rubbish in the other. She drags a drawer along on each of her subsequent trips. When she finishes, she rests for a while in the café on Balmes and has milk chocolate with a sugar bun while she watches the cars drive by, hooting their horns. Then she goes home, takes off her coat, puts on her apron, drinks a glass of water and gathers up the hangers where he'd hung his jackets, shirts and trousers and sticks them in a big bag. She takes the toolbox from the sideboard and puts it on the kitchen top. She uses a screwdriver to remove the doors from the wardrobe. She puts on her coat and drags the doors as far as the elevator. It takes her two journeys to get them downstairs. She returns home, carries the chairs to the elevator and takes them down in four journeys. She also makes one trip per armchair. She goes straight back home, takes off her coat, puts on her apron, turns the table over and unscrews the legs. As it is school-leaving time, she decides not to make any more trips, because from now on, for a few hours at least, there will be a constant stream of parents and kids. She piles everything up in the hallway and waits for evening so she can take off her apron, tidy her hair, put on lipstick, and take it all out to the street.

She orders a plateful in the café on Balmes: fried egg, chips, and a tomato sliced down the middle. She goes home, takes off her coat, puts on her apron, strips off the counterpane, bed linen top and bottom, pillows, and pillowslips. As well as what's in the wardrobe. She sticks part in the sack where she'd put the hangers; the others in two more sacks. She takes off her apron and puts on her coat. She puts all three sacks in the elevator and pushes the foam mattress until she gets it in as well. She finds an old man waiting on the ground floor by the elevator who gives her and her cargo a look of surprise and says "Good night." She replies with a "Good night," pulls out the mattress and leans it against the wall. "Leave that, leave that, I'll help you," the man tells her. "No, really, there's no need," she responds as she takes the sacks out of the elevator and puts them next to the mattress. She has to make three trips to the dumpster, one with the mattress, the second with two bags and the third with just one. She also takes the television and the rocking chair down. When she is back home, she takes off her coat, puts on her apron and dismantles the window that looks over the square. She puts it in the hall. She extracts a hammer and chisel from the toolbox in the kitchen and spends a while attempting to prise the window-frame from the wall. She starts levering with the chisel in the small crack she has managed to make after a few minutes. She gradually chisels pieces out, until the absence of one of the four sides enables her to lever the other three out more easily. When—after putting on her coat—she takes it all to the dumpster it is nighttime with few people in the street. She goes to the café on Balmes, but they have already pulled down the metal shutters and switched off the lights. They are hard at it inside: putting chairs on tables, sweeping and washing up. She goes home, brews coffee, shuts off the water supply and, with the spanner, unscrews the screws holding down the toilet bowl. Then she detaches it from the pipes and finally, after a few kicks, the bowl gives ways and falls on to the floor. She drags it to the hallway. She also unscrews the taps from the washbasin, and the basin falls on the floor and cracks. The shower tray also cracks, because she has to wrench it out with the chisel. She drags it to the landing, takes off her apron, puts on her coat and gradually stuffs everything in the elevator, and from there—in several trips—takes it to near the dumpster, because the dumpster has been full for hours, and all around it is choc-a-bloc too. Then she goes home, takes off her coat, puts on her apron and starts levering out the tiles. First, from the bathroom walls. Then, from the kitchen walls, and every single floor tile. Many tiles crack, because she often misses the chisel and the hammer smashes against the tiles. Very few emerge intact. Shortly, the city police come and tell her a neighbor has complained about the noise. She apologizes, and when the police have gone, she heaps the tiles in the hallway: then she takes off her apron, puts on her coat, loads the tiles into her shopping trolley—because the sacks can in no way take the weight—and has to make trips throughout the night. Sometimes she thinks: maybe this isn't the time to be making so much noise. But she doesn't want to wait till morning; she wants everything to be sorted by sunrise. But it is too much work for her to finish before daybreak. When there isn't a single tile left in the flat, she wrenches the front door from its hinges. She takes off her apron, puts on her coat and, when she is dragging the door down to the dumpster, the black of the sky is beginning to be streaked with dark blue. She goes home, takes off her coat, puts on her apron and starts scraping the paint from the dining room with a scraper. Then, the bedroom walls. Then, what used to be the kids' bedroom. Then, the hallway. Then, the passage. When the plaster on all the walls is exposed, she sweeps up the paint scrapings, sticks it in sixteen sacks and—after combing out the dust that had got into her hair, taking off her apron and putting on her coat—she takes the sixteen sacks down to near the container. She knocks the dust off her hands, goes to the café on Balmes and, as it is now open again, has a coffee, three donuts and a glass of *anís*. She goes home, takes off her coat, puts on her apron, sits in one corner, and stares at the bare walls, ceiling, and floor. It is daytime now and the light gradually spreads through the rooms. It is Saturday and that is why it is silent everywhere. On the stairs, in the other flats, and out on the street. Almost everybody is still asleep. She puts her hands into her apron pocket and plays with the scissors. She takes them out and jabs the sharpest point at the skin on the thumb of her left hand, near the nail, and once she has finally made an incision, she puts the scissors down and with her right hand gradually starts to pull the skin away. Now and then she stops and wipes the blood on her apron.

The Same Voice, Always

Yves Bonnefoy
Translated by Marc Elihu Hofstadter
French (France)

Born in 1923 in Tours, Yves Bonnefoy became famous with the 1953 publication of his first volume of poetry, *Du mouvement et de l'immobilité de Douve* (*On the motion and immobility of Douve*). In this book, the mythic, mysterious female presence "Douve" presides over a world of violence, heartache, despair, and illumination. Since *Douve* Bonnefoy has published seven more books of poems, in addition to many volumes of essays about literature, art, and myth. He is the preeminent French translator of Shakespeare, and has also published translations of Yeats, Keats, and Leopardi. His poetry has changed over the years from fairly compact, lyrical forms through loose, dramatic ones to mixtures of poetry and prose in shapes that are unlike anything else in French poetry. The inheritor of the great French Symbolist tradition of Baudelaire, Rimbaud, and Mallarmé, Bonnefoy expands and contracts lines and images with the highest of goals: to convey something of the essence of reality. He is a spiritual poet without a God—his trajectory is that of one who seeks what Rimbaud called "*la vraie vie*" ("true life"). His verse exhibits an incredible intensity of feeling and perception.

"The Same Voice, Always" is the second-to-last poem in Bonnefoy's second book of poems, *Hier régnant désert*. In this, the blackest of Bonnefoy's books, a kind of "dark night of the soul" is passed through and finally left behind. The simple bread, fire, water, and sea-foam are carriers of a kind of tenderness toward reality that is earned by the speaker, who has gone through suffering, irony and depression to reach it. The "evening bird" is a symbol that suggests (as birds so often do in Bonnefoy's world) purity, harmony, and peacefulness.

The challenge for the translator in bringing across Bonnefoy's poems stems from the differences between the French and English languages, the former having fewer words that, characteristically, define essences, the latter being more concrete and particular. The translator must convey the elegance and high tone of the originals while placing them in a tongue that is not used to such elemental thinking. I have tried in my translation to employ simple diction that matches that of the original, and to suggest the sweet, poignant comfort of the poem.

Original text: Yves Bonnefoy, "La même voix, toujours," from *Hier régnant désert*. Paris: Mercure de France, 1958.

La même voix, toujours

Je suis comme le pain que tu rompras,
Comme le feu que tu feras, comme l'eau pure
Qui t'accompagnera sur la terre des morts.

Comme l'écume
Qui a mûri pour toi la lumière et le port.

Comme l'oiseau du soir qui efface les rives,
Comme le vent du soir soudain plus brusque et froid.

The Same Voice, Always

I am like the bread you will break,
Like the fire you will build, like the pure water
That will accompany you in the land of the dead.

Like the foam
That ripened the light and the port for you.

Like the evening bird who erases the shores,
Like the evening wind suddenly rougher and colder.

Two Poems

Rafael Acevedo
Translated by Erica Mena
Spanish (Puerto Rico)

A defining voice of his poetic generation, Rafael Acevedo is a poet, novelist, playwright and professor of literature at the University of Puerto Rico. He has six books of poetry and three novels, and his poems have been included in several anthologies of Latin American and Puerto Rican poetry.

Acevedo's work exhibits a remarkable breadth, fusing the politics inherent in the poetic tradition of a colony, the oldest colony in the world, with deep rhythmic and lyric sensibilities. These poems, taken from Acevedo's somewhat experimental and often political collection published in the mid-'90s, indicate two important movements in his work: the intimacy of a romantic quotidian and the intimacy of the political. Acevedo's broad gaze encompasses the sensual world and fuses it with the political, from a distinctly Caribbean perspective. Like many Puerto Ricans, Acevedo is bilingual in English and Spanish, and has written a novel in English. But these poems are deeply rooted in the tradition of Puerto Rican poetry, a lineage that includes Luis Muñoz Rivera and Clemente Soto Vélez and Julia de Burgos, poems that have a simultaneous inward and outward gaze, one that is both insular and global.

In "Measuring Instruments" Acevedo makes an overt, yet deeply personal, criticism of the U.S. policy towards Puerto Rican *independaentistas.* This poem is difficult particularly because of its structure: a single, long sentence that moves recursively, always gesturing backwards while moving forwards in a frenzied free-fall of political injustice. The anaphoric repetition of place and name creates a rhythmic structure to the poem that holds the syntax, constantly threatening to slip away, just barely together. This accretion is vital to the poem. Of course, there's a bigger elephant in the translation—all of the references are likely totally unknown to an English reader. But the power of the poem lies in the fact that the reader doesn't need to know exactly who all these people are, because the fact of their existence, and their imprisonment, is enough to be dizzying.

"Mirror" is quieter, slighter, but no less challenging for that. Things aren't always what they seem to be, there is a slipping away of reality into reflection or dream, perception is troubled, but all this is concentrated in a moment of utter banality. The challenge is in preserving the oppositional relationships constructed in each line, and the sympathy in tone among the first three lines, while allowing the last two lines to flatten without sinking the whole poem.

Original text: Rafael Acevedo, "Espejo" and "Instrumentos de medición" from *Instrumentario.* San Juan: Isla Negra Editores, 1996.

Espejo

Tampoco el otro lado del sueño es el mundo.
Tampoco desde el cielo se ven las estrellas de mar. Tampoco
la lluvia es el animal exactamente enemigo de la llama.
Por eso a ella no le basta mirarse en el espejo
y me pregunta.

Mirror

The other side of *dream* is not the world either.
Neither can you see starfish from the sky. Neither
is rain the exact animal enemy of flame.
And so it is not enough for her to see herself in the mirror
and she asks me.

Instrumentos de medición

El gobierno de los estados unidos
tiene instrumentos de medición p.e.:
conflictos de baja intensidad kilómetros cuadrados
país amigo foráin pólici habitantes por milla cuadrada
y se equivoca al medir la nación boricua y se equivoca
con las cárceles para los prisioneros de guerra
boricuas que son
de San Lorenzo como Alejandrina Torres
que se mudó a Nuevayor luego a Chicago
y está presa en California que son
de Lajas como Adolfo Matos artesano que se mudó
a Nuevayor y está encarcelado en California
que son de Yauco como Antonio Camacho
que tiene cuatro hijos
y está preso en Pensilvania que son
de Ponce como Elizam Escobar que pasó por Nuevayor
es pintor bueno y está preso en Oclajoma que son
de Chicago como Edwin Cortés que estudió y estudió
y está encarcelado donde está Antonio que son
de San Sebastián como Ricardo Jiménez
que estudió y estudió y ahora está preso en la misma cárcel

Measuring Instruments

The government of the United States
has measuring instruments, e.g.:
low-intensity conflicts squared kilometers
friendly governments *foráin pólici* population by square mile
and it makes mistakes measuring Puerto Rican and it makes mistakes
with the cells of prisoners of war
boricuas who are
from San Lorenzo like Alejandrina Torres
who moved to Nuevayor and later Chicago
and is locked up in California; who are
from Lajas like Adolfo Matos artisan who moved
to Nuevayor and is incarcerated in California;
who are from Yauco like Antonio Camacho
who has four children
and is jailed in Pennsylvania; who are
from Ponce like Elizam Escobar, who passed through Nuevayor,
is a good painter and is jailed in Oklahoma; who are
from Chicago like Edwin Cortés, who studied and studied
and is incarcerated where Antonio is; who are
from San Sebastián like Ricardo Jiménez
who studied and studied and now is jailed in the same prison

en la que está Edwin que son de Arecibo
como Carmen Valentín que la fueron chiquita
a donde se fue Alejandrina
y está encarcelada en el mismo sitio
que son compueblanos
como Oscar López compueblano de Ricardo
aislado sin atención médica en la unidad de control
de Marion Ilinois que son
de donde es Carmen
como Haydée Beltrán que está recluida por donde está Antonio
que son por donde pasó Elizam
como Dylcia Pagán
que hizo trabajos
en la eibísi sibiés enbisí pibiés de la televisión
cosas para niños que tiene un niño que nació
en clandestinaje que está presa donde está presa Alejandrina
que es donde está presa Ida Luz Rodríguez que nació
en Las Marías
que tiene una hermana Alicia Rodríguez que nació
compueblana de Edwin y que grita
viva Puerto Rico libre en corte
y está encarcelada por donde está preso Oscar que está preso
por donde está preso Luis Rosa compueblano de Alicia
que es lejos de la cárcel
donde está Alberto Rodríguez de Nuevayor
que tiene un nene y una nena
y está en la cárcel donde está Ricardo que es lejos de la cárcel
donde está Roberto José Maldonado de Santurce
que está preso en Tejas
que es lejos de la cárcel
donde está Juan Segarra de San Juan
que está preso en Florida
que es lejos de la cárcel

as Edwin; who are from Arecibo
like Carmen Valentín, who they sent young
to where Alejandrina went
and is incarcerated there;
who are compatriots
like Oscar López, compatriot of Ricardo,
isolated without medical care in the control unit
of Marion Illinois; who are
from where Carmen is
like Haydée Beltrán who is locked up where Antonio is;
who are where Elizam passed through,
like Dylcia Pagán,
who made shows
for ai-bi-ci, ci-bi-es, en-bi-ci, pi-bi-es on television,
things for children, who has a child that was born
in secret, who is jailed where Alejandrina is jailed,
who is where Ida Luz Rodríguez is jailed, who was born
in Las Marías,
who has a sister, Alicia Rodríguez, who was born
a compatriot of Edwin, and who screamed
viva Puerto Rico libre in court
and is incarcerated where Oscar is jailed, who is jailed
where Luis Rosa is jailed, who is compatriot to Alicia,
who is far from the prison
where Alberto Rodríguez from Nuevayor is jailed,
who has a boy and a girl
and is in the prison where Ricardo is, who is far from the prison
where Roberto José Maldonado from Santurce is,
who is jailed in Tejas
which is far from the prison
where Juan Segarra of San Juan is,
who is jailed in Florida
which is far from the prison

donde está Carlos Alberto Torres de Ponce

que está preso en Alabama

que es lejos de donde nadie sabe donde está Filiberto Ojeda

que resistió el arresto y sus compueblanos

lo absolvieron en la corte

que es donde nunca irá Víctor Gerena vecino de jalfor

y ahora nadie sabe donde está

que si se sabe donde está

Guillermo Morales de Nuevayor

internacionalmente reconocido como perseguido político

y en justa guerra por la liberación de la nación

que los instrumentos de medición

del gobierno de estados unidos

no pueden medir

la patria es larga místeres.

where Carlos Alberto Torres of Ponce is,
who is jailed in Alabama
which is far from where…no one knows where Filiberto Ojeda is,
who resisted arrest and his compatriots
absolved him in court,
which is where Victor Gerena neighbor of Hart-ford will never go
and now nobody knows where he is,
if you know where
Guillermo Morales of Nuevayor is,
internationally recognized and politically persecuted,
and in the just war for national freedom
the measuring instruments
of the government of the United States
can't measure

homeland is the greatest guide.

The Niche Desired

Fanny Rubio
Translated by Rebecca Kosick
Spanish (Spain)

Fanny Rubio's collection of poems, *Reverso*, was first published in 1987, less than fifteen years after Franco's death. And though I would not characterize the collection as a book only about the dictatorship, I will say that it is a book about contemporary life in Spain and the reality of living and writing in the time that follows an historical silencing of writers and writing. Rubio's generation was among the first since Franco to be able to write openly about everyday life in Spain, and *Reverso* works to give voice to the complexity of its moment.

The poems in *Reverso* push against historical and other silences, beginning with the first poem, which opens onto a scene of a wordless, but crowded plaza. As the book continues, Rubio plays with the question of what is speakable, and we see one important approach to this question in "The Niche Desired."

The poem just before it, "Root," ends with the line "here we don't speak these things." This line is, of course, the culmination of that poem, but it also serves as a silence which "The Niche Desired" interrupts via its pronunciation of some of the most private, hidden, topics of quotidian life—topics until then rarely spoken of outside the home, and historically left silent in what some considered to be the "exalted" space of poetry.

One way of thinking about translation is as a process of giving voice, or of enabling a voice to speak in new language. In translating "The Niche Desired" I had the chance to be an apprentice to Rubio's voice, to learn from the way she intervenes in the silence that precedes all writing.

This poem, for example, not only addresses the question of voice thematically, but also works formally, especially through the use of repetition, to give voice to the many silent routines that drive the, at times, monotonous rhythm of daily living. These routines, in turn, drive the rhythm of the poem and translating them provides the opportunity to think about the ways form can work with content to emphasize a poem's project and, also, to consider the challenges, responsibilities, and joys of taking part in its voicing.

Original text: Fanny Rubio, "El nicho deseado" from *Retracciones y Reverso*. Madrid: Ediciones Endymion, 1989.

El nicho deseado

*(sin ruidos y con un consumo
muy ajustado)*

La manera de cerrar una cafetera dis-
tinta y particular en cada uno de los
casos o el tiempo de estancia en el re-
trete es lo que marca el ritmo cotidia-
no. Las intermitentes meadas del bebé:
*ya huele, está mojado, es que no sabes
cuidarlo, está escocido.*

Los sorbos, cuatro, siete, del desayu-
no. El mismo número de pasos el lu-
nes, el martes, el miércoles, el jueves y
el viernes te dejan cara de repetido
cuando te afeitas: tienes cara de pro-
ducto de supermercado.

El choque del agua contra los azule-
jos: unos marcianos que se duchan al
otro lado del tabique; una llamada de
ascensor a la derecha y llega al nivel
de las tuberías, a la altura de los ra-
diadores de la calefacción, el elemento

The Niche Desired

*(quiet and with reasonable
association fees)*

The manner of closing a coffee pot
distinct and particular in each case or
the time spent on the toilet is what
marks the quotidian rhythm. The
intermittent pisses of the baby: *the
baby smells, the baby's wet, it's that
you don't know how to take care of
the baby, the baby has a rash.*

The swallows, four, seven, of breakfast. The same number of steps on
Monday, on Tuesday, on Wednesday, on Thursday and on Friday give
you a face repeated when you shave:
you have a face of a supermarket product.

The shock of water against the blue
tiles: some Martians showering on the
other side of the wall; a push of the
button on the right and the elevator

más respetado del inmueble, estera, doble espejo, a horas fijas: las siete treinta y cinco, las ochos diecisiete, las nueve menos cuarto. Por más que te cubras la cabeza, te enrolles con la almohada, cierres a piedra y lodo, es inflexible: a las siete treinta y cinco, a las ocho diecisiete, a las nueve menos cuarto sube el representante de la circulación del edificio, baja y sube con el mismo peso, se saludan los que se encuentran de la misma manera en el portal, en la puerta de la calle, en el aparcamiento: una especial manera de abrir o de cerrar la puerta a una hora poco frecuente puede marcarse en el silencio de las veinte personas que te rodean: cuarto derecha, cuarto centro, tercero izquierda, quinto izquierda. Una especial presión en el interruptor de la luz y es como si llamaras, si es de noche, a toda la urbanización.

arrives to the level of the pipes, to the height of the radiators, the most respected part of the building, doormat, double mirror, at fixed hours: seven thirty-five, eight seventeen, quarter to nine. However much you cover your head, roll up in your pillow, shut out the world, it's inflexible: at seven thirty-five, at eight seventeen, at quarter to nine the building circulation representative comes up, goes down and comes up with the same weight, the people who see each other say hello to each other in the same way in the entryway, in the doorway, in the parking lot: a special way of opening or closing the door at an infrequent time can imprint itself on the silence of the twenty people who surround you: fourth right, fourth center, third left, fifth left. A special touch of the light switch and it's like you're calling, if it's nighttime, to the whole development.

Seven Days to the Funeral

Ján Rozner
Translated by Julia Sherwood
Slovak (Slovakia)

Sedem dní do pohrebu (Seven Days to the Funeral), a fictionalized memoir by Slovak journalist, critic, and translator Ján Rozner (1922–2006) is an account of the first week following the death of his first wife, Zora Jesenská, an eminent translator of Russian literature. Following the Soviet-led invasion of Czechoslovakia in August 1968, both husband and wife, active proponents of the Prague Spring, were blacklisted and banned from publishing. When Jesenská died of cancer in 1972 her funeral turned into a political event and everyone attending it faced recriminations.

However, *Seven Days to the Funeral* is much more than a fictionalized memoir—it is also a historical record of the period of so-called normalization and of the devastating impact of politics on people's characters. Writing the book in the third person enabled Rozner to describe the events from a distance: the author-narrator is brutally honest in reflecting on his own feelings, past mistakes, and personality flaws. With its ruthless and caustic portraits of key figures of Slovak culture *Seven Days to the Funeral* presents a fascinating panorama of the cultural history of Slovakia between 1945 and 1972. The book is also a moving love story of an unlikely couple—she the scion of one of the oldest Slovak literary families, a Lutheran from Central Slovakia; he, 13 years her junior, the son of an impoverished German mother and Jewish intellectual father who grew up on the periphery of the then-trilingual capital, Bratislava.

Although Ján Rozner started working on the book soon after emigrating to Germany in 1976, it was left unfinished upon his death in 2006. Sensitively edited by his second wife Sláva Roznerová, the book was published posthumously in 2009, becoming an instant literary sensation and hailed by many as the best book of the year.

Knowing that the author, a family friend, had devoted nearly 30 years to the writing of this book, meticulously calibrating every single word, the main challenge I faced as a translator was balancing faithfulness to the original with the very different cadences and stylistic conventions of Slovak and English. Moreover, I was acutely aware that as someone with scores of translations under his belt and an extremely sharp and critical eye, Ján Rozner would have applied the same exacting standards to my translation.

Original text: Ján Rozner, *Sedem dní do pohrebu*. Bratislava: Albert Marenčin Vydavateľstvo PT, 2010.

Sedem dní do pohrebu

VEČER

Vrátil sa domov okolo siedmej, o niečo neskôr ako v posledné dni, hlavu mal prázdnu z napätej pozornosti, ktorú musel vynakladať posledné hodiny, bol aj hladný a z toho všetkého podráždene zlostný. Rozhodol sa, že si teraz nezačne krájať chleby, natierať ich maslom a syrom a potom ich pomaly prežúvať, pchal ich do seba na raňajky a na večeru už aspoň druhý týždeň. Keď bol naposledy v samoobsluhe, kúpil si nejakú mäsovú konzervu, podľa návodu stačilo dať ju neotvorenú na päť či desať minút do vriacej vody.

Postavil na plynový šporák kastról s vodou. Prichystal si tanier a príbor, a z tašky, ktorú doniesol so sebou, vybral prázdne fľaše od minerálky a ovocnej šťavy a dve hrubé knihy. Knihy vráti zajtra do knižnice a vyberie nejaké dve iné. Fľaše odložil do kúta kuchyne, knihy odniesol do izby, a keď sa vrátil do kuchyne, voda v kastróle už sipela, vložil do nej mäsovú konzervu a až teraz si spomenul, že si neprečítal, či má byť vo vode päť, alebo desať minút. Ale už ju nevybral. Sadol si na lavicu v kuchynskom jedálenskom kúte, a keď sa mu zdalo, že čakal už dosť dlho, vypol plyn, rýchlo vybral konzervu z horúcej vody, otvoril ju, polovicu z nej vyklopil na tanier a odkrojil si kus chleba, hoci medzi mäsom v omáčke nechutnej farby videl aj nadrobno nakrájané zemiaky. . . .

Seven Days to the Funeral

DAY ONE: EVENING

It was around seven o'clock by the time he got home, somewhat later than in the previous few days, his head empty from hours of the intense effort to stay alert but also feeling hungry and, as a result, angry and irritable. He decided that this time he wouldn't just cut a few slices of bread, spread them with some butter and cheese, and proceed to chew on them the way he'd been stuffing himself at breakfast and dinner for over a week now. On his last visit to the supermarket he'd bought some canned meat; on the can it said that all you had to do was put it into boiling water, unopened, for five or ten minutes.

He filled a pot with water and set it on the gas stove. He laid out a plate and cutlery, and removed empty bottles of mineral water and fruit juice and two thick books from the bag he had brought home. Tomorrow he would take the books back to the library and choose another two. He left the bottles in the corner of the kitchen and carried the books into the living room. When he returned to the kitchen he found the water in the pot already hissing so he placed the can in the water and it was only then that he remembered he hadn't checked whether you were supposed to leave it there for five or ten minutes. But he didn't take it out. He sat down on a bench at the kitchen table, and when he thought he'd waited long enough he turned off the gas, quickly took the can out of the hot water, opened it, tipped half the contents onto a plate, and cut himself a slice of bread even though he could see small bits of potatoes floating in the unappetizing looking sauce among the pieces of meat.

The canned meat was lukewarm. It tasted disgusting and sticky like industrial rubber but that made sense, it made sense, fitting into everything else that had conspired against him.

Lately he'd taken to talking to himself—only short sentences though, mainly curses (directed at himself) and questions (so what else was I supposed to do?) meant to conclude a particular chain of reminiscences. This time, too, he felt the urge to give loud, succinct, and strong expression to his annoyance with the foul-tasting canned meat, which was why he followed each gulp with a loud and accusatory scream at the wall opposite:

"Damned canned meat!"—"Fucking life!"

The screaming helped him to calm down a bit and made him realize how ridiculous it was for him to swear, especially using words he normally never used. But at least it was a way of unburdening himself to someone invisible. He was fully aware that it wasn't the fault of the disgusting canned meat and that there was nothing stopping him from tipping the contents of the plate into the toilet and making himself a sandwich with some cheese from the fridge, but it was doing him good to berate everything that couldn't be tipped into the toilet and so, after swallowing each chewy piece of the disgusting canned meat, he continued insisting to himself, only now more calmly—as if he had discovered the immutable nature of things—and much more quietly, over and over:

"Damned canned meat."—"Fucking life."

The repetition turned his swearing into some feeble-minded child's game and as he continued mindlessly, he suddenly heard the telephone ring.

He remained seated for a while, not interested in hearing what someone might want to say to him on the phone. What if it's something else though, he thought, as the names of three or four friends flashed through his mind but then again, as he began to walk toward the phone in the living room, he thought: this had to be it, irredeemably, definitively.

He crossed the living room, picked up the phone and spoke into it. Since a voice on the other end asked who was speaking, he introduced himself. The voice said its name was "Doctor Marton." It flashed through his mind that there was a time when he used to hear this name more often, he thought it belonged to a urologist and for a moment he wasn't so sure he was going to hear the news he was expecting, but once the voice on the telephone started explaining "I'm calling from the oncology ward, I just happen to be on night duty here tonight," he was quite certain again he would hear what he'd been expecting.

Actually, he wasn't expecting it at all; it's just that sometimes it had vaguely occurred to him that this call might come, perhaps the day after tomorrow, in a week, or in a couple of weeks. But he wasn't expecting it just yet…

However, the voice on the other end of the phone didn't continue with the news he was fearing but proceeded instead to give him a detailed account of how he hadn't been able to find his name in the telephone directory, and that's why he had to call at least three people who he thought might know him, but none of them had his number, and only then had he remembered a fourth person from whom he finally got the number. That was why he hadn't called earlier.

The voice on the other end of the phone paused, so, just to say something, he offered: "Yes, my name isn't listed in the phone book." Then the doctor moved on to the crux of the matter: "The thing is, your wife's condition has deteriorated. The situation is critical."

Again, he just said "yes," as if to encourage the doctor to say more but the doctor digressed once again: "I'm sure you remember that before we admitted her we told you that something like this couldn't be ruled out… that you had to be prepared for it."

What does he mean by "we," he thought, annoyed; he had talked to the chief physician and nobody else was present at the time. But out loud he just said "yes" again and then finally, as he'd been expecting, the doctor moved on to the reason why he was calling: "And that's why it would be a good idea for you to come straight away."

Again, he repeated mechanically, "Yes, I'll be there straight away," to which the doctor added: "It would be a good idea for you to bring someone along."

He didn't understand why he should bring someone along just because his wife's condition had deteriorated, but again he just repeated his "yes" but this time the voice on the other end of the telephone quickly went on, like someone who had inadvertently forgotten to mention something important: "Obviously you have to be prepared for the fact that your wife is already dead."

Now the voice at the other end of the line had nothing more to announce, and he repeated his "yes, I'll be there straight away" and put the receiver down.

For a moment, he stood by the telephone without moving, as if the last sentence had to be chewed first and then swallowed, like another chewy piece of the disgusting canned meat. But he hadn't swallowed it yet. He focused on something that had nothing to do with the content of the telephone conversation. Like an editor or a dramaturge editing other people's texts he reviewed the doctor's last few sentences, as if proofreading a manuscript on his desk. Where's the logic in this—first he tells him about the situation getting critical and then he ends by saying the critical situation is over. And then this "obviously you have to be prepared..." Obviously! He didn't mind that it was an ugly word but it bothered him that in this sentence it didn't make any sense. Surely the doctor didn't mean to say "obviously"; what was so obvious about it, surely he wanted to say "of course," in the sense of "but": "but you have to be prepared for..."; there would have been some stylistic logic in that.

Having finished his proofreading he went back to the kitchen, slowly and deliberately, as if carrying a secret. Once in the kitchen he sat down on the bench again to ponder something and it took him a while to realize he wasn't thinking of anything, and that all he had to do was go to the hospital and take someone along. So he got up, picked up the plate so that the smell of the canned meat wouldn't linger in the kitchen, tipped the rest into the toilet, flushed it down, put everything away, and sat down on the kitchen bench again, as if he now needed a little rest before leaving.

He sat there with his shoulders drooping, his hands in his lap. He would no longer have to... yes, there were quite a few things he would no longer have to... think about what she might like in hospital and what he would say to her... or to think, as he had done so often over the past two weeks, whether she would ever come back to this apartment... and if she did, for how long. He no longer had to be petrified, nothing would change, everything had settled down. She simply was no longer. He was unhappy with himself for not feeling a sudden alarm that was supposed to shake him up. But then again, could it have ended any other way? She was likely to have been thinking the same way. And maybe she'd even wanted it. Nonsense. But still, sometimes over the past few days these ideas had crossed his mind. The thought had lodged itself in his brain and now he felt ashamed to think that she, unlike him, had come to terms with it... and she had left him here alone. Surely she must have known he wouldn't be able to cope by himself. He'd be left sitting in this huge apartment from morning till night. Surrounded only by an immutable silence. And a vast emptiness. Suddenly he seemed to have gotten a grip, noticing his mind had gone blank again and that he had to go to the hospital. The doctor had ordered him to come. Although right now it no longer mattered if he went there straight away or if he went on sitting here. He wasn't going to the hospital to see her anyway; he was only going there because of her.

The Foam of Nights
in Trois-Rivières

Rosa Alice Branco
Translated by Alexis Levitin
Portuguese (Portugal)

Rosa Alice Branco lives in Porto, in northern Portugal, but this poem commemorates in a rather playful way a poetry festival she attended in Trois-Rivières, situated halfway between Montreal and Quebec. This city is home to Les Écrits des Forges, the publisher of Branco's collection *Epeler le jou* (Spelling Out the Day), published in 2007. This poem is a frolicsome excursion into jazz, booze, and the unrestrained pleasures of a poetic interval in a foreign land in a changing season. The imagery suggests the poet's awareness that any art, whether verbal or musical, must earn its way through a certain abandon to primordial creative forces. Hence the Dionysian touches: "soaked in wine," "high temperatures," "heat increases," the sweat of midnight," "a line of poetry that hits you in the stomach," "pugilistic verses," "the sax explodes in our teeth," "splinters of glass," "the foam of letters broken in the breaking of the waves." This last image to me is more a reminder of the poet's Portuguese seafarer identity than a reference to waves in the St. Lawrence River.

After all the Bacchanalian play tinged with threat, there remains the purity of art sor of memory: "And in the ring not a trace of blood!" In the translation, I have tried to convey a sense of fun spiced with danger: "some splinters of glass." I can assure the reader that beyond this single poem the great pleasure of collaborating over the years with Rosa Alice Branco springs from the agon of poet and translator, struggling together to wrestle the living breath of Portuguese into the living breath of English.

Original text: Rosa Alice Branco, "A espuma das noites em Trois-Rivières" from *O mundo não acaba no frio dos teus ossos*. Vila Nova de Famalição: Quasi Edições, 2009.

A espuma das noites em Trois-Rivières

No chão há folhas do frio a caminhar
para o inverno. À noite as cores de cada uma
embebem-se de vinho,
e do sax saem temperaturas tão altas
que o piano vem temperá-las de azul. O calor
aumenta com a hora, o suor da meia-noite
encostado às vozes, às línguas, ao silêncio
que se enrosca nelas com um copo a caminho
e um verso que pega o estômago desprevenido.
Há versos pugilistas. Cada murro que desferem
é como se estivéssemos de costas. O sax explode
nos dentes. Também ele sabe que ninguém sai vivo
do poema. Estalidos de vidro, língua cor de vinho,
espuma de cerveja roçando um verso, espuma
de letras desfeitas na rebentação. Último round,
fundo do copo, último verso. O verão indiano
ficará atrás das asas do avião até sermos todos
comidos pelo frio. E no ringue nem sinais de sangue!

The Foam of Nights in Trois-Rivières

On the ground there are leaves of cold headed
towards winter. At night the colors of each one
are soaked in wine,
and from the saxophone such high temperatures emerge
that the piano comes to temper them with blue. The heat
increases with the hour, the sweat of midnight
leaning against voices, tongues, silence
curling around them with a glass on the way
and a line of poetry that hits you in the stomach unaware.
There are pugilistic verses. Every punch they let fly,
it's as if our backs were turned. The sax explodes
in our teeth. He knows as well that from a poem no one
can escape alive. Splinters of glass, a tongue the color of wine,
beer foam rubbing against a verse, the foam
of letters broken in the breaking of the waves. Last round,
bottom of the glass, last line of poetry. Indian summer
will remain behind the wings of the plane till we are all
eaten by the cold. And in the ring not a trace of blood!

Summer, Landscape

Shamshad Abdullaev
Translated by Valzhyna Mort
Russian (Uzbekistan)

Shamshad Abdullaev, the author of seven books of poems, was born in the town of Fergana in East Uzbekistan, a sun-lit valley swept by the parching dry wind and enclosed by mountains, where a multiplicity of cultures were brought together by the Stalin repressions. He became one of the first poets to verbalize the language of the surrounding Asian landscape, and is usually distinguished as the father of the Fergana school of poetry. Fergana poets, even though writing in Russian, do not stem from the Russian literary tradition, but bypass it, and orient their poetry in line with the Western tradition, Anglo-Saxon and American free verse, hermeneutic in its poetics.

In his poems, Abdullaev takes you outside—he observes his characters from a dusty street, a balcony, or from a veranda, black with flies. Pacing slowly through the scenes of provincial life in the heart of Asia, Abdullaev meditates indiscriminately on French cinema, Western philosophy, and his elderly toothless neighbor. If all poetry is a lie, his is rather a mirage hanging in the dry air of Fergana. English gives him a helpful hand here: after all, "image" is an anagram of "mirage." Abdullaev's mirage-images are the natural language of his Fergana landscape, where the mirages of the West become images, while the images of the East turn into mirages.

From the first word the poem "Summer, Landscape" works on

the reader like a spell that dissolves with the poem's last line. Consequently, the main translation challenge is to obtain the sensation of being put under and out of a spell in English. I begin the poem in English with monosyllabic words, balancing the first two verb-less sentences with a narrative structure "it's sunny and stuffy," which opens the central image of the poem. The scene of the young butcher cutting the sheep's throat takes up seven lines of this rather short poem and is held together in a single sentence through a sequence of enjambments. The poem ends with a line of monosyllabic words, which announce the break of the spell.

Original text: Shamshad Abdullaev, "Leto, Landshaft" from *Nepodvizhnaya Poverhnost*. Moscow: Novoye Literaturnoye Obozreniye, 2003.

Лето, Ландшафт

Солнечный удар, мальчик на раскаленной площади, свет
и тень. В руке
старой женщины блеснули четки. Крикнула птица
в лиловом оперенье, вспорхнула и вдалеке
прошуршала тихим проклятьем. Светло и душно, будто сейчас
молодой полуголый мясник, затаив
дыхание, дожидается, когда
из горла черного барана сама –
в пароксизме нетерпеливой жертвенности – вытечет кровь,
как песнь во славу южного солнца; и
темнеющая струйка (пот), чуть позже, раздвоит
четкий мужской сосок. Но
кто всколыхнет нас?
Кто расколдует молчанье?
Земля, твои губы, красная птица.

Summer, Landscape

Sunstuck, a boy on a red-hot square, light
and shadow. Beads
in the hand of an old woman. A bird
with lilac feathers screams, flies up, and from afar
whispers its quiet curse. It's sunny and stuffy, as if at this moment
a young half-naked butcher, holding
his breath, were waiting for blood
to stream by itself–in the paroxysm of impatient
sacrifice–from the throat of a black sheep
like a song of praise for the Southern sun; and
later, a dark trickle (sweat) would cut
a well-defined male nipple. But
who would move us?
Who would break the spell?
The earth, your lips, a red bird.

BRAZIL

At Your Feet

Ana Cristina Cesar

Translated by Brenda Hillman and Helen Hillman

My mother and I embarked on translating a few poems by Brazilian poets while my father was healing from heart surgery in 2011. My mother was born in Brazil and is still fluent in Portuguese. I have only a smattering of that beautiful language from two childhood years spent in Rio. My mother and I are doing this long-distance, by phone. She does the literal versions and I try to make something that sounds good in English. My mother and I started with a few poems by Manuel Bandeira (whose work we love) but we wanted to translate Brazilian women poets, especially those who have an eco-feminist perspective.

I fell in love with the work of Ana Cristina Cesar when I read a few in Michael Palmer's wonderful anthology of Brazilian poetry, *Nothing the Sun Could Not Explain: Twenty Contemporary Brazilian Poets* (1997). Cesar was born in 1952, so we were tiny children at the same time in Rio. I feel very drawn to her language experiments; *A teus pés* (At your feet) is a mix of poetry and prose. It is experimental syntactically, formally, and in its lexicon, but has a wide emotional range—dramatic shifts of emotion, images, abstract statement, and fragmentary notes. Cesar's work reminds me of the work of a more structurally innovative Plath, and alas, she also committed suicide in her 30s. The main challenges my mother and I faced had to do with different lineation we find in different versions of the texts, and with Cesar's wild vocabulary.

Original text: Ana Cristina Cesar, *A teus pés*. São Paulo: Editoria Atica, 2010.

A teus pés

O tempo fecha.
Sou fiel aos acontecimentos biográficos.
Mais do que fiel, oh, tão presa! Esses mosquitos
que não largam! Minhas saudades ensurdecidas
por cigarras! O que faço aqui no campo
declamando aos metros versos longos e sentidos?
Ah que estou sentida e portuguesa, e agora não
sou mais, veja, não sou mais severa e ríspida:
agora sou profissional.

At Your Feet

The weather closes down.
I'm so faithful to the biographical happenings.
More than faithful, oh, such a prisoner. These mosquitoes
don't let go. My longings have been drowned out
by cicadas! What do I do here in the country
reciting long metrical verses with feeling?
Ah, I'm melancholy and Portuguese, and now I'm not
any more, look, I'm not severe and sharp,
now I'm professional.

An English Gent

João Gilberto Noll
Translated by Stefan Tobler

João Gilberto Noll was born in Porto Alegre, Brazil, in 1946. He has published over 15 books including *Harmada, Hotel Atlantico, Lorde* and *A céu aberto,* which have received numerous accolades, including five Jabuti awards, Brazil's most important literary prize, and three of his works have been adapted for cinema. Prior to publishing primarily as a novelist, Noll worked as a journalist, and has taught courses on Brazilian Literature at the University of California, Berkeley.

Lorde was published in 2003. In the tone of a spy thriller, the novel tracks a man as he undergoes a surgical operation, breaks apart, and becomes a new character during a visit to London. The rhythms of the book sometimes reflect hardboiled crime fiction, but the book as a whole refuses to adhere to a single, ascertainable style. When not under the influence of anesthesia warmly welcomed for relieving his "need to do anything to attribute continuity to things," the narrator moves through London in a freewheeling, improvised way. In this passage and in the book as a whole, Noll introduces sudden unexpected shifts in tone and event, and interjects mysticism at unforeseen points such as when the narrator reflects upon his mysterious operation: "They had kept me there for a reason that I didn't know. I would use it to be born."

As a translator, I found that Lorde presented a number of fascinating challenges related to retaining the different tones and allusions that rotate throughout this passage.

Original text: João Gilberto Noll, from *Lorde*. Brasilia: Editora Francis, 2004.

Lorde

Na manhã seguinte o inglês bateu à minha porta. Acordei. Pediu que eu não me preocupasse, mas que me levaria ao hospital para ver se estava mesmo tudo bem. Pedi um instantinho para trocar de roupa. Pegamos o 55, descemos na altura de Bloomsbury. Dava para ouvir nossos passos, o silêncio total. Vi por uma placa que passávamos pelo Museu Britânico. Quis comentar alguma coisa, por exemplo que Rimbaud freqüentava a biblioteca do Museu. A voz não saiu porque tinha certeza de que tudo o que dissesse soaria como tergiversação — o homem a meu lado estava preocupado e não fazia nada para esconder.

Preenchi a ficha na portaria. Entremos numa enfermaria. O inglês parecia um funcionário do hospital tamanha a sua desenvoltura pelos seus interiores. Pediu que eu sentasse numa cama vaga. Sentei. Até aparecer o que parecia ser o médico. Que começou a me examinar. "É," falou com certa dureza. E pediu que eu deitasse. Chamou uma enfermeira. Ela lhe passou uns instrumentos. E o médico enfiou uma agulha na minha veia. Não me lembro de ter sentido tamanha satisfação em toda a minha vida. Não que a medicação que estava sendo introduzida surtisse algum efeito entorpecente a me tirar do ar. Nas próximas horas eu não precisaria fazer nada para atribuir continuidade às coisas. E mais, sem medo algum do meu destino dali ...

An English Gent

On the following morning the Englishman knocked at my door. I woke up. He told me not to be concerned, but that he would take me to the hospital to see if everything was all right. I asked if he could wait a moment while I got changed. We took the 55, getting off in Bloomsbury. We could hear our footsteps, the total silence. I saw on a sign that we were passing the British Museum. I wanted to say something, for example that Rimbaud used to go to the Museum's library. Not a word came out because I was sure that anything I said would sound like procrastination—the man at my side was worried and did nothing to hide it.

At reception I filled out a form. We entered a ward. The Englishman seemed to be on the staff, so at ease was he inside the hospital. He asked me to sit on an unoccupied bed. I sat. Until the person who seemed to be the doctor arrived. He started to examine me. "It is," he said with a certain harshness. And he asked me to lie down. He called a nurse. She passed some instruments to him. And the doctor inserted a needle in my vein. I don't remember ever having felt such satisfaction in my whole life. Not because the medication being introduced had a numbing effect that left me out of it. In the following hours I wouldn't need to do anything to attribute continuity to things. And was, what's more, without any fear of my destiny from here on, which

JOÃO GILBERTO NOLL | STEFAN TOBLER 195

would be the normal response in a patient about to undergo a medical procedure in any hospital ward. I just didn't believe that anything worse could happen, that's all! I trusted the opposite would be true: that during that whole stay in the hospital the man who was starting to throb inside me and who I still didn't really know would have a better chance to surface. That when I woke from the anaesthetic I would start to live with another hypothesis about myself and that I would work on it in secret, so that not even my own English friend would be able to notice any change in my character or on the surface of my body. They had kept me there for a reason that I didn't know. I would use it to be born.

I died for the time I was sedated. Waking up, I saw a nurse with a sour face. She just said that everything was fine and that I could go. They had cleared up some question about my health. What test did they do? I asked. She didn't understand me or preferred to keep quiet. I exited onto a square in Bloomsbury. I didn't live in the area, as I would have liked to, but that was where they put me to bed, for how long I didn't know. Maybe to see if I showed any sign of health problems that would affect whether or not I stayed on the official programme of a Brazilian outside his country. Or would there be an unofficial reason, some by-product of minds with parallel powers? I was stuck in some pulpy spy novel, now inoculated with some substance which would make me even more submissive to them—I, my mind clouded, for that reason in particular, would provide them with a key that I was in no position to predict. I was the idiot in the global citadel. I would serve for every job whose sense was beyond me. But I was not going to cry, to bemoan my lot. Catching a plane back to Brazil wasn't an option.

The vein where I had been jabbed was hurting, and standing on a corner I flexed my arm, thinking about what to do next. If I returned to the house in Hackney, would it continue to be mine? Would the key in my hands open it? The wind whipped my neck. I turned up the collar of my jacket. If I phoned the Englishman, I'd end up on his damn answering machine. In my eyes, I'd always been from London. There was no other city, no other country. With my own hands I could drown the child that had preferred to go on counting his days rather than drown should a single image of my Brazilian childhood come back. My childhood had passed in these very streets where I was now shivering with cold. Puberty, youth, adulthood until now. Not that I had any special love of all this, which was always the same. It was raining and I was dribbling. I wasn't managing to keep my saliva in my mouth. Maybe it was some consequence of the hospital procedure I'd been submitted to. I was like a child who doesn't have the strength to express himself, just dribbles. If I were hungry, cold, thirsty or in pain, none of that would require me to expose myself to anyone, if only because in this country I only had the English guy to expose myself to, and now I had serious doubts as to whether he was still there for me at all. Perhaps I was very sick and they no longer had any use for me. Who knows. But that hypothesis seemed somewhat distant.

That was when I went into the British Museum. Tourists on all sides. I went as far as Egyptian civilization. I admired its remote gods. And I was enchanted by what might be the Museum's smallest image, minuscule. Apis, the bull god. Exactly what I was to those English who wanted to make me fall ill. Yes, now I truly saw myself in a mirror. They couldn't get me. I no longer needed the mirrors in public toilets, nor in my own house, I was Apis, I could walk through London if I felt like it—down every alley, prowl round all the parks and could even fast, as they no longer knew what to do.

I could go into a pub, not to inebriate myself or eat something, because I hadn't put anything in my mouth for days, except for a glass or two of water to keep the bull on his feet. I went into one that was appropriately called The Bloomsbury. Let people look at me, see someone else in me. The fact that I wasn't eating or drinking, was sitting there looking at nothing, might make someone wake up to me. The waiter could come. I'd say, I just want to rest, I've just come from the hospital and I need to rest. All right, there was the chance I'd need to get a mineral water for the waiter to leave me alone. But I'd just stand there, not wanting to sit down. This was what I had been needing in London. The attention of someone who wasn't that Englishman who had gone missing who knows how many days ago, since I had fallen into that indeterminate unconscious time in the hospital. A drunk came to talk. He complained about his wife. I sipped at my mineral water as if I were savoring the voice directed at me, even if he was not really noticing me in the midst of all the other people. We're talking about a drunk after all. I received the alcohol on his breath like the only bath I wanted to take. I didn't interrupt him, didn't stick my oar in, although I really thought that his wife was a hopeless case. Everything instilled in me the impression of a medieval tavern. There was a sourness in the air, the bodies smelled bad, particularly mine, which had not seen a change of clothes for an unspeakable amount of time. My genitals were itching, my chest, my hairy scalp still burnt from the hair dye. Oh, I had forgotten to check my appearance in a mirror, to see whether I continued to be the same person who had already changed so much, whether I was another person, or whether the hospital had given me back my old features, which I had left in Brazil. Where had I lost the power of evocation? The only thing that concerned me was where I was, the city of London in winter, and in this instant the pub with the drunk recounting with delight the extramarital conquests of his youth, suddenly his daughter dead in the arms of his tearful wife, the convulsion that made him grab my throat as if he were about to strangle me, like this, his finger on my jugular, suddenly my heart on fire—I drop the glass of water, it breaks, everyone looks: this is my only reaction; I'm saved, so lost I'm saved again.

Saved and dribbling. Maybe this lack of salivary control offers no solution. Yes, everyone in the pub is looking at me, just as I wanted. No longer because I knocked over my glass and was about to be strangled. But because I'm dribbling and yet still have the cheek to frequent pubs. I could ask: what makes me into that man who has no civic decorum for a night with possible drinking pals? I could ask, but I don't for one reason: tomorrow none of this will matter, when I'll be able to live the life of that man who is still lying in the Bloomsbury hospital bed, who stayed there as I made this little escape, motivated by the nurse's bad intentions. There lies a part of me that has stopped, without any thought of controlling the world or what goes on inside itself, a waiting stone. I'll go back in the dead of night, I'll lift up the sheet and lie down. And when the Englishman comes back, I'll see that the experiment has worked. I'll be that man again, ready to hold forth in public spaces on the questions that afflict his students who stubbornly refuse to show themselves.

Two Poems

Sérgio Capparelli
Translated by Sarah Rebecca Kersley

Sérgio Capparelli is a prolific poet, translator, journalist, and speaker. He has won numerous national awards over the past 30 years, including The Jabuti Prize (Brazil's biggest literary award) four times. Best known in Brazil for his poems and stories for children, he has also published extensively about the role of television in society, and in recent years, has developed several digital poetry projects. Capparelli lived in China from 2005 to 2007, and on his return to Brazil published Portuguese translations of Chinese short stories for children (*Contos sobrenaturais chineses*, L&PM, 2010, compiled and translated by Capparelli and Márcia Schmaltz), and translations of the Chinese poets Wang Wei, Du Fu, Li Qingzhao, Li Bai, Bai Yuchan, plus a selection of female Chinese poets (available at www.capparelli.com. br). He now lives in Italy.

These two poems come from the project *Wang Wei in São Paulo*. It is a graphic-digital project wherein Tang Dynasty Chinese poet Wang Wei (699-759) takes a trip around the São Paulo metro system, conceiving a poem at each location. On a metro map, the reader clicks on a station to read the Wang Wei/Capparelli reflection of that place. In his transportation of the Buddhist Tang Dynasty poet to modern-day São Paulo, Capparelli mirrors many features of the real Wang Wei's poetry, in relation to form and also semantic content. The poems echo many of Wang Wei's themes, such as nature, corruption, friendship, nostalgia, and love. And throughout the collection there is also a strong sense of Capparelli's own identity, with reflections on his native Brazil, the city of São Paulo, and natural and urban landscapes. In the English versions, my principal aim was to reproduce this double voice: the implied voice of Wang Wei—often with inferences to specific poems—and that of Capparelli himself. Additionally, as is my aim with any translation, to create an independent text, accessible to English-language readers and with a tone recognizable to those familiar with the city of São Paulo. When working on the translations, I referred to English versions of Wang Wei's poetry in an attempt to make the poems "sound like" Wang Wei, or rather, sound like the voice previously given to him by English translators.

Original text: Sérgio Capparelli, "SAÚDE: Saúde" and "BRESSER: Pôr do Sol em Bresser" from *Wang Wei em São Paulo*. www.amaisnaopoder.com.br.

SAÚDE: Saúde

Olho para frente
e assim evito torcicolos
voltando ao que passou.
Passado é passado,
tiro minhas conclusões
E sigo em frente,
Com o sol nos dentes.

SAÚDE: Health

I face forward
and avoid a twisted neck
returning to what's passed.
What is done is done.
I draw my conclusions
and go forward,
my teeth in the sun.

BRESSER: Pôr do sol em Bresser

Cansado de muriçocas, de dor de ouvido,
e da vida pacata de ovelhas, bois e galinhas,
Vim pra São Paulo para uma vida mais pura.

Agora num andar alto, de concreto e vidro
Assisto da sacada um pôr do sol de néon,
em um telão panorâmico de tevê.

Delícia! Tudo clean, visto do alto
Ou uma vertigem e agito, lá de baixo:
Alternâncias dessa boa nova de asfalto!

BRESSER: Sunset in Bresser

Tired of mosquitoes, earache,
and the quiet life of sheep, cows and chickens,
I came to São Paulo for a purer life.

Now, on a high-up floor made of concrete and glass,
I watch, from the window, a neon sunset
on a widescreen TV.

Wonderful! Totally sharp, seen from up here
Either this or madness and bustle, down there:
Alternations from this new story of asphalt.

The Spies

Luis Fernando Verissimo
Translated by Margaret Jull Costa

Luis Fernando Verissimo is one of Brazil's best-selling authors, whose regular column is syndicated in many Brazilian newspapers. In addition, he has published a series of humorous novels, some featuring a provincial psychiatrist and others an inept detective, as well as five darkly comic novellas.

In his fifth novella, *The Spies*, Verissimo turns his satirical gaze on publishing, provincial life and literary pretensions, but I think the book is also about our strange willingness to be duped by a fiction—about the allure of the imagination and of lies.

As a writer, Verissimo has a deceptively simple style, but he uses language very precisely. One example: the narrator refers to "*a enxurrada de autores*" ("the deluge of authors") sending their unsolicited manuscripts to the publishing house he works for. The primary sense of "*enxurrada*" is "deluge" or "flood," but it also has the subsidiary sense of "*jorrada de imundícies*," i.e. "stream of filth," which is how the narrator perceives both authors and manuscripts. There doesn't seem to be one neat English word that describes all that, and so I have added the adjective "festering" to capture the vaguely excremental whiff of that secondary sense and the narrator's distaste. Verissimo's seemingly straightforward prose is full of such subtleties.

Original text: Luis Fernando Verissimo, *Os espiões*, Alfragide: Publicações Dom Quixote, 2009.

Os espiões

1

Formei-me em Letras e na bebida busco esquecer. Mas só bebo nos fins de semana. De segunda a sexta trabalho numa editora, onde uma das minhas funções é examinar os originais que chegam pelo correio, entram pelas janelas, caem do teto, brotam do chão ou são atirados na minha mesa pelo Marcito, dono da editora, com a frase "Vê se isso presta." A enxurrada de autores querendo ser publicados começou depois que um livrinho nosso chamado *Astrologia e amor — Um guia sideral para namorados* fez tanto sucesso que permitiu ao Marcito comprar duas motos novas para sua coleção. De repente nos descobriram, e os originais não param mais de chegar. Eu os examino e decido seu futuro. Nas segundas-feiras estou sempre de ressaca, e os originais que chegam vão direto das minhas mãos trêmulas para o lixo. E nas segundas-feiras minhas cartas de rejeição são ferozes. Recomendo ao autor que não apenas nunca mais nos mande originais como nunca mais escreva uma linha, uma palavra, um recibo. Se *Guerra e paz* caísse na minha mesa numa segunda-feira, eu mandaria seu autor plantar cebolas. Cervantes? Desista, homem. Flaubert? Proust? Não me façam rir. Graham Greene? Tente farmácia. Nem le Carré escaparia. Certa vez recomendei a uma mulher chamada Corina que se ocupasse de afazeres domésticos e poupasse o mundo da sua óbvia demência ...

The Spies

1

I'm a literature graduate and seek oblivion in drink. But I only drink
on weekends. From Monday to Friday, I work for a publishing company, where one of my tasks is to vet the unsolicited manuscripts that
arrive in every post; they come in through the windows, drop from
the ceiling, push up through the floorboards, or are dumped on my
desk by Marcito, the owner of the publishing house, with the words:
"See if this is any good." This festering deluge of authors wanting
to be published began after a little book of ours, entitled *Astrology
and Love—A Sidereal Guide for Lovers*, proved such a success that
it allowed Marcito to buy two new motorbikes for his collection.
All those would-be writers suddenly became aware of our existence,
and the torrent of manuscripts hasn't stopped since. It falls to me
to read them and decide their future. On Mondays, I always have a
hangover, and any typescripts that arrive then go straight from my
trembling hands into the bin. And on Mondays, my rejection letters
are particularly ferocious. I not only advise the author never to send us
anything else, I also suggest that he or she never writes another line,
another word, not even a receipt. If *War and Peace* were to arrive on
my desk on a Monday, I would tell its author to take up gardening.
Cervantes? Give it up, man. Flaubert? Proust? Don't make me laugh.

Graham Greene? Try a career in pharmacy. Not even Le Carré would escape. I once advised a woman called Corina to concentrate on her housework and spare the world her demented belief that she was a poet. One day, she barged into my office, brandishing the rejected book, which had ended up being published by someone else, and hurled it at my head. Whenever anyone asks me where I got the small scar over my left eye, I say:

"Poetry."

Corina has since published several books of poetry and *pensées* with great success. She makes a point of sending me invitations to her various launches and signing sessions. I understand her latest publication is a collection of her complete poetry and prose, four hundred pages of the stuff. In hardback. I live in dread that one day she'll turn up at the office and throw that great brick at my head too.

A more immediate threat, at the time, came from Fulvio Edmar, the author of *Astrology and Love*, who had never received any royalties for his work. He had paid for the first edition himself and felt that he should receive full royalties for all the editions printed after the book took off. Marcito did not agree, and I was the one who had to respond to Fulvio Edmar's ever more outraged demands. For years, we exchanged insults by letter, although we never met. He once described to me in great detail how, if ever we did meet, he would put my testicles where my tonsils are. I, in turn, warned him always to carry a knuckle-duster in his pocket.

However, even my most violent rejection letters, my Monday-morning diatribes, end with a charming PS. On Marcito's instructions. If, however, you would care to pay for the publication of your own book, the publisher will be delighted to review this evaluation etc. etc. I've known Marcito since we were at school together. Two spotty fifteen-year-olds. He knew that I was the best in class at writing essays and invited me to pen some dirty stories, which he then stapled together to make a book entitled *The Wanker*, which he rented out to anyone who wanted to take it home with them, on condition that they return the book the following day—unstained. After we left school, we didn't see each other for years, until, that is, I sought him out on hearing that he had started his own publishing house. I had written a novel, for which I needed a publisher. And, no, it wasn't a dirty book. We had a good laugh about *The Wanker*, but Marcito said that, unless I paid for the publication costs myself, there was no way he could publish a spy story about a fictitious Brazilian nuclear program sabotaged by the Americans. The publishing house was only just getting started. His partner in the company was an uncle of his, who owned a fertilizer factory, and whose sole interest in the enterprise was the publication of a monthly almanac to be distributed among his customers in the interior of Rio Grande do Sul. Marcito, however, made me an offer. He had plans to start a real publishing house and needed someone to help him. If I went to work for him, he would, eventually, publish my novel. He couldn't promise me a large salary, but... At that point, I recalled how he had never shared the rental money from *The Wanker* with me. He was doubtless going to exploit me again. But I was seduced by the idea of working for a publisher. I was, after all, a literature graduate and, at the time, working in a shop selling videos. I was thirty years old and had recently married Julinha. João (Julinha wouldn't allow me to call him Le Carré) was about to be born. So I agreed. That was twelve years ago. My first task was to copy out an encyclopaedia article about chameleons for inclusion in the almanac. A prophetic choice: the chameleon is a creature that adapts to any situation and merges into the background. That is precisely what I've been doing ever since. I read typescripts. I write letters. I come up with most of the copy for an almanac intended to boost the sales of fertilizers. I feel sorry for myself and I drink. And, very slowly, I'm merging into the background.

The publishing house grew in size. I discovered that Marcito wasn't simply the cretinous rich kid I had always imagined him to be. He had a taste, which I would never have suspected in a collector of motorbikes, for Simenon. After the success of *Astrology and Love*, we started publishing more books, mostly paid for by the authors themselves. If we're lucky or if the author has a large family, some of these books even sell quite well. Occasionally, I recommend that we publish one of the unsolicited manuscripts that arrive on my desk, especially if it arrives on a Friday, when I am full of good will towards humanity and its literary pretensions, because I know that I will end the day at a table in the Bar do Espanhol, where my weekly booze-up begins, my three days of consciousness numbed by the *cachaça* and beer with which I cut myself free from me and *mi puta vida*—my wretched life. My most frequent companion at that table in the Bar do Espanhol is Joel Dubin, who comes into the office twice a week, on Wednesdays and Fridays, to edit the text of the almanac or check the proofs of any forthcoming books. They say that, despite his short stature, his blue eyes thrill the girls at the sixth-form college where he teaches Portuguese. He swears blind that he has never had it off with any of his students, although he does promise wild nights of love to those who manage to pass the university entrance exam. I know little about Dubin's real sex life, except that it must be better than mine. Even the chairs in the Bar do Espanhol have a better sex life than I do. Dubin always used to fall in love with entirely unsuitable girls. Once, he was in the middle of an argument with one such girl when she asked the waiter if they had any sparkling wine without the bubbles. He decided there and then that she wasn't safe to be out on her own in the world and they very nearly got married. He wrote poems, bad poems. He introduced himself as "Joel Dubin, minor poet." He used to recite one of these poems to any potential girlfriend, something about a hypotenuse in search of a triangle. He called this his "geometrical chat-up line." Any girls who understood the poem or smiled just to please him would immediately be rejected, because he loathed intellectuals. He preferred girls who bawled: "What?!"

Dubin and I had long arguments, at the office and at our table in the bar, about literature and grammar, and we disagreed radically about the placement of commas. Dubin is a legalist and says that there are rules regarding the use of commas and that these should be respected. I am a relativist: I think that commas are like hundreds and thousands, to be distributed judiciously wherever they are needed and without spoiling one's enjoyment of the cake. It's not uncommon for me to re-revise Dubin's revision of a text and either cut out any commas he has added or add a few of my own in defiance of the rules, wherever I think fit. In the bar, our conversations used to begin with the comma and then branch out to take in the human condition and the Universe. They would become increasingly vitriolic and strident the more we drank, until the Spaniard who owned the bar—hence the name—would come over and ask us, please, to keep the noise down. We would heap ever more rancorous insults on every writer in the city. I still don't know if Dubin accompanied me down into the depths of my weekly plunges into unconsciousness. I don't even know how I got home on Friday nights. Perhaps Dubin, having drunk rather less, actually carried me. I've never asked. On Saturday evenings, we would find ourselves back at the same table in the Bar do Espanhol, where we would start getting drunk all over again and resume the same insane conversation. It was a way of dramatizing our own inescapable mediocrity, a way of mutual flagellation through banality. Dubin called our endless arguments "Pavannes for the living dead." Once, we spent almost an hour yelling at each other over some grammatical query or other:

"Enclisis!"
"Proclisis!"
"Enclisis!"
"Proclisis!"
"Enclisis!"
"Proclisis!"

Until the Spaniard signalled to us from behind the bar to keep the noise down.

I also don't know how I managed to get home in the early hours of

Sunday morning. I spent all of Sunday sleeping, while Julinha and João went to lunch at her sister's house.

I was left alone with Black the dog. The sweet Julinha whom I married when she became pregnant had disappeared, never to be seen again, inside a fat, embittered woman of the same name. On Sundays, she only left food for the dog. If I wanted to eat, I had to negotiate with Black. She hardly spoke to me at all. João, who was twelve, didn't talk to me either. The only one who did was Black. At least his eyes seemed to say "I understand, I understand." On Sunday evenings, I would return to the Bar do Espanhol to meet up with Dubin. The Spaniard, by the way, isn't Spanish. His name is Miguel, but Professor Fortuna started calling him "Don Miguel" and then "the Spaniard." Equally, Professor Fortuna is not a professor. He was a regular at the bar, but never sat at our table. He said that he didn't like to mix, not with us personally, but with humanity in general. He explained that he called the Spaniard the Spaniard because he reminded him of Miguel de Unamuno, whom he had, in fact, met. Now, as far as we knew, Unamuno had never visited Porto Alegre and the Professor had never left Porto Alegre. Sometimes we wondered if he had ever even left the Bar do Espanhol. Besides, the ages didn't match, even though the professor is a lot older than me or Dubin. "A bluffer," was what he called Unamuno. We suspected that the Professor had read none of the authors on whom he had such definite opinions. He used to say:

"Nietzsche is the man. All the others are rubbish."

"And what about Heidegger, Professor?"

He would rub his face with both hands, the invariable prelude to one of his categorical statements.

"A fake."

Marx?

"He's washed up."

Camus?

"A queer."

Professor Fortuna was always unshaven and, regardless of the time of year, wore an overcoat the colour of a wet rat. He's not an ugly man, but it was easier to believe in the sexual adventures he recounted ("I learned all I know in India") than to believe, as he claimed, that he could read Greek. He said that any day now he would hand over for publication the book he was writing, a response to *The Critique of Pure Reason*, which had the provisional title of *Anti Kant*. We knew almost nothing about his life, but we were sure of two things: that book did not exist and he had never read Kant. Or Nietzsche. Dubin and I frequently involved him in our discussions, even when his table was far from ours and we had to shout so that he could hear us.

"What's your position on the comma, Professor?"

And he would answer:

"I'm against them!"

The Professor's thesis was this: you can put a comma wherever you like. The true test of a writer is the semi-colon, which, according to him, no one has yet mastered. With the possible exception of Henry James, whom he clearly hadn't read either. A recurring topic of debate was: Can detective or spy fiction be good literature? I said it could, Dubin wasn't sure, and the Professor declared roundly that it was arrant rubbish. He reacted to my evidence to the contrary with dismissive noises. Graham Greene. Pf! Rubem Fonseca? Ugh! Raymond Chandler? Huh! Once I asked him if he had bought a particular book by John Le Carré.

"What for? I have toilet paper at home."

The only reason I didn't get up and hit him was because I couldn't. It was Saturday night, and I was already halfway down to the bottom of the pit.

But why am I telling you all this? Take it as a plea either for mercy or for punishment. An attenuating or perhaps aggravating factor for what is to come. My defence or my condemnation. This is what I was before the first white envelope arrived. This is what we were. Garrulous but innocent members of the living dead. I swear we were innocent. Or take it merely as a description of the background into which I was gradually merging when the story began, like a chameleon. First chapter, first scene, colon: a sulphurous swamp, a lake of lamentations, upon which, one day, a white envelope alighted like a lost bird.

It's all over now, what the stars ordained would happen happened, and we are no longer innocents. Or, rather, we are not the same innocents. Nothing can be done or undone, all that's left is the story and our lingering guilt. Curse us, please. Be kind and curse us.

The first envelope arrived at the publisher's one Tuesday in the post. I was still suffering the effects of Monday's hangover and very nearly threw it in the bin unopened. There was something about the handwriting, though, that stopped me. Something appealing, almost supplicant about those capital letters, written in a tremulous, childish hand, made me open the envelope. Inside were four sheets of paper bound together between transparent covers by a spiral binding. On the first sheet of paper was a title, "Ariadne," written in ballpoint pen, with a little flower above the 'i' instead of a dot. The one thing I never understood about this whole story was that little flower. If I *had* understood it, the story would never have happened and we would all have been spared. Between the first and second sheet was a note folded in two. It was from someone signing themselves "A friend," explaining that the author of those sheets of paper did not know that they had been xeroxed and sent to a publisher. They were the first pages of a diary or an autobiography or a confession. The "friend" asked that we read the text "kindly." If we were interested in publishing it, she would send us the rest of the book when it was ready. A "yes" from the publisher would help persuade the author to finish what she had begun with those few pages. "Please say Yes!" said the note in conclusion.

I read the first lines of that handwritten page.

"My father met a painter in Europe who was obsessed with Ariadne. I owe my name to a stranger's obcession. I sometimes think my whole life has been ruled by other people's obcessions. At least the obcession that will kill me will be mine alone because nothing is as self-indulgent or as solitary as suicide. But not yet not yet."

"Obsession" was spelled incorrectly, but that didn't make me throw the pages in the bin as I had with Corina's poems, when she wrote "lusid" instead of "lucid." I continued reading. "Ariadne" was twenty-five. She would not commit suicide at once because "I need to close myself up gradually like someone closing up a house before setting off on a journey. Window by window room by room. My heart first." Only with her heart closed could she avenge herself for what they had done to her and to someone she called "the Secret Lover." To avenge herself on those who had destroyed everything "our past the living room in the old house with the candles burning on the floor the corner of the ruined garden where he said that if the moon smiled she would resemble me and I cried 'Are you calling me "Moonface?!" and he kissed me on the mouth for the first time." Only with her heart closed could she exact a just revenge for what they had done to her father too, "the poor distracted man probably doesn't even know he's dead." In those first four pages there was no explanation as to who "they" were, the people on whom Ariadne would take her revenge before committing suicide. Nor what form that vengeance or that suicide would take. The pages ended with the author evoking "the house of the catalpa tree," home I presumed to the living room with the candles burning on the floor and the ruined garden where she and the Secret Lover met.

I found those four pages fascinating. Not because of their literary value—that smiling moon was a bit too much for me to stomach, well, I still hadn't quite recovered from the weekend's drinking. I don't really know what it was I found so enchanting, which means that I cannot explain this whole story. It was more like being dazzled, in the sense of being in the presence of a light that dissolves all shadows. It was a sudden incursion into the darkness in which I lived. Ariadne had invaded my mind along with the light emanating from her words. In an instant, I imagined her so entirely and so intensely that my next feeling was an absurd twinge of jealousy for that Secret Lover. Or perhaps what attracted me was the imminent tragedy she described, my identification with a co-suicide in the making. Or perhaps it was just the complete absence of commas.

I looked at the back of the envelope. The return address was a P.O. box number in the town of Frondosa.

Marcito's secretary is called Bela. She's a tall, buxom, blonde Italian with rosy cheeks. We work in the same room. Whenever Dubin came into the office, he would sing "Bela, Bela Giovanella," and she would roll her eyes and sigh, weary of the effect she had on foolish men. In response to little Dubin's invitations to go to some smart café in the country ("My dream is to possess you somewhere that serves seven different types of jam," he would say), she would suggest he come back when he had grown up. Lovely Bela has a lover who is older than her, although we don't know what exactly goes on in Marcito's office when he calls her in and shuts the door. Whatever it is they do behind that door, they do it in silence.

She and I were alone on the afternoon that the white envelope arrived and I asked her if she knew where Frondosa was.

"Frondosa, Frondosa… Hmm, it's certainly nowhere near where I come from."

Until she was fifteen, lovely Bela had lived in an area in the interior of Rio Grande do Sul that had been colonised by Italians. Dubin claimed to have erotic fantasies about the lovely Bela walking barefoot among the pigs. He dreamed about her muddy calves. He said he had a thing about the calves of adolescent country girls. He used to ask the lovely Bela if the parish priest used to sit her on his knee and stroke her calves, and wanted to know all the details. The lovely Bela was not amused.

"Túlio will know where it is," she said, pointing at the white envelope.

Túlio is a salesman for the fertiliser factory owned by Marcito's uncle. He travels all over the state. He's the one who delivers the firm's almanac to the factory's customers. He was bound to know everything about Frondosa.

"He'll be here tomorrow," said the lovely Bela, before returning to her copy of *Hello* magazine.

Ariadne. With a little flower above the "i." Was it a fictitious name? Her father, whether fictitious or not, had chosen the name. How did the myth of Ariadne go now? She was the daughter of Minos, King of Crete. She fell in love with Theseus, to whom she gave a ball of thread so that he could find his way out of the labyrinth once he had killed the Minotaur. Ariadne had stood at the entrance of the labyrinth, holding the end of the thread for her lover. Now there was another Ariadne, whether fictitious or not, holding the end of a thread in a place called Frondosa. The other end of the thread was there before me. A tiny thread. A mere nothing. Just a P.O. box number in an unknown town, on the back of a white envelope. A beginning.

2

"I think I've read that phrase somewhere before," said Dubin.

"Which phrase?"

"If the moon smiled she would resemble you. And it wasn't on a lavatory wall either."

It was Wednesday. Dubin had arrived, given his usual greeting—"Bela Bela Giovanella"—and read the four manuscript pages, having first perused the accompanying letter. His hunch was that the "Friend" of the letter and the "Ariadne" of the text were one and the same. You could tell by the absence of commas in both documents. He liked the diary-cum-autobiography though. The author was obviously a keen reader, despite the errors in punctuation and spelling. He didn't believe it had been written by a potential suicide.

Not a real suicide.

"It's a fiction. Phoney literary despair. You get a lot of it in the those small towns."

Dubin had invented a town in the interior called Santa Edwige dos Aflitos—St. Edwige of the Afflicted—which was a summation of his affectionate scorn for anyone who didn't live in the capital. Now and again, he would supply us with new information about the town, which had "the best carnival in the whole Piruiri valley," Piruiri being a river he had invented too. It was the largest producer of hay in Brazil and every year, they held a National Festival of Hay, known as the HayHoedown, during which the queen and the princesses of the festival were chosen at dances held in the Clube Comercial, where, on the occasion of a rare appearance by Agnaldo Rayol, the prefect's wife had made a complete spectacle of herself by clinging to the singer's legs. According to Dubin, there was a local Academy of Letters with 127 members and a football team that was at the bottom of the state's bottom division and was awaiting the creation of another division so that it could be relegated still further. The local Academy of Letters would be full of Ariadnes like ours, perhaps a little older and less gifted at writing. But no real suicides.

Túlio arrived and greeted us with his usual enthusiasm ("Gentlemen! *Signorina!*"), but this time I interrupted his swift passage through our room to Marcito's office and asked if he could tell us anything about a town called Frondosa. He didn't even have to think.

"Frondosa? Galotto."

"Galotto?"

"The Galotto factory. The owners of the factory own the town."

"Are they very powerful?"

"Powerful and rich. The most powerful company in the region."

"Where is Frondosa?"

"Have you got a map handy?"

I had. Túlio's finger hovered over one area of the map for a few seconds before finding the right place to land. There it was: Frondosa. "It's a very pretty area, although the town's no great shakes. Apparently, it takes its name from a big, leafy tree that used to stand in the square."

Túlio is a burly fellow, nearly six foot six tall and with a pleasant, swarthy, rather Arab face. He travels all over the state selling fertilizer and distributing our almanac, so he has contacts everywhere. Did he know anyone in Frondosa?

"Let's see… The people I have most to do with there are the staff at the agricultural cooperative. No, wait, I do know a Galotto."

"One of the owners of the factory?"

"No, the factory doesn't belong to the Galotto family any more. They kept the name, but it's under different ownership now. The man who started the business was Aldo Galotto, a tinsmith. He passed it on to his son, whose name I forget now, but who made the business into a real force to be reckoned with. But the son of that son wanted nothing to do with the business, he was a painter. He lived for a long time in Europe and mixed with all kinds of artists. The factory ended up in the hands of his son-in-law, Martelli, and the Galotto family were left with nothing. I don't know how the Galotto fellow I know manages to live. I guess his sister gives him money. He's a nice fellow, a good talker, but an idle so-and-so. He spends all his time playing snooker. And he drinks like a fish."

"So the artist only had one son and one daughter?"

"I'm not sure. I think there's a younger brother too, or was. Something happened to him. I can't quite remember what… Or perhaps that was another member of the family. I don't recall."

"Do you know the sister's name?"

"The one who's married to Martelli? No, but I can find out. Why do you want to know all this?"

Dubin answered:

"We're looking for new authors."

Túlio undertook to find out the sister's name. It was unlikely she was *our* Ariadne. Only the reference to the artist father who had known other artists in Europe connected her to the Galotto family. And if she was the same person, she would hardly be using her own name. We needed to investigate. First step: reply to the letter from the "Friend." I wrote saying that we were very impressed by the sample she had sent us of Ariadne's work and would like to see more. It would help if she could give us more information, about herself and about the author. If the rest of the book was as good as the sample, we would seriously consider publishing it, but we needed names so that we knew who we were dealing with. We would also require a photo of Ariadne. For some reason, I signed the letter with a pseudonym, Agomar Peniche, Editorial Director. Second step: I went into Marcito's office, flung the four sheets of paper down on his desk and said: "*This* is good." He didn't even look at them. He asked what they were. I told him and said they were worth investing in. This provoked a pained look.

"How much?"

"I don't know," I said. "I don't know how long the book's going to be."

Marcito continued to suffer.

"Do you think it will sell?"

"I believe we will be launching a fine new writer, who will bring prestige and critical acclaim to the publishing house. Or are we only interested in earning money?"

"I don't know about you, but that's all I'm interested in."

"The story might be true though. In which case it could turn out to be a *succès d'escandale.*"

Marcito dismissed me with a gesture, irritated less by my pushiness than by my French. I interpreted this as a yes.

That Friday, I took the manuscript to the Bar do Espanhol, to get Professor Fortuna's opinion. His thesis was that literature, like stevedoring and Formula 1 racing, was not a suitable career for women. Whenever I cited examples of great women writers, he would shake his head and smile a demoniacal smile. According to him, the only thing women achieved with their literature was to drive themselves and those around them mad. He said women writers had ruined the lives of more men than prostitutes and gambling. He had serious doubts about the wisdom of teaching women to write at all and advised strong corrective action at the first sign of literary ambitions in young girls. That's why we were surprised when he read the four pages and said:

"Not bad."

"You mean you liked it, Professor?"

"As I said, it's not bad."

"Virginia Woolf or Madame Dely?"

"More like Ivona Gabor."

Dubin and I looked at each other. Ivona Gabor?

"Hungarian," said the professor. "You wouldn't know her, of course."

"What did she write?"

The professor sighed and made a vague gesture. We could hardly expect him to summon up, just like that, the works of Ivona Gabor, which were, apparently, legion.

"Is she dead?"

"Oh, she died a long time ago, killed herself, but not without first sending her husband and her whole family mad. Yet another example of the imprudence of the indiscriminate teaching of literacy."

My letter to the P.O. box in Frondosa had been sent on the Thursday. We reckoned that a reply and possibly more pages would arrive on the Wednesday of the following week. Until then, all we could do was wait. We spent the rest of that Friday re-reading and discussing Ariadne's manuscript. Dubin even went so far as to take a pen from his pocket, but I stopped him before he started spattering the text with commas. Could our Ariadne have anything to do with the story of the Galotto family in Frondosa? It would be a huge coincidence, but it was an attractive hypothesis. We sought more information about Frondosa from our immediate surroundings, namely, the other regulars at the Bar do Espanhol. Tavinho, who knows everything about football, the only subject that seems to interest him, told us that Frondosa had a football team, but for *futebol de salão*, Brazilian five-a-side. And the team was supported by some local industrialist whose name he had forgotten. Galotto? Yes, that was it! Did anyone else in the bar know anything about Frondosa? No one. Most didn't even know the town existed. We only knew that the author's father had been to Europe where he had met a painter obsessed with the mythical figure of Ariadne. Her father must be the artistic Galotto, who wanted nothing to do with the factory. This would make Ariadne, his daughter, Martelli's wife. And she had cheated on Martelli with the Secret Lover.

"Martelli found out and killed the lover."

"That's the story she's writing."

"The book will be her revenge."

Dubin gleefully rubbed his hands together. His fictitious Santa Edwige dos Aflitos had known only one crime of passion in its entire history. And that was years ago. The affair had ended with a geography teacher being castrated and an heiress banished to a convent. The history of Frondosa promised far more. Always assuming, of course, that it wasn't just another fiction.

"De Chirico," said Tavinho suddenly.

We looked at him, surprised.

"What?"

"The painter obsessed with Ariadne. His name was De Chirico. He was a major influence on the surrealists."

We stared at him, openmouthed. How did Tavinho, who only ever talked about football, know that? He knew more too.

"De Chirico died in Rome."

"How do you know?"

"I support Lazio," said Tavinho, as if this explained everything. "I know all there is to know about Rome. Would you like me to list the names of all the Popes?"

We spent the rest of the evening speculating about Ariadne's manuscript and the real or imagined drama she would reveal to us. Only at midnight did I realise that I had drunk only one glass of *cachaça*. The Inaugural Drink, I call it. Ariadne had so filled my mind that I had forgotten to drink and had gone no further than that first inaugural shot of rum. I arrived home sober. Black the dog looked at me, astonished, but said nothing.

The Move

Graciliano Ramos
Translated by Padma Viswanathan

"The Move" is the first chapter, or story, from *Vidas sêcas*, a 1938 novel by Brazilian writer Graciliano Ramos (1892–1953) about a hard-luck family from the Brazilian interior, displaced by one of the many droughts to scourge the Northeast. The storytelling in the piece also migrates between the characters' minds, from Fabiano, the father, to Vitória, his wife, and even to their dog.

Vidas sêcas is one of Ramos's best-known works, but there is only one previously published English translation, by Ralph Dimmick. While I must acknowledge a debt to that 1961 version, I also found infelicities and omissions that made me want to retranslate.

A few examples: Dimmick interprets and forecasts when he calls the book *Barren Lives*, and this story "A New Home." *Vidas sêcas* means, literally, *Dry Lives*, while the original title of his story is "Mudança," which means a move, almost always to a new home, though Ramos didn't name a destination. "The Move," I think, has an equivalent resonance for English readers. Dimmick refers to "the drought victims," where Ramos called them "*os infelizes*." "*Infeliz*" simply means "unhappy" or "unfortunate." I call them "wretches." Then, the dog, "*Baleia*," or "Whale," goes entirely unnamed in Dimmick's translation, diminishing the writing's often pointed irony. These are but a few examples, and surely future readers will find faults and errors in my own translation! My wish, regardless, is that it gives this deserving book new life.

Graciliano Ramos, "Mudança" from *Vidas sêcas*.
Rio de Janeiro: José Olympio Editora, 1938.

Mudança

Na planície avermelhada os juázeiros alargavam duas manchas verdes. Os infelizes tinham caminhado o dia inteiro, estavam cansados e famintos. Ordinàriamente andavam pouco, mas como haviam repousado bastante na areia do rio sêco, a viagem progredira bem três léguas. Fazia horas que procuravam uma sombra. A folhagem dos juàzeiros apareceu longe, através dos galhos pelados da caatinga rala.

Arrastaram-se para lé, devagar, sinhá Vitória com o filho mais nôvo escanchado no quarto e o baú de fôlha na cabeça, Fabiano sombrio, cambaio, o aió a tiracolo, a cuia pendurada numa correia prêsa ao cinturão, a espingarda de pederneira no ombro. O menino mais velho e a cachorra Baleia iam atrás.

Os juàzeiros aproximaram-se, recuaram, sumiram-se. O menino mais velho pôs-se a chorar, sentou-se no chão.

— Anda, condenado do diabo, gritou-lhe o pai.

Não obtendo resultado, fustigou-o com a bainha da faca de ponta. Mas o pequeno esperneou acuado, depois sossegou, deitou-se, fechou os olhos. Fabiano ainda lhe deu algumas pancadas e esperou que êle se levantasse. Como isto não acontecesse, espiou os quatro cantos, zangado, praguejando baixo.

A caatinga estendia-se, de um vermelho indeciso salpicado de manchas brancas que eram ossadas. O vôo negro dos urubus fazia ...

The Move

On the reddening plain, the jujube trees spread in two green stains. The wretches had walked all day. They were tired and hungry. They typically walked less, but after a good rest on the sands of the dry riverbed, they had managed a full three leagues. For hours now, they'd been looking for shade. Through the bare branches of the scrubland, the jujubes' foliage appeared far away.

They trudged toward it, slowly: Miz Vitória with the younger boy straddling her hip, and the tin trunk on her head; sullen, bandy-legged Fabiano with the thistle-fiber game bag slung across his chest, the drinking gourd hung from a strap hooked to his shoulder strap, and the flintlock on his shoulder. The older boy and the dog, Whale, followed behind.

The jujubes came close, receded, vanished. The older boy, breaking down in tears, sat on the ground.

"Move, Goddamn you!" his father shouted at him.

This had no result. He hit the boy with the scabbard of his knife, but the little fellow kicked and balked, then quieted and lay down, eyes closed. Fabiano kept hitting him in hopes he might get up. This didn't happen. He looked this way and that, swearing angrily under his breath.

The scrubland spread in every direction, an uncertain red sprinkled with the white stains of skeletons. Vultures in black flight made high circles around dying animals.

"Move, you disgrace!"

The kid didn't budge. Fabiano wanted to kill him. His heart was heavy, and he wanted someone to blame for his misery. The drought seemed to him an unavoidable fact, and the child's stubbornness aggravated him. Clearly, this tiny obstacle wasn't to blame, but he made the going tough, and the cowhand needed to arrive, even if he didn't know where.

They had left the roads, which were full of thorns and pebbles, and had been walking for hours along the river's edge, where the dry, cracked mud scorched their feet.

The backlander was troubled briefly by the thought of abandoning his boy in that desert. He thought of the vultures and bone heaps, scratching his dirty, red beard indecisively and looking at his surroundings. Miz Vitória pointed with her lip, vaguely indicating a direction, and grunted, suggesting they were close. Fabiano sheathed his knife and put it in his belt as he crouched to grab his son's wrist. The boy shrank, knees to his stomach, cold as a corpse. Fabiano's rage vanished into pity. He couldn't possibly abandon his little angel to the beasts of the wild. Trusting his rifle to Miz Vitória, he loaded his son onto his back and stood, grasping the thin, limp little arms that fell across his chest. Miz Vitória approved this arrangement, and grunted again, guttural sounds to indicate the invisible jujube trees.

So the journey dragged on, ever slower, ever more miserable, in the enormous silence.

Without her buddy, Whale took the lead. Back bowed, ribs jutting, she ran, panting, tongue hanging out. From time to time, she waited for the people, who lagged behind.

Just the night before, there had been six of them, counting the parrot. Poor thing, it died on the river bank, where they had rested beside a puddle: hunger was pinching the migrants, and with no sign of food anywhere. Whale dined on the feet, the head, and the bones of her friend, and had no memory of this. Now, whenever they stopped, she would look over their belongings with bright eyes and find it strange not to see, on top of the tin trunk, the little cage where the bird would awkwardly perch. Fabiano also sometimes missed it, but then the memory would return. They had hunted in vain for roots, they had used up the last of the flour, they heard no lost cattle lowing in the scrubland. Miz Vitória had been sitting on the burning-hot earth, her arms crossed firmly on her bony knees, thinking on old events in no particular order: wedding parties, rodeos, novenas, all a jumble. Roused by a harsh cry, she saw, close by, reality and the parrot, pacing furiously, feet spread, in a ridiculous attitude. She decided then and there to make a meal of it, and justified this by declaring that the bird was useless anyway. It didn't even talk. It had never had a chance to learn to talk. The family itself barely ever talked, and since the disaster, they had lived in silence, save for occasional, brief words. The parrot floated along like a buoy, hollering at non-existent cattle, barking in a parody of a dog.

The jujube tree stains again appeared. Fabiano sped up, forgetting his hunger, fatigue and injuries. The heels of his sandals were worn out and the ropes had worn painful cracks between his toes. His heels, hard as hooves, were split and bleeding.

At a bend in the road, he spied the edge of a fence. It filled him with the hope of finding food. He felt like singing. His voice came out hoarse and horrible-sounding, and he shut up so as not to lose it altogether.

They left the river's edge, following the fence up a rise, and arrived at the jujubes. It had been a long while since they had seen shade.

Miz Vitória made her sons comfortable. They collapsed in heaps, and she covered them with rags. The older boy, now recovered from the vertigo that had felled him earlier, curled up on a pile of dry leaves. His head resting on a root, he dozed and wakened. When he opened his eyes, he made out a hill nearby, some stones, an ox-cart. The dog, Whale, was nestled in beside him.

They were in the yard of a deserted ranch. The corral was empty, as was the ruined goat pen. The ranch hand's house was closed up. Everything signaled abandonment. Surely the livestock had died and the occupants fled.

Fabiano listened in vain for the sound of a cowbell. He went up to the house, knocked, and then tried to force the door open. Finding it resistant, he broke into a small garden full of dead plants, rounded the hut, and arrived at the backyard, where he saw an empty clay pit, a stand of blighted *catingueiras*, a Turk's-foot cactus, and the extension of the corral fence. Climbing up on the corner post, he looked out on the scrubland, where the bone heaps and vulture-darkness had grown. Getting down, he pushed on the kitchen door. Discouraged, he returned and lingered an instant on the porch, considering whether to lodge his family there. But on returning to the jujubes he found the children asleep and didn't want to wake them. He gathered kindling, bringing from the goat pen an armload of wood half-eaten by termites, tore up some clumps of *macambira* roots, and arranged it all for the fire.

At this point, Whale pricked up her ears and pointed her nose into the wind, catching the scent of guinea pigs. She sniffed for a minute, located them on a hill nearby, and took off running.

Fabiano followed her with his eyes and startled: a shadow was passing over the top of the hill. He touched his wife's arm and pointed at the sky. The two dared to squint into the sun's brightness for a time. Wiping away tears, they went and squatted close to their sons, sighing and making themselves small, worried that the cloud might have some defect and be vanquished by the terrible blue, that blue that dazzled people and drove them mad.

Days came and days went. The nights covered the earth unexpectedly, an indigo lid falling, a darkness broken only by the redness of dusk.

Tiny, lost in the burning desert, the fugitives clung to each other, tallying their misfortunes and terrors. Fabiano's heart beat together with Miz Vitória's, a tired arm drew up their tattered covers. Resisting their weakness, they pulled back, ashamed, without the heart to face again the hard light, fearful of losing the hopes they nourished.

They grew sleepy and were awakened by Whale, who brought, in her teeth, a guinea pig. Everyone got up, yelling. The older boy rubbed his eyes, which were pebbly with sleep. Miz Vitória kissed Whale's snout. It was covered with blood, which she licked up, making the most of the kiss.

It was a measly catch, but it put off the group's death. And Fabiano wanted to live. He looked at the sky with resolution. The cloud had grown, and now covered the entire hill. Fabiano walked with confidence, forgetting the cracks that split his toes and heels.

Miz Vitória rummaged in the trunk and the boys went to break off a rosemary branch to use as a spit. Whale, ears pricked, sat up, begging, watchful, waiting for her share, probably the bones and perhaps the hide.

Fabiano took the gourd, went down the slope and walked along the dry riverbed, where he found, in the animals' watering hole, a little damp spot. He dug in the sand with his nails, waited for water to bubble up, and leaning over the ground, drank deeply. Sated, he fell, maw up, and watched the stars come alive. One, two, three, four, there were so many stars, more than five stars in the sky. The dusk was covered with high, wispy clouds, and a crazy happiness filled Fabiano's heart.

He thought of his family and felt hungry. On the march, he had moved as though he were a mere object, hardly different from Mr. Tomás's mill wheel. Now, lying down, his belly tightened and his teeth chattered. What had become of Mr. Tomás's mill wheel?

He looked again at the sky. The clouds gathered, the moon rose, huge and white. It was sure to rain.

Mr. Tomás had fled as well. With the drought, the mill wheel had stopped. And he, Fabiano, was like the mill wheel. He didn't know why he was, but he was. One, two, three, more than five stars in heaven. The moon had a halo the color of milk. It would rain. Good. The scrubland would come back to life, the seed of the cattle would return to the corral, and he, Fabiano, would be the cowhand of this dead ranch. Cowbells with bone clappers would enliven the loneliness. The children, fat and ruddy-cheeked, would play in the goat pen, Miz Vitória would wear flashy floral skirts. Cattle would fill the corral and the scrubland would grow totally green.

He remembered his sons, his wife, and Whale, who were still up top, under the jujube, thirsty. He remembered the dead guinea pig. He filled the gourd, rose and edged away slowly, so as not to spill the brackish water as he climbed the slope. A warm breeze shook the lupines and the cereus, a new heartbeat. He felt it, a shiver of excitement passing through the scrubland, a resurrection of twisted branches and dry leaves.

He arrived. He put the gourd on the ground, propping it up with stones. That would take care of his family's thirst. Then he squatted, rummaging in the game-bag, pulled out the flintlock, lit the macambira roots, and blew on them, puffing out his hollow cheeks. The flames trembled and rose to tint his sunburnt face, his red beard, his blue eyes. Minutes later, the guinea pig twisted and sizzled on the rosemary spit.

They were all happy. Miz Vitória would wear a ruffled, flowered skirt. Her withered face would grow young, her spindly haunches would fill out, her scarlet dress would be the envy of the other *mestizas*.

The moon grew, its milky shadow grew, the stars were exhausted by the this whiteness that filled the night. One, two, three, now there were fewer stars in the sky. At close range, the cloud darkened the hill.

The ranch would revive, and he, Fabiano, would be the cow hand, which was as good as saying he would be the boss of this world.

Their paltry things were gathered on the ground: the flintlock rifle, the game bag, the water gourd, and the painted tin trunk. The fire crackled. The guinea pig sizzled over the coals.

A resurrection. The colors of health would return to Miz Vitória's sad face. The children would loll in the soft earth of the goat pen. Cowbells would tinkle all around. The scrubland would be green.

Whale wagged her tail, looking at the coals. And because she didn't worry about such things, she waited patiently for the moment when she would chew the bones. Afterwards, she would sleep.

post-op poem

Angélica Freitas
Translated by Hilary B. Kaplan

Angélica Freitas's *Rilke Shake* (2007) takes a cosmopolitan spin on the Brazilian and world poetry canons in the age of identity, internet, and innovation after the 20th-century vanguards. Freitas's roots in southern Brazil, combined with years spent in São Paulo and abroad, inflect the poems' language. The book has been translated into German and selections have been published in English, Romanian, Spanish, and Swedish. Currently, Freitas lives in her native Pelotas, Rio Grande do Sul, where, as a recipient of a Programa Petrobras Cultural writing fellowship, she is completing her second book.

The compact "post-op poem" enacts the struggle to blend personal and poetic identities using humor, colloquial language, and concrete imagery. In this poem about extraction, the idea of economy in words becomes particularly resonant to its translation. The second and third stanzas are sites of several tradeoffs between Portuguese and English. The efficient *daí* becomes a whole stanza, while other, lengthier Portuguese constructions tighten up. A few words provide good challenges: *desentranhadas* refers to what's been taken out of the subject of the poem, but it is also a poetry term, referring to a poem constructed from lines from another work (as in a cento) like Manuel Bandeira's *"Poema desentranhado de uma prosa de Augusto Frederico Schmidt"* and Carlito Acevedo's *"Na noite física (desentranhado de um poema de Charles Peixoto)." Gaita de boca* is a harmonica, also known as a mouth harp, which preserves the reference to the body part and creates visual symmetry with the previous line, filling the gap between the parentheses, and the hole left by the removal of some essential persons/parts.

Original text: Angélica Freitas, "poema pós-operatório" from *Rilke Shake*. São Paulo: Cosac Naify; Rio de Janeiro: 7Letras, 2007

poema pós-operatório

ex
em latim
fora de

daí algumas criaturas
parecem ter sido

desentranhadas
de você

você passa na rua
e as reconhece

ei, ali vai minha
oitava costela!

era minha!

e aponta pra lacuna
no lado esquerdo

post-op poem

ex
in latin
former

so that's why
it feels like

you've had a few critters
harvested

you walk down the street
recognizing them

hey, there goes
my eighth rib!

mine, i say!

you point to the lacuna
on your left side

(cabe uma gaita
de boca)

olha só!

(it could hold
a mouth harp)

look!

The Summer of Chibo

Vanessa Barbara and Emilio Fraia
Translated by Katrina Dodson

Vanessa Barbara and Emilio Fraia co-wrote their debut novel, *O verão do Chibo* (The Summer of Chibo), over the course of three years and countless emails. Both of these young São Paulo writers, each of whom turned thirty this year, are incredibly active in the world of Brazilian letters. Barbara's book chronicling her stint working the information booth at Latin America's largest bus terminal, *O Livro Amarelo do Terminal* (The Bus Terminal Yellow Pages, 2008), won the prestigious national Jabuti Award for journalism. She has translated Gertrude Stein and F. Scott Fitzgerald into Portuguese and writes for the *Folha de São Paulo* newspaper, among other publications. Fraia has also worked as a journalist for national magazines and is currently a literary editor at Cosac Naify. Both writers have graphic novels forthcoming in a series from Companhia das Letras.

O verão do Chibo is more experimental and absurdist than the realist fiction of Barbara and Fraia's Brazilian contemporaries, perhaps a reflection of the creative momentum of collaborative projects. The story, likewise, is driven by the collective imaginations of four young boys, whose friendship grows and unravels through their improvised plots involving insects, secret agents, and mysterious objects found on the corn plantation where they spend their summers. The novel opens with the disappearance of Chibo, the narrator's older brother, and this excerpt leads into reminiscences of happier summers that contrast with the group's present threat of dissolution. The narrative is striking for its humor and highly visual quality. Its evocation of comic books, cartoons, old Westerns and noir films transitions naturally into American English. These influences mix with Brazilian childhood references, like the "yellow cow" contest (page 258), based on the rhyme that lays down a challenge for who can be silent the longest: "Yellow cow / shit in the pan. / Whoever talks first / eats up all its poo!" ("*Vaca amarela / cagou na panela. / Quem falar primeiro / come toda a bosta dela!*")

The biggest challenge for translation was finding a voice to match the seven-year-old narrator's register, which veers between a rambling São Paulo vernacular and a more literary, nostalgic tone. Though I tried to stay close to the original Portuguese, the authors' linguistic playfulness invited me to be similarly inventive in English, coming up with words like "hard-shells" as an alias for beetles ("*cascudos*") and "Moptop" for the chubby kid nicknamed "*Cabelo*" because of his shaggy hair.

Original text: Vanessa Barbara and Emilio Fraia, *O verão do Chibo*.
Rio de Janeiro: Objetiva Alfaguara, 2008.

O verão do Chibo

Lembro da primeira vez que vi a plantação. O Chibo me trouxe pela mão, me colocou sentado numa pedra. Pediu para eu não sumir de vista, nem sujar a bermuda, e foi com o Bruno para a beira do laguinho apostar corrida de besouro. O sol, alto e mole, castigava o Cabelo que tinha o nariz coberto de pomada. Ele era o juiz e me olhava desconfiado entre um grito e outro da torcida. Tão logo os cascudos cruzaram a linha de chegada (vitória do Chibo sob vaias do Bruno), o Cabelo veio e perguntou se eu sabia o que era uma bolha de sabão. Fiz que não e ele achou graça. Depois me ensinou sua careta favorita, a boca um pouco mais torta, o olho virado, assim, e em pouco tempo eu e o Cabelo tínhamos nosso próprio besouro, que era o mais rápido e desbancou todos os outros do milharal.

Com o Bruno foi diferente. No início ele mal falou comigo, não me queria por perto. Ou então duvidava que eu pudesse entender o que ele dizia (daí ficava quieto). Depois isso melhorou, mas não muito. Tinham coisas que ele só contava ao Chibo ou em voz alta quando saía entre os pés de milho. O Cabelo também era carta fora, mas a verdade é que ele não dava a mínima: estava ocupado demais com o nosso besouro campeão. O Cabelo era dedicado: adestrava o cascudo Bob falando enrolado. Botava o bicho na parte de cima da mão, prendia uma pata pra ele não fugir e começava a pregar a palavra...

The Summer of Chibo

I remember the first time I saw the plantation. Chibo led me by the hand, sat me down on a rock. He told me not to leave his sight or get my shorts dirty and went with Bruno to the edge of the pond to bet on beetle races. The sun, high and draining, punished Moptop, his nose all covered in sunscreen. He was the judge and looked at me suspiciously amid all the shouts and cheers of the fans. As soon as the hard-shells crossed the finish line (victory for Chibo under Bruno's jeers), Moptop came and asked if I knew about soap bubbles. I shook my head and he thought it was funny. Then he taught me his favorite silly face, your mouth a little more twisted, one eye rolled up, like this, and in no time Moptop and I had our own beetle, the fastest of all, who put every other bug on the cornfield to shame.

With Bruno, it was different. He barely spoke to me at first, didn't really want me around. Or he didn't really think I could understand what he was saying (so he kept quiet). Later it got better, but not by much. There were things he'd say only to Chibo or in a loud voice as he was leaving, headed into the corn plants. Moptop was also an odd man out, but honestly he didn't care at all: he was too busy with our champion beetle. Moptop was dedicated: he used to train Bob the Beetle, babbling to it softly. He'd put the bug on top of his hand, hang onto a leg so it wouldn't escape and start to hold forth: *bloash-bloblo-bloarsh-bloblof.* He'd bring his face close to hear its response and answer *bloarsh* as though he were teaching the beetle to enunciate syllables. For the whole summer that we first found Bob napping under a leaf, Moptop would spend his afternoons in long beetle discussions, taking his mascot to meet Bruno, and putting the little critter close to different things to teach it what they were. Finally, one day he stopped hanging onto the beetle's leg and it became the fastest of the cornfield's Coleoptera. Bob would wander up Moptop's shoulders and his back, complaining about life. Bob was ours, Bob belonged to the two of us and he always beat all the other bugs (except in the triathlon competitions). I remember Bruno leaving bread crusts at the Bobsean abode, located in a hollow in the tree house, I remember the supply of cookie fillings that Chibo and I would scrape together for him, a zigzagging pile of chocolate and strawberry. Never was there a beetle like Bob. Bruno and Chibo spent days collecting hard-shells and trying them out one by one in the races, but none were as good. Besides all this, Bob glistened in the sun, was very green and round, and looked like an underworld ladybug. Moptop taught Bob to rub his legs together when he wanted to eat, trained Bob in the twenty-inch dash, with and without obstacles, crumblifting, spit-puddle swimming, twig jump. Moptop made Bob friendly: he'd stay still in your hand, used to sunbathe at Bruno's side, would come wagging his tail whenever we opened his jar.

It's funny to think that Bob almost never flew. Sometimes he'd glide, in a leisurely way, but he didn't care for it much. He preferred athletic training or enjoying Moptop's performance of the song "I'm a Little Rice Ball" (before bedtime). When fully rested, our Bob could make the dash in 6.8 seconds, a time never before recorded in the entire history of the plantation. The other competitors would run in circles, burrow into the dirt, fly away, or arrive years later, lethargic and moldy smelling. Bob would cross the racecourse with flair, fluttering his wings for show and swinging his majestic carapace back and forth. Moptop would wait at the finish line with a towel, me with five different cheers, and we'd go on jumping and shouting while Bruno and Chibo glared at their own team—a pile of bugs with the same stony faces, summer after summer.

After Bob died of coronary disease, or of indeterminate abdominal problems (he simply stopped and didn't move again), we dropped the races because they weren't fun anymore. We still kept trying to poke Bob with a twig, whisper *bloarsh-boblof* in an impatient tone (arms wide open), but he'd gone to sleep. He was tired. As soon as Bruno confirmed the passing of our hard-shell, comforting Moptop with a pat on his shoulder, we observed a minute of silence. But Chibo didn't let anyone stay sad for long, and what followed was the grandest funeral ever seen this side of the red-all-over-tree: my brother gave a long speech, I wore my shorts inside out to look cleaned up and Moptop sang "I'm a Little Rice Ball" in a loud voice and without crying, mustering all the respect that only truly great personalities inspire. We raised the national flag and placed an inscription next to the tree where Bob was buried, inside an empty box of chocolates: "To great men, the grateful homeland."

During the speech, Chibo said many beautiful things, destiny, homeland, the hard law of the stars (along with other things I didn't understand), but he was interrupted by a clamor of locusts that got louder and surrounded us. The same thing happened earlier today, when my arm was burning and I got the hiccups. Locusts. It was impossible to know where the buzzing came from, it came from everywhere and nowhere. I thought of a bunch of different enemies; Indians, pirates, geckos. Or it wasn't any of them either, and I ran without really knowing why (maybe Chibo and Bruno are in the dark, laughing at me from the other side), or because I'd been exposed and hit by the stars. Or chased by the Dead Guy, who isn't working alone, but as part of an invisible organization; the Dead Guy who controls the stars.

The hard law of the stars: right hand on the waist, the other pointing to a thin cloud. Standing on the stage made from the tree house's left-over planks, Bruno was the human cannonball. "Respectable public," Chibo faced the audience of rocks and little boats, and grabbed Bruno by the legs, "help me out with this." Moptop and I each took an arm. We propped the Bruno-package this way and that until Chibo gave the order. We heave-hoed. Bruno cried out. He rose high up then crashed down onto a pile of leaves that we'd prepared, a perfect landing. The curtain fell and was pierced by bursts of applause (Moptop had rushed down there to pump up the chorus). Moptop looked good in a top hat. Returning to the stage, he put on a pair of white gloves. It was the first time I'd seen the coin trick. Some finger acrobatics and ta-da: they disappeared. They'd turn up—sometimes larger—inside my shoe or in the mane of the magician himself, who thanked the gentlemen and ladies with an exaggerated salaam to the ground. One or two of the coins would fall out of his hair during this bow, but Moptop wouldn't even care. He'd pull a persimmon from his top hat, saw invisible people in half, and was always game for whatever task in the role of Bruno's assistant.

Bruno was the locust tamer: he'd tuck three of them into his shirt and then release them onto the stage, challenging the beasts with a branch. Bruno would jump from great heights into the elephants' trough, swing on the trapeze that Chibo had made for the tree house and launch himself into the air to land on both feet (applause), or on top of Chibo (cries of pain). As for me, I didn't do anything—until one day Chibo gave me three very ripe persimmons to practice juggling with. The result was so bad, oh so bad, that Bruno came over personally to ask if I knew how to clap. Under Chibo's angry glare, he decided instead to teach me how to wrap my foot up behind the nape of my neck. He also turned me into an expert statue.

On show days, we'd wake up really early and eat bread all day. Chibo would set up the stage while it was still dark and I'd remain seated on a box, swinging my feet, stuffed so full of bread I could barely move. One time, Moptop was afraid I'd never move again, just like Bob, so he came running at me with an invisible camera, breathing strangely. He said he was going to take my portrait, so I held still, and he launched a faucet at my head. It's true, I couldn't see straight for awhile, but I didn't care. A few days later, I suggested, with the best of intentions, that he try swallowing fire, and we called it even.

From a distance, I spotted the red-all-over tree. It was a tiny dot and grew larger and larger until I recognized Bruno there, under the leaves. When he wanted to, Bruno really knew how to lie. He really did. He felt like I couldn't ever understand what he was saying—so he lied. He did it because sometimes it was probably just too complicated to explain things (they pass so quickly through our heads) or because we never really got what he said. Today, Bruno lied: there was no way he'd made it to the red-all-over tree before me. According to the plan, he was supposed to make a sweep of the pond area (I checked the map), which was situated on the outer side of the Ferris wheel—that is, on the other side. But only when the weather's clear. Because if the rain comes down hard, the lines on the map get smeared, the cornfield gets all messed up (west corresponds to north and the center is next to the eastern border) and no one moors their ships. Then the dances on the ship decks drift out to sea but continue into the day, shining brightly, with floating flaming cocktails, an opera singer and the sound of vibraphones. At these parties, the queen of Bulgaria shows off her outrageous hairdos, some bearing a strong resemblance to shoes, others like birds from some eastern forest. The coolest are the ones that pay homage to the Bulgarian nobility, with State symbols or the face of some ancient king sculpted into the queen's hair with a lifetime's worth of patience. (She's fat and a good dancer.)

I turned my hand into a spyglass. It really was Bruno leaning against the red-all-over tree, alone, looking like a scarecrow. The edges of the field had dried up a little (a pack of vultures coming from the direction of the road swooped down into the tops of the cornstalks) and there was no sign of Moptop. In the Bulgarian spy's pocket, I guessed, were the ring and the lighter. These things seemed to have lives of their own and were now controlling Bruno.

❖

A banana-flavored gumdrop. A ring, a lighter, a fork, a persimmon, a sneaker with no laces, the Kingdom of Bulgaria, the forbidden zone of the plantation.

Bruno's feet were sunk into the dirt and he was trying to imagine bigger and bigger things, in ascending order, until they got so big they didn't fit into ideas anymore. Then he'd stop existing. Because people don't die just from standing still—no, that can't be right—people die from their heads exploding, from keeping everything bottled up inside, five raised to a hundred, twelve-thousand nine hundred and fifty-four, ten times a billion, until it all goes completely… empty. But it was hard to go past seventeen galaxies, especially on such a hot day. Bruno had no idea what could be bigger than seventeen galaxies except for eighteen (all lined up), and couldn't stop thinking about the Dead Guy's lighter.

Bruno, leaning against the tree, his feet stuck in the dirt, had made a fool of us all. Even from a distance I knew he hadn't spent the afternoon investigating the pond area. I bet he'd sent us off to different ends of the plantation while he dug a hole under the wire fence: Bruno had been exploring the forbidden zone. They used to talk about that place a lot. When we'd all go off to rest somewhere in the shade together after running around all day, the conversation would gradually work its way over to the off-limits area. Starting to get freaked out and trying not to lose it, I'd pretend that the dead zone was far away from the cornfield. Chibo would laugh softly. I'd make myself think of it as a strange region, something that had nothing to do with me, totally far away and no fun at all. But no. Bruno and Chibo insisted that the off-limits area was right there, nearby… inside. It stretched out close to the main road, and its vegetation-covered spaces, its empty corners and corridors, were practically the same as the plantation's. Bruno compared the forbidden zone to a hurt wrist, a wound that opened and closed, opened and closed, opened and—that always hypnotized me. Three hundred steps south of the red-all-over tree, and there it is, Bruno used to say. He made it sound like the promised land, where eighteen galaxies would fit and where the day was always just beginning, even at four in the afternoon, at noon or at six in the morning.

Thinking back on it now, that's where Chibo must've gone the past few summers, whenever the tree house stood empty. But I never paid much attention (Bob was having an incredible season and got even better after Moptop and I got through the *Crumb-Lifting Manual: Techniques for Improved Distribution of Weight in the Hind Legs, Variations on Breathing, and Tips on How to Work the Wing Muscles*.) Now what I wanted most was to run and run and find Moptop, to say that maybe Chibo had been hiding out in the off-limits area the whole time and that Bruno had tricked us and that's where he'd been today. He'd most likely gone to meet Chibo. The two of them had probably turned up the air-conditioning to the coldest cold, ordered takeout over the phone, and spent hours chewing on alliances and plans, criticizing the foreign policy of Her Majesty's government.

Bruno didn't notice me approaching. He kept his feet buried, looking at the lighter, imagining monumental distances, calculating gigantic sums. I remembered something Moptop had told me once: cows in the forbidden zone have humps on their backs. At times like these, I felt Chibo's absence more desperately, and I clung to him, as he laughed.

Trying to forget the fact that Chibo used to laugh silently until going totally purple, I sat down next to Bruno without making a sound. I didn't want to disturb him. He continued looking at a point floating in the ether, far away from our beetle races—a forbidden zone—and squeezing the lighter as if his thoughts were there: inside that lighter, polished with t-shirt, spit, t-shirt. I let myself get bitten by some flying things because we all were lazy like that and put a little more dirt into my pocket. And then a little more. Silently. Sometimes I go months without saying a word but I keep hanging around until everyone forgets I'm there. I like being with other people, but I just don't understand why they always have to say something—as if they were all in the dark. While searching for signs of intelligent life in the mound of dirt in my pocket, I was suddenly struck by the thought that I could win any yellow cow contest in the world—this boy, honorable judges, hasn't spoken since the previous judges' parents were born. I'd start a round of applause for myself and trip over my own very long, white beard, then give the announcer a few pats on the back and shuffle back to my tree mansion. I'd live like a king. Maybe I'd even win a little brother since I'd have already won all the possible prizes and I wouldn't really know what to do with a leather three-seater sofa, then I'd tell my youngest brother that no one had to speak at the lunch table or think up things to say, never ever. Bruno probably didn't hear my footsteps, that's why he didn't turn around, or could it be that he was a dead gecko? I found a few larvae of some beige thing in my pocket pile of dirt, two or three snails, some of my snack. Yes, I'd stuffed dirt into the same pocket as the bread. I insulted myself for my own stupidity and realized then that Bruno had noticed me; he started unburying his feet and came out of his trance. Out of the corner of his eye, he saw me pouring the rest of the dirt back into my pocket but didn't say anything. In an unspoken gentleman's agreement, we exchanged a knowing look as if to say it's no big deal and put our hands in our laps. With our eyes, we both followed one of those large ants that was moving almost as slowly as we were. Bruno leaned over the ant and surrounded it with the Dead Guy's ring. It froze for an instant, looked up and scaled the obstacle with a snotty tsk-tsk, not knowing this would cost it its life. The tragedy was inevitable, I was sure: if, one day, Moptop were to decide to sneak through the hole in the wire fence (with a snotty tsk-tsk) to explore the secret area of the plantation, something terrible would happen—Bruno took the lighter and I looked up at the sky.

When I looked back again, the giant ant had been killed in an arson attack that also decimated a few lengths of vegetation. Bruno gave me the lighter, "for you."

No joke. It was the first time Bruno had given me anything. I was so happy that I even forgot about the carbonized ant. I clutched the lighter to my chest breathlessly, like someone who suddenly rises to the surface, forgetting what's still there, thrashing and clawing at him from the depths below. In any case, people are made from a head, a trunk, and a bunch of things—the things mix with the people, the people mix with the things, and it all gets confused. The lighter, for example, was a living part of the Dead Guy (or he was a dead part of the lighter).

"Did you find anything?" Bruno asked me while dumping out a pile of dirt from his sneaker. I shook my head, annoyed. I had to hold my tongue to not say anything about his lies— (because I knew everything: no way had he really investigated the area by the pond, fat chance)—much less mention my hunch that agent Dead Guy could still be alive. "Don't look at me like that," Bruno insisted, "nothing in the pond area either," and he started walking in circles. He stomped with the heavy footfalls of someone running up steps. He was all worked up ("have you seen Moptop?"), and I knew he was hiding something. I showed him some dirt to avoid answering, the dirt I'd been collecting all day and had stored in a special, indestructible receptacle (also known as my pocket).

He waved off the offer with an angry gesture, and a bunch of dust got lost in the space between our fingers. I really wanted to understand Bruno. He stopped circling the tree and mumbled, before turning his back on me: "No, *you* analyze this sample, there's a strainer in the tree house, lemme know if you find anything." When he walked away, I followed. Bruno turned around, stopped, and lifted his hand to tell me something, then gave up and continued walking. He was heading south, in the direction of the forbidden zone.

So: if they call me an ant and Moptop is a three-banded armadillo, there's no denying the fact that Bruno's a beetle. Everybody knows that beetles are the most intelligent animals of the living kingdom. Beetles carry a wisdom twenty times greater than their body weight, and that's why they suffer from constant headaches. Their shells are as tough as Bruno's forehead—nothing goes in, nothing goes out. According to the scientific community, "there's no way to understand the beetle, without being one," which makes it the saddest creature ever since that one-eyed gecko we found in the pond two summers ago.

Encouraged by the lighter in my back pocket, possibly, I started following Bruno in stealth mode, pretending I was no more than a giant ant.

I tried guiding myself by the sight of his feet, since the plantation had already risen far above my head. I walked in a crouch, without taking my eyes off that pair of sneakers dozens of cornstalks ahead of me; I didn't want Bruno to disappear around a corner because then I wouldn't know which way to go. I sped up. I dropped to all fours to avoid the stalks and leaves, while he walked straight ahead, cool and composed like a member of the Bulgarian nobility. I still didn't know whether Bruno was leaving just to play a trick or if it was time to start panicking, I also wasn't sure if he'd be mad when he found out I'd disobeyed his express orders to go get a strainer. But hey, he'd thought it fair enough to get rid of a friend by telling him to go after a strainer miles away. No doubt, it had been a highly elegant gesture to dispatch someone with the mission of analyzing a mound of dirt or finding some Dead Guy. But I had a lighter in my pocket and didn't plan on playing clean either (I adjusted my imaginary hat on my head for effect). Who knew, maybe Bruno actually wanted someone to follow him. That would explain why he'd now begun to count his steps aloud (one hundred and twelve, one hundred and thirteen) and then stopped suddenly, probably for effect.

I braked too, with my hands on the ground. I tried to see better through the plants and could swear he was thinking hard, in the way you can tell when someone's stopped on purpose to think (hard). Then he went on: minus one hundred and eighty-seven, minus one hundred and eighty-six, minus onehundredeightyfive. It was a relief to know that Bruno was still Bruno, as he rigorously counted down the number of steps left to get to three hundred. Still, his voice was different. Why didn't he ever tell us anything?

My knees scraped against the dirt and I held my breath as I mentally repeated the same three words four times. Then I let out my breath and went back to thinking (now with an empty chest): "horse," "noise," "race." These were my favorite, but there were others too. Chibo told me to breathe this way whenever I got confused; lungs full, lungs empty. He said that the pauses in between were good for releasing ideas and unclogging our heads. It was true, what he said, to the point that it gave a certain order to things. But the empty spaces always filled up with "horse," "noise," "race," and with a whole gang of old gamblers crowded around an old yellow TV, shouting with a handful of money in their hands; total chaos. To be honest, as much as my brother insisted, I almost never breathed this way. Because I liked doing the opposite of what he told me. But now that the plantation went on without Chibo, I caught myself repeating his habits. Poking at knee scrapes, for example—boy, did he love doing that. And me, a kid who always hated messing with dried-up blood (because it hurts), spent the next hour picking off all my scabs. I was afraid that Chibo's absence would go unnoticed, especially by me. I put a piece of scab into my mouth and felt a bitter, reddish taste; a brother is a strange sort of friend. It's just like our own names. We go for years without really noticing them, then suddenly realize we have a name and repeat it a million times before falling asleep and… when I opened my eyes, Bruno, there was no sign of Bruno. I'd lost his trail, but the off-limits area was probably nearby. The central command's periscope didn't show anything, the vegetation grasped spears and swords that scratched out and erased the path. A gust of sea wind bit my face. I pulled the lighter from my pocket and decided that the biggest fire in the history of the plantation was about to begin.

Three Poems

Flávio de Araújo
Translated by Rachel Morgenstern-Clarren

Zangareio, Flávio de Araújo's powerful 2008 debut poetry collection, explores the world of the *caiçaras*—a traditional fishing community with Portuguese, indigenous, and African roots that inhabits the southeastern coast of Brazil. Born in Paraty in 1975, Araújo comes from a family of caiçara fishermen. *Zangareio* captures the daily and seasonal rhythms of his ancestral home in Praia do Sono; relationships between people and the natural world are at the center of his work.

In addition to masterful storytelling, buoyant imagery, and caustic humor, *Zangareio* is intriguing for its use of the caiçara dialect. This vocabulary stems from the influence of the native Tupi-Guarani languages on the Portuguese, and the caiçaras' many fishing-related words. The poem "Portion," for instance, refers specifically to the portion of the total catch that each person receives; if there's only one fish, that fish is divided equally. *Craro de lua* is the period between peak fishing times (the new and full moon phases), when fish just "watch the nets." Many words reappear in different poems. One such word is *samburá*—a basket used to store fish, woven from bamboo or philodendron root. The book is divided into five sections whose names designate tackle or gear (*Zangareio, Puçá*), artisanal traps (*Caiçara, Cerco*), and the hold of the ship (*Porão*) where the catch is stored on ice. Zangareio itself is the name of a multi-hook squid jig. Araújo includes a caiçara glossary at the back of the book.

Depending on the rhythm of the poem, and the significance of the word or phrase, I have kept the caiçara language in some places (like *craro de lua*), and used variations in others (such as substituting *natiê* blue with the sonically resonant navy). I have attempted to maintain the lyricism and accessibility of the originals, without simplifying or eliminating the caiçara elements that make Araújo's poetry so unique.

Original Text: Flávio de Araújo, "Craro de Lua," "Observations Aboard a Ferry," and "Portion" from *Zangareio*. São Paulo: OFF FLIP Press, 2008.

Craro de Lua

Colcha de retalhos em nanzuque
azul de natiê
pra mode de amar.

A moça deita
refestelada.
A faca amolada na pedra
descansa sobre o jirau
e os pargos no samburá
aguardando os lanhos.

Enquanto acompanha com olhos
flutuantes algumas
formigas de réiva
espera quem lhe roube
o cabelo desfeito o tecido,
cheirando a babosa.

O fumeiro doce na casa
o vento silvando o reboco
ondas que quebram

Craro de Lua

A navy blue
nainsook patchwork quilt
ready for love.

The girl lolls
across the bed.
The knife sharpened against stone
rests on the kitchen rack
and snapper in the *samburá*
anticipates its slicing.

As her eyes flutter
concentrating on brave
ants, she waits
for the one who'll steal
her loosened strands
smelling of aloe.

Sweet smoke in the house
wind whistling through plaster
waves that break

e retornam a se fazer.

Então ele chega com pouco dinheiro
com relógio de cigano
e ouro nos dentes.
É craro de lua.
E os pescadores se aportam
em colchas de retalhos em nanzuque
azul de natiê
pra mode de amar.

only to form anew.

Then he arrives with no money
with a gypsy's watch
and gold teeth.
It is *craro de lua*.
And the fishermen dock
on navy blue
nainsook patchwork quilts
ready for love.

Observações a bordo de um ferry-boat

Ela é toda açúcar e dentes
em seu vestido salsaparrilha
e quando anda
parece um navio.

Seu cabelo de sisal
seu hálito de nuvens brancas
mais que uma mulher simples
quando fala sobre coisas.
Puro perfume de tempero
sobre os pés
e quando anda
parece um navio.

Toda precisão de mulher
bem quista
para projetos matrimoniais
definitiva quando diz sim
indutiva no talvez.
De beleza que constrange
e quando anda

Observations Aboard a Ferry

She's all sugar and smiles
in her sarsaparilla dress
when she glides past
like a ship.

Her sisal hair
her white-cloud breath
she's more than a simple woman
when she speaks about things.
A sweet scent
about her step
when she glides past
like a ship.

She speaks with all the precision
of a woman pursued
by many suitors.
Firm in saying yes
meaning maybe.
A beauty that puts you to shame
when she glides past

parece um navio.

Ela é toda espelhosa
refletindo no futuro
o retrato da sagrada família.

Ela é toda açúcar e dentes
e quando anda,
sim,
parece mesmo um navio.

like a ship.

She's all mirrors
reflecting the future
portrait of the holy family.

She's all sugar and smiles
and when she glides past,
yes,
she's just like a ship.

Quinhão

À mesa, como num tribunal
sob o juízo de nossa mãe
disputávamos, com fervor,
os melhores pedaços
da magra galinha.

As irmãs menores,
cada qual com suas asas,
balbuciavam qualquer coisa
de bom
voando entre os dentes.

O impasse era sempre
com as coxas.
Duas
para três admiradores.

Fora o confronto
tomei predileção

Portion

At the table, as in a tribunal
subject to our mother's judgment,
we bitterly contested
the best pieces
of scrawny chicken.

My younger sisters,
each one with her wings,
chattered—
any tasty pieces
catching in their teeth.

The impasse always came
at the thighs.
Two
for three admirers.

Only I
developed a preference

por peitos.

O que Freud explicaria
com a teoria das perdas.

for breasts.

Which Freud would attribute
to the theory of loss.

Crow-Blue

Adriana Lisboa
Translated by Alison Entrekin

Born in Rio de Janeiro in 1970, Adriana Lisboa is one of Brazil's foremost contemporary writers, with works translated into several languages and a number of important literary prizes to her name, including the José Saramago Prize for her novel *Symphony in White*.

The first thing that struck me about *Crow-Blue*, from which this excerpt is taken, was its cross-cultural appeal and translatability (I always look for these things as I read because much of what I translate suffers from differing degrees of un-translatability). I took an immediate liking to the veritable diaspora of characters that dances across the pages of this powerful novel about modern-day families and sense of place. In it, Lisboa writes from the in-between world of migrants, who teeter on the cusp of belonging but who are forever outsiders at the same time. Perfect, I thought, for a book about to be translated, as its characters—and writer—are themselves in an ongoing process of self-translation.

As for the translation itself, there isn't too much to tell. Gregory Rabassa famously said that the most celebrated book he ever translated, *One Hundred Years of Solitude*, was also the easiest, precisely because it was so well written. I found this to be the case with *Crow-Blue*, which has not been difficult so far (knock on wood), with but a few hair-splitters. Nothing too dire, all in a translator's day's work, but enough to give pause for thought.

I remember leaving the phrase "*um verão irmão da água*" (literally "a summer brother of water") in the middle of the text for quite some time as I translated everything around it, trying to work out a way to render the derivative sense of *irmanar* (to join, link, unite), while retaining the familial aspect of *irmão* (brother) and the lyricism of the original. The solution, "a summer wed to water" only came to me on the last day, with my back up against a wall, as is often the case with solutions.

I re-invented the little lamb poem so that it would rhyme in English, as I felt that a literal translation would fall flat, and hemmed and hawed for quite some time over Elisa's term of endearment for Evangelina: "*preta preta pretinha*" ("black black little black girl"), which is actually from the song, "Preta pretinha" by the group Os Novos Baianos. References to skin color are so natural to Brazilians and mostly unencumbered by concerns with political correctness, besides which, the character isn't even black. She is just deeply tanned. After talking it over with Adriana, who is herself an accomplished literary translator into Portuguese, I decided on "little caramel girl."

Original text: Adriana Lisboa, *Azul-Corvo*. Rio de Janiero: Editora Rocco, 2010

Azul-corvo

Crotalus atrox

Foi ela quem me ensinou inglês e espanhol. Era o que ela sabia fazer. Se fosse professora de ioga, teria passado doze anos me ensinando ioga, e se trabalhasse na lavoura eu teria uma enxada antes mesmo de aprender a falar. Era o que ela sabia fazer, e achava um desperdício não deixar para mim, de graça, como herança em vida, qualquer conhecimento que fosse.

Eram inglês e espanhol porque ela havia morado nos Estados Unidos, nos estados do Texas e do Novo México, durante vinte e dois anos, e porque se há algo que vinte e dois anos num lugar te impõem é o domínio da língua local, mesmo que você não tenha nenhum talento especial para isso.

Minha mãe aprendeu formalmente o inglês na escola. Com os *tejanos*, informalmente, o espanhol.

E eu aprendi as duas línguas com a minha mãe, me entregando às aulas com uma resistência que nunca teria condições de competir com a resistência dela.

¿Es el televisor?

No, senōr (señorita, señora), no es el televisor. Es el gato.

Once upon a time there were four little Rabbits, and their names were —

Flopsy...

Crow-Blue

Crotalus atrox

She was the one who taught me English and Spanish. It was what she knew how to do. If she'd been a yoga teacher, she'd have spent twelve years teaching me yoga, and if she'd worked on the land I'd have had a hoe before I'd even learned to talk. It was what she knew how to do, and she thought it a waste not to pass on to me, for free, as an inheritance in life, some kind of knowledge.

It was English and Spanish because she'd lived in the United States, in Texas and New Mexico, for twenty-two years, and if there's one thing that twenty-two years in a place impose on you it is mastery of the local tongue, even if you don't have any special talent for it.

My mother had learned English formally at school. Spanish, informally, with the *tejanos*.

And I learned both from my mother, surrendering to her lessons with a resistance that was never any competition for hers.

¿Es el televisor?

No, senōr (señorita, señora), no es el televisor. Es el gato.

Once upon a time there were four little Rabbits, and their names were—

Flopsy,

Mopsy,

Cottontail,

and Peter.

(Later on I saw Peter Rabbit in supermarkets at Easter. I remembered my mother. I also remembered Flopsy, Mopsy and Cottontail, who were very good little rabbits and thus escaped life's punishments, though they lacked Peter's heroic charm.)

The mothers in this family die young. By the age of nine my mother had lost her mother, and went to Texas with her geologist father. A work opportunity for him, which he'd gotten through his contacts' contacts' contacts.

My mother grew up in Texas. One day, and she never told me why, and somehow I didn't think I should ask, she severed ties with her father and moved to New Mexico.

My mother liked severing ties with men and disappearing from their lives. The tendency began there, with my geologist grandfather.

She found a little house in Albuquerque, near Route 66 with its old-fashioned charm, more than a decade before I was born. One of those little adobe houses, with a flat roof resting on wooden beams that ran horizontally through the walls.

She still lived in this house when I was born. We lived there until I was two. I visited it much later, with Fernando and Carlos, my improbable pair of travel companions, one icy November day. It was a small house of the most absolute simplicity, as if it had sprung from the ground itself.

My mother made her living teaching English to Mexicans migrating back to New Mexico—some time after the Americans had migrated there, as she liked to say. Who was foreign there, who was a local? What language did the land speak? (In essence, it didn't speak English or Spanish, because the people who were there when the explorers and conquistadores arrived were Navajo and Anasazi and Ute. And others. And others before them. But none with the surnames Coronado or Oñate, no one known as Cabeza de Vaca. Or Billy the Kid.)

My mother also taught Spanish to Americans. University students sometimes sought her out. Some, very few, wanted to learn Portuguese. By this time, it was the least fluent of her three languages. But because of her students she delved into Brazilian music and films and books. The few Americans interested in Brazil made my mother rediscover Brazil, which she did perhaps a little clumsily at first, with the awkwardness of the not-at-all prodigal child who returns home with their hands in their pockets and drooping ears. But a short time later they are crossing their feet on the table and flicking cigarette butts into corners.

I don't remember my early childhood in Albuquerque, of course. When I travel back in time, it feels as though I was born in Rio de Janeiro. More specifically, on Copacabana Beach—right there on the sand, among the pigeons and the litter left behind by beachgoers. I think of Copacabana. I close my eyes and even if I'm listening to Acoustic Arabia and burning Japanese Zen-Buddhist temple incense, what reaches my senses, via memory, is a vague whiff of sea breeze, a vague taste of fruit popsicles mixed with sand and salt water. And the sound of the waves fizzing on the sand, and the popsicle vendor's voice under the moist Rio sun.

I remember the light, my fingers digging tunnels and building castles in the wet sand, patiently. There were other children around, but we were all the beginning, middle and end of our own private universes. We played together, that is, sharing space in a kind of tense harmony, but it was as if each child was cocooned in his or her own bubble of ideas, sensations, initiatives, and state-of-the-art architectural projects involving wet sand and popsicle sticks.

So I was born at the age of two on Copacabana Beach, and it was always summer, but a summer wed to water, and my tools for changing the world, for altering it and shaping it and making it worthy of me, were a little red bucket and a yellow sieve, spade and rake.

And further along was a horizon I gave no thought to. The imaginary line where the sky and sea parted company, liquid to one side, not liquid to the other. A kind of concrete abstract.

I left the horizon in peace and preferred to dream of islands, which were real, and which maybe I'd be able to swim to if I ever got serious about swimming, and separated by a world of different shadows, a world where speed and sounds were different, where animals very different to myself lived. The world of fish, of algae, of mollusks, of crow-blue shells—like those I would read about in a poem, much later. A whole other life, other register, but a human being could actually swim between them, observe them, dive to the ocean floor in Copacabana and touch the intimacy of the sand, there, so far from the popsicle sticks and volleyballs and empada vendors. The intimacy that was completely oblivious to the customary chaos of the neighborhood of Copacabana, where people hurried along or dawdled in the elderly gait of the retired or mugged or got mugged or queued at the bank or lifted weights at the gym or begged at traffic lights or pretended not to see people begging at traffic lights or looked at the pretty woman or were the pretty woman with the tiny triangles of her bikini top or tallied up prices on the supermarket cash register or collected garbage from the sidewalks and streets or tossed garbage on the sidewalks and streets or sold sex to tourists or wrote poems or walked their dogs. The drama of the city didn't even figure in the subconscious of the ocean floor. It wasn't important or relevant. It didn't even exist there.

The horizon was the leitmotif of those who yearned for the impossible. So they could keep on yearning, I suspect. I've always thought searching for something you're not going to find a convenient position. Pondering the poetry and symbolism of the horizon wasn't for me. I preferred to ponder islands and fish.

Or, better yet, the architecture of the castle I was building that morning, which was not going to crumble this time. I was making some improvements to the project, which had already failed several times.

There were children and adults around me; I was aware of their existence more or less peripherally. We could get along well if we didn't bother one another, if we interacted as little as possible. The beach was large and free of charge, the sun was for everyone.

In Rio, my mother also taught English and Spanish. And Portuguese to foreigners. She said it was a Wild-Card Profession, and she said it like she meant it. Anywhere in the world, there would always be people wanting to learn English and/or Spanish. And Portuguese— Portuguese would increase its sphere of influence after Brazil showed the world what it was made of.

You'll live to see it, she'd say, straightening her back and lifting her chin as she spoke, defying the very air in front of her to contradict her.

When we went to live in Brazil, she became a nationalist. Advocate of all things Brazilian, among them the language we had inherited from our European colonizer and acclimatized, and which she came to consider the most beautiful in the world.

It was the 1990s and she *voted in the presidential elections.* All Brazilians of age *voted in the presidential elections.* They were still getting used to this degree of democracy, but they'd get there one day, she'd say. We'll get there. If I hadn't been such a small a child at the time, I might have asked how, if the first thing that the first democratically elected president in three decades had done, on his first day in office, was confiscate the money in the people's savings accounts. He promised it would be returned at a later date. This happened a year before we returned to Brazil and my mother hadn't felt the brunt of it, but Elisa no doubt ranted and raved and uttered swear words that I could have remembered for future reference if I'd been present and able to understand her. But, all said and done, they were adults and should have known what they were doing, electing, confiscating, swearing.

My mother and I never returned to Albuquerque together. In fact, we never returned to the United States together.

Firstly, because she no longer got paid in US dollars for her lessons, and in Brazil human resources were pretty cheap, even perfectly trilingual human resources—as such, the trip was too expensive for our new green and yellow more-or-less-underpaid pockets.

Secondly, because my mother wasn't one to retrace her steps. When she left, she left. When she walked out, she walked out.

In the long summer holidays, we always went to Barra do Jucu, in the state of Espírito Santo, where my mother had friends. We'd climb into her Fiat 147 and some seven hours later we'd arrive, weary and happy, and along the way my mother would listen to music and sing along, and we'd stop at luncheonettes that smelled of grease and burnt coffee to use bathrooms that smelled of urine and disinfectant, where a very fat employee sat crocheting and sold crocheted doilies and underwear next to a cardboard box that said TIPS PLEASE.

My mother would play Janis Joplin and turn up the volume and stick her head out the window of her Fiat 147 and sing along, as if she was in a film:

Freedom's just another word for nothing left to lose,
Nothing don't mean nothing honey if it ain't free, now now.

Even when I didn't understand the words, I was hypnotized by my mother's trance. She seemed like another woman, which fascinated and frightened me. Her voice had a hoarseness exactly like Janis Joplin's and I wondered why some people became Janis Joplin and others became my mother.

You sing just as good as Janis Joplin, I once told her.

The only thing we have in common is that her dad worked for Texaco, she replied. You know. Oil.

When I was informed that Janis Joplin had died in 1970, almost two decades before I was born, I was indignant. I'd thought Janis Joplin was my contemporary, and that she was singing "Me & Bobby McGee" somewhere on the planet, while my mother, who was everything Janis Joplin hadn't been, who was her opposite, her antimatter in another dimension, stuck her head out the window of the car that wasn't a Porsche painted in psychedelic colors and belted out what she could to the scalding-hot asphalt of the highway.

In Barra do Jucu, my mother sometimes went out dancing at night, or to meet someone for a few beers.

Two of these someones became boyfriends, who lasted a few summers. One of them came to visit us in Rio. The other one lived in Rio, was a surfer and had a five-year-old boy whom I envied, secretly and angrily. In Rio and Barra do Jucu, my mother's boyfriend started teaching me to surf, but then things between them ground to a halt. He called me for a few months to ask how things were going and to try to discover, between the lines, if my mother had met someone else, and if this someone else seemed more likable than him, and why. I became the surfer's ally, but it was no good. One day he stopped calling, and I stopped surfing.

My mother's friends in Barra do Jucu also had young kids. We liked watching the crabs in the mangrove swamp right behind the house—the crabs held a terrible fascination for me and, though horrified and disgusted, I couldn't keep my eyes off their slow, muddy walk, those lone monks in their long meditative trances. The other kids and I changed from pajamas into beachwear and from beachwear into pajamas, after a hose-down at the end of each day. Someone always butted in with a bar of soap and a bottle of shampoo: growing up is a drag. But I was violently happy there, and returned from Barra do Jucu when the holidays were over with skin the color of dark wood, almost like the jacaranda table in our living room.

Elisa used to call me her little caramel girl. Elisa was my mother's foster sister.

My family's genealogy is confusing and simple at the same time. My grandmother brought up Elisa as if she were her own daughter. Later my mother was born and then my grandmother died, and when my mother went to Texas with my grandfather, Elisa stayed in Rio. She was all grown up, sixteen years old, and had a job and a fiancée who would never become her husband but was a fiancée nevertheless and that was better than nothing. Unlike his real daughter, she never severed ties with the man who'd brought her up, but never saw him again either, because there was an entire continent between them, and when my retired-geologist Brazilian grandfather died of a Texan snakebite on Texan soil at the age of 67, she was the one who broke the news to my mother, all the way from the southern hemisphere.

Elisa was the daughter who had accidentally sprung from the womb of my mother's mother's maid. There was no father in the picture. The mother died in childbirth.

I'll bring her up, said my grandmother, and that was how Elisa came into the family.

But she'd always be the maid's daughter, and this original sin, this hybridism with the dark world of the servant class, in a caste system deeply rooted in Brazilian society from day one, set her apart from my mother, who went to the United States, while Elisa stayed behind after my grandmother's death. If she nursed any hurt feelings like tiny secret jewels at the bottom of a drawer, she never let on to me. Later she studied to be a nurse and got a job in the public service and broke off her engagement because her fiancée kept stalling. According to Elisa, it was better to be alone than in a dead-end relationship.

As for me, when someone asked me what I wanted to be when I grew up the only things that occurred to me were occupations that took place on a strip of sand with waves breaking against it. Empada vendor? Thus, the year spent in Copacabana and Barra do Jucu, with the powerful machine known as the Fiat 147, was one hundred percent convenient. And except for a living Janis Joplin, I wanted for nothing, ever.

But there were the Spanish and English lessons and putting up resistance was useless. This way you'll get work anywhere in the world, my mother used to say.

And I'd mentally recite:

¿Es el televisor?

No, señor (señorita, señora), no es el televisor. Es el gato.

I didn't want to work anywhere in the world explaining to people that cats weren't TVs. But putting up resistance to the transmission/

imposition of knowledge was useless.

My mother told me stories about her mother. About her father, she only said the barest minimum.

I imagined my grandmother as a very thin woman with tiny feet who collected postcards from places with suggestive names like Hanover and Islamabad. She had a cat that lay in her lap and bit everyone else. An eccentric cat, who preferred his teeth to his claws. One day the cat fell out the apartment window and died, sprawled across the sidewalk. People said the cat had committed suicide.

My mother told me that she'd told them that cats don't commit suicide.

How do you know? I asked her.

Cats don't commit suicide, she repeated.

I imagined my grandfather in a cowboy hat, selling his geological knowledge to oil companies in Texas. And one day getting bitten by a lethal rattlesnake called *Crotalus atrox*. He had a blue suit jacket and a roll of fat at the nape of his neck.

My grandparents had names. My grandmother was Maria Gorete, a name I've never seen on anyone else. There must be other Maria Goretes in the world. But for me Maria Gorete is synonymous with grandmother, and a specific grandmother. My grandfather, her husband, was Abner, which was something biblical, with the usual biblical grandiosity.

Maria Gorete and Abner were Elisa's foster parents and my mother Suzana's parents for real. They were my grandparents for real, even though I never met them. And not the grandparents of the children that Elisa never had.

This was my family tree until I was thirteen years old. One man and four women in three generations. Odd arithmetic, tied up like colorful handkerchiefs inside a magician's top hat. A family tree lacking roots, which, in the place of certain branches only had rather vague gestures, indications, suggestions, forget-about-its.

If you look at it from another point of view, however, things were very simple.

After all, sometimes people vanish.

But sometimes other people go looking for them. They pull their colorful handkerchiefs out of their top hats, dragging out rabbits, doves and even a burning torch, to the audience's astonishment.

Maria Gorete, my grandmother, liked to play with dolls even as an adult. She liked to sing a song about a lamb, which never failed to make my mother cry. *I used to have a little lamb, Jasmine was her name. Her wool was fleecy white, and when I called she came.* When she had visitors over and wanted to show off her daughter, Maria Gorete would say, "Do you want to see her cry?" And she'd sing. *A hunter in the flowering fields* (my mother's eyes would already be brimming over) *shot her down one day.* And Maria Gorete would recite: *When I got to her she was dead, and I cried in dismay.*

And my mother would cry.

"How cute," visitor no. 1 would say.

"She's so sensitive," visitor no. 2 would say.

"No, she's just silly," Maria Gorete would say.

My mother would tell me this story and I secretly agreed with Maria Gorete: how silly to cry over a lamb in a song. But my mother always cried again when she sang the song to me and I knew that she wasn't asking my opinion and that it was better not to say anything. Besides which, I also thought it was silly of Maria Gorete to play with dolls as an adult. And I thought it was the height of silliness for Maria Gorete to show off her daughter to visitors by making her cry, and over such an unworthy thing. I decided they deserved each other.

Maria Gorete fell ill and died. Two years before Janis Joplin. My mother inherited her dolls, and when she thought she was too big to play with dolls, now living in the United States, she donated them all to a Presbyterian orphanage in Dallas. All but one, Priscila, which she kept and when I was big enough gave to me as a present. Which was a mistake. I still wasn't big enough and did Priscila's makeup with a pen and washing her was useless. She was left with a smudged, end-of-party look for the rest of time.

The day I arrived from Brazil, I hung the clothes I had in the closet. There weren't many. In the front entrance of Fernando's house in Lakewood, Colorado, there was a closet for coats and shoes. I put Elisa's high-heels, which I was never going to use, in it. The heels half-closed their eyes and there they stayed, like a Hindu ascetic going to meditate in a cave.

When you come inside, take your shoes off, Fernando told me. That way the house stays clean longer.

Then he went to his room and came back with a bag.

Here, Evangelina, I bought these for you. They're to wear around the house.

In the bag was a pair of checkered slippers that were fleecy on the inside. I thought they looked like granny slippers, but I didn't say anything.

They're not for now, of course, he said. They're for when it gets cold.

You can call me Vanja, I said.

Fernando's house had two bedrooms. He got the sofa bed ready for me in the spare bedroom. Later on we'll have to buy you a coat and some boots, he said. There's a shop with some good stuff at the outlet. But it doesn't have to be right away.

It wasn't necessary. It was unimaginable that at some point I was going to feel cold there. Boots? He had to be kidding.

But contrary to all of my expectations and everything that pointed to permanent dryness and to a new world one hundred percent untouched in its desert rigidity, it started to rain every now and then.

The first rain fell during the night. I woke up and everything was wet, but it didn't last. The sun re-confiscated all of the water possible on the ground, on the heroic plants. And it was as if nothing had happened. It was as if someone had committed a faux pas at dinner and everyone present had hurried to forget it.

The second was in the afternoon, a fine rain, and I had the impression that it gave up and evaporated halfway between the clouds and the earth. An odd rain, that didn't wet the ground.

The third was a storm that lasted nineteen minutes, accompanied by lightening and thunder. I observed the miracle from the window, fascinated.

It's raining quite a bit this summer, said Fernando. And one Saturday, when everything was dry again, he got his red 1985 Saab and took me down Highway 93, flanking the mountains, to the city of Boulder. Along the way I saw a drag racing track. In Boulder, he bought two tire tubes and blew them up at a gas station and we rode down a section of the river with our backsides in the holes, hollering and overturning on the rocks and grazing our knees.

Then I sat in the shade by the river's edge and watched skaters, uniformed cyclists, labradors, and a bum with dreadlocks go past.

One day I went to my future school on roller skates and for the first time I felt real fear, the sort that can send shivers through you even when outside waves of heat are lifting up off the asphalt like something supernatural. It was the hottest time of day and the public school was closed for the holidays, and its muteness evoked something secret and dangerous. Maybe military research was carried out or political prisoners were arbitrarily held in there.

One morning, a month from then, I would walk through those doors together with new and old students. I was still in my early teens, but I already suspected that adolescence was more or less like a declared war between me and adulthood.

Later I discovered it wasn't exactly the case; rather, the simple, mundane fact that my ideas were suddenly clear in my mind, and in my mind only, while everyone else made one mistake after another.

Everyone else wore the wrong clothes, listened to the wrong music and said the wrong things at the wrong time, read the wrong books, drove the wrong way, sniffled and used toothpicks, had family lunches on Sundays, got married, got divorced, died, was born, and check out the moustache on that man, and check out that woman in those awful soccer-players' shorts.

My messianic wave would come and go, for lack of disciples, or the wrong marketing strategy. It would be brief. But before I realized that I personified a secular combination of Jesus, Buddha, Muhammad, and Deepak Chopra, to then succumb to the weight of responsibility and give it all up, Fernando had already let me know what he thought about school and its dangers.

Careful about this thing of being popular, he said. Run from the word. Popular. Also run from the word loser. Don't say these things. Don't think them. Don't divide the world into popular and unpopular people, winners and losers. All that crap.

Then he apologized for saying crap.

After three weeks of school Aditi Ramagiri and I were already saying how Jake Moore was a loser. A big time loser. A mega-loser. Such a complete and utter loser that there was no possible salvation for him. It wasn't even worth growing up and becoming an adult. He'd be a loser as an adult too. I don't remember exactly why, but I remember that when Jake Moore went past, Aditi and I would look at one another and whisper: loser.

I found out on my own, a little later, that the opposite of loserhood, the disease that all losers have, was my dentist. He had a photo of his whole family on his desk. They all wore matching clothes—in red and white, against a backdrop of snow-covered pine trees, in a Christmas pose. It was the first time I´d seen a family all together for a thematic photograph. They were all blonde, good-looking and smiling. Especially smiling, obviously.

That photo made me feel embarrassed: I had no family. I was American too, according to my papers, but in essence I was really a Latin product. It was on my face—and the rest of me—with all that insistent melanin in my skin. And I wore a coat from an outlet to top it off. Almost all of my clothes were from outlets. The styles that would definitely be in the no-no columns of fashion magazines.

But there was hope. The photo seemed to suggest that if he was my dentist maybe one day I'd have teeth like his family's, and teeth like his family's could deliver me from all evil and make me of use to the world. Janis Joplin's good aspects + my mother's good aspects, carefully picked. *Life is Good.*

Meanwhile, the mollusks in the sea at Copacabana drowned out the world in their crow-blue shells. And crows flew over the city of Lakewood, Colorado. Shell-blue crows.

Editors

2011 American Book Award winner **Camille T. Dungy** is the author of three books, including *Smith Blue* and *Suck on the Marrow*, editor of the anthology *Black Nature: Four Centuries of African American Nature Poetry* and co-editor of *From the Fishouse: An Anthology of Poems that Sing, Rhyme, Resound, Syncopate, Alliterate, and Just Plain Sound Great.* Dungy's honors include a National Endowment for the Arts fellowship, two Northern California Book Awards, and two NAACP Image Award nominations. She is a Professor in the Creative Writing Department at San Francisco State University.

Daniel Hahn is a writer, editor, and translator, with some thirty books to his name. His translations (from Portuguese, Spanish, and French) include fiction from Africa, Europe, and Latin America, and non-fiction by writers ranging from Portuguese Nobel laureate José Saramago to Brazilian footballer Pelé. He has both judged and won the *Independent* Foreign Fiction prize award; not, obviously, in the same year. A past chair of the UK Translators Association, he is currently national program director of the British Centre for Literary Translation.

Contributors

Elliott batTzedek began translating while studying in Drew University's MFA in Poetry in Translation, where she worked closely with Ellen Doré Watson. Her own poetry shares many of themes with Shez, and has appeared recently in the journals *Armchair/Shotgun, Adana Literary Journal, Naugatuck River Review, Trivia, Poetica* and *Poemeleon.*

Dan Bellm teaches literary translation at Antioch University, Los Angeles, and New York University. He has translated poetry and fiction from Spanish and French for *American Poetry Review, The Ecco Anthology of International Poetry,* the *Kenyon Review, Pleiades,* the *Village Voice,* and other journals and anthologies. His three books of poetry include *Practice* (Sixteen Rivers), winner of a 2009 California Book Award. He lives in Berkeley, California.

Matthew Brennan earned his MFA in fiction from Arizona State University. He is a novelist, translator, short-story writer, and freelance editor, and his short fiction has received several awards and fellowships. His work has appeared in several dozen journals, most recently in *Pure Slush, Fiddleblack,* and the *Eunoia Review,* and is forthcoming from *Recess Magazine.* Brennan serves as an assistant fiction editor for the *Hayden's Ferry Review* and *Speech Bubble Magazine*.

Peter Bush translates literature in Barcelona. Previously he directed the British Centre for Literary Translation in Norwich. Recent translations are *Tyrant Banderas* by Ramón del Valle-Inclán, the classic novel of dictatorship in Latin America; Lorca's first book *Sketches of Spain:Impressions and Landscapes*; and *Uncertain Glory* by Joan Sales, a Catalan classic set behind the lines during the civil war.

Alex Cigale's poems have appeared in *Colorado*, *Green Mountains*, *Tampa*, and the *Literary* reviews, and online in *Asymptote* and *Drunken Boat*. His translations are online in *Ancora Imparo* and *Brooklyn Rail InTranslation*, and in print in *Literary Imagination*, *Modern Poetry in Translation*, *PEN America*, *Cimarron* and *Washington Square* reviews. He is currently Assistant Professor at the American University of Central Asia in Bishkek, Kyrgyzstan.

Lydia Davis, a 2003 MacArthur Fellow, is the author, most recently, of *The Collected Stories of Lydia Davis* (Farrar, Straus & Giroux, 2009), as well as the translator of Flaubert's *Madame Bovary* (Viking Penguin, 2010) and Proust's *Swann's Way* (Viking Penguin, 2003), among other works. She lives near Albany, New York, and teaches at SUNY Albany and NYU.

Katrina Dodson is from San Francisco and has previously lived in Rio de Janeiro, most recently as a Fulbright scholar. She is a PhD candidate in Comparative Literature at the University of California at Berkeley, and her writing has appeared in *McSweeney's Quarterly*, *Qui Parle*, and on her blog *Weird Vegetables* (www.weirdvegetables. blogspot.com).

Alison Entrekin has translated a number of works by Brazilian authors into English, including *City of God*, by Paulo Lins, *Near to the*

Wild Heart, by Clarice Lispector, *The Eternal Son*, by Cristovão Tezza, shortlisted for the 2012 International IMPAC Dublin Literary Award, and *Budapest*, by Chico Buarque, which was voted one of the ten best books published in the UK and a finalist in the *Independent* Foreign Fiction Award in 2004. She was a finalist in the New South Wales Premier's Translation Prize & PEN Medallion in 2009 and 2011.

Forrest Gander's newest book, *Core Samples from the World*, is a National Book Critics Circle Finalist. His most recent translations are *Watchword*, the Villaurrutia Award-winning collection by Pura López Colomé (Wesleyan, 2012), and *Fungus Skull Eye Wing: Selected Poems of Alfonso D'Aquino*, forthcoming in 2013 from Copper Canyon Press.

Willem Groenewegen is a bilingual Dutch-English literary translator. He has translated many poets from the Netherlands and Flanders since 2001, for publishers like Shearsman, Arc and Seren, and for magazines like *Fulcrum Annual, Poetry Review, Poetry London* and *Ambit*. In 2007, his translations of Rutger Kopland's poetry were shortlisted for the Popescu Prize of European Poetry in Translation.

Elizabeth Harris has translated various authors from Italian, including Mario Rigoni Stern, Domenico Starnone, Giulio Mozzi, and Marco Candida. Her translations appear in journals like *Words Without Borders*, the *Kenyon Review*, and the *Missouri Review*, and her translations have also appeared in Dalkey Archive Press's *Best European Fiction 2010* (Mozzi) and *Best European Fiction 2011* (Candida). Her translation of Rigoni Stern's novel *Giacomo's Seasons* is forthcoming with Autumn Hill Books and her translation of Mozzi's story collection *This is the Garden* is forthcoming with Open Letter Books. She teaches creative writing at the University of North Dakota.

Brenda Hillman is the author of eight collections of poetry, all published by Wesleyan University Press, the most recent of which is *Practical Water* (2009). With Patricia Dienstfrey, she edited *The Grand Permission: New Writings on Poetics and Motherhood* (Wesleyan, 2003). Hillman teaches at St. Mary's College where she is the Olivia Filippi Professor of Poetry.

Helen Frances Hillman was born in São Paulo, Brazil in 1924 and spent her youth in Porto Alegre. During World War II, she came to Texas to attend Mary Hardin Baylor College, where she majored in botany. She married Jimmye Hillman in 1947 and has worked as a teacher, a translator, a homemaker and an avid gardener. Mother of three children and three grandchildren, she lives in Tucson where she is known for her extensive knowledge of local wildlife.

Marc Elihu Hofstadter was born in New York City and earned his PhD from the University of California at Santa Cruz. He has taught at the University of California at Santa Cruz, the Université d'Orléans, and Tel Aviv University, and has published five books of poetry and one of essays. He lives in Walnut Creek, California.

Margaret Jull Costa has been a literary translator from Spanish and Portuguese for over twenty-five years, translating authors such as Eça de Queiroz, Fernando Pessoa, Bernardo Atxaga, Ramón del Valle-Inclán and José Saramago. She is currently translating Javier Marías's latest novel *Los enamoramientos* (The Infatuations).

Hilary B. Kaplan received a 2011 PEN Translation Fund award for her translation of *Rilke Shake*. Her translations appear in *Litro, PEN America, World Literature Today,* and elsewhere. She holds an MFA from San Francisco State University and is completing a PhD in comparative literature at Brown University.

Sarah Rebecca Kersley was born and raised in Britain and now lives in northeast Brazil. She is an independent translator specializing in academic translation, and creative adaptation of poetry. Her versions of Brazilian poems have been published in magazines and journals in Brazil and the USA.

Rebecca Kosick's poems and translations have appeared in, or are forthcoming from, such places as the *Iowa Review, Reunion: The Dallas Review*, the *Awl*, and the *Recluse*. In addition to writing and translating, Rebecca is currently pursuing her PhD in Comparative Literature at Cornell University.

Alexis Levitin's translations have appeared in well over 200 magazines and have resulted in 31 books to date, including Clarice Lispector's *Soulstorm* and Eugenio de Andrade's *Forbidden Words* (both from New Directions). In September, Milkweed Editions is bringing out his translation of *Blood of the Sun*, by prize-winning Brazilian poet Salgado Maranhao.

Michael McDevitt was runner-up in the inaugural Harvill Secker Young Translator's Prize. His work has appeared in TWO LINES: World Writing in Translation, the *White Review, New Spanish Books*, and *El Dodo*. He lives in Madrid.

Erica Mena is finishing the MFA in Literary Translation at the University of Iowa. Her poems and translations have appeared with *Vanitas*, the *Dos Passos Review, Pressed Wafer, Arrowsmith Press, Words Without Borders*, the *Iowa Review, the Kenyon Review, PEN America*, and *Asymptote*, among others. She co-hosts the Reading the World Podcast and is founding editor of Anomalous Press.

Philip Metres has written a number of books, most recently the chapbook, *abu ghraib arias* (Flying Guillotine, 2011) and *To See the Earth* (Cleveland State University Poetry Center, 2008). His work has appeared in *Best American Poetry*, and he teaches literature and creative writing at John Carroll University in Cleveland, Ohio.

Rachel Morgenstern-Clarren is an MFA candidate in poetry and literary translation at Columbia University. Her poems have appeared in journals such as *Nimrod, Calyx, New Delta Review*, and *Upstairs at Duroc*. More of her translations of Flávio de Araújo's *Zangareio* are forthcoming in *Asymptote*.

Valzhyna Mort was born in Minsk, Belarus and moved to the USA in 2005. She's the author of two collections of poetry, *Factory of Tears* (Copper Canyon Press, 2008) and *Collected Body* (Copper Canyon Press, 2011). Mort was the recipient of the Lannan Literary Fellowship and the Bess Hokin Prize from Poetry Magazine.

Denise Newman is a poet living in San Francisco. Her third collection of poems, *The New Make Believe*, was published by The Post-Apollo Press. New Directions published her translation of *Azorno* by the late Danish poet Inger Christensen, and she is also the translator of Christensen's novel, *The Painted Room*, which is distributed by Random House, UK. She teaches at the California College of the Arts.

Victor Pambuccian is professor of mathematics at Arizona State University. His primary concern is the axiomatic foundation of geometry, in which he has published over 90 papers. His English translations of Romanian poems by Tzara, Fundoianu, Blecher, and Celan have appeared in *Words Without Borders* and *International Poetry Review*. He was the guest editor of the Fall 2011 issue of *International Poetry Review*, dedicated to contemporary poetry from Romania, and has translated most of the poems written in Romanian or French, and all those written in German in that anthology. His translations of the Swiss poet Vahé Godel have appeared in TWO LINES. He has also co-translated Armenian poetry into German.

Susanne Petermann is a writer living in Medford, Oregon. Her translations of Rainer Maria Rilke have been published in many journals, including *AGNI* and the *Jung Journal of Culture and Psyche*. While she prepares her translations for publication in several volumes she works as a personal organizer.

Dimitri Psurtsev is a Russian poet and translator of British and American prose-writers and poets. His two books of poetry, *Ex Roma Tertia* and *Tengiz Notebook* were published in 2001; his poems can be found at http://www.stihi.ru/avtor/exroma. Dimitri teaches translation at Moscow State Linguistic University and lives with his wife Natalia and daughter Anna.

Anna Rosen Guercio is a translator, poet, and higher educator. Her work has appeared in anthologies and journals, including the *Kenyon Review Online, Pool*, the *St. Petersburg Review, Painted Bride Quarterly, Anomalous Press, Eleven Eleven*, and *Words Without Borders*. Her translation of José Eugenio Sánchez's suite prelude *a/hɪnɪ* is available from Toad Press and her collection of original poetry, *By Way of Explanation*, from Dancing Girl Press.

Nathaniel Rudavsky-Brody is a translator living in Brussels. He studied math in Chicago and medieval French and Occitan literature in Poitiers and Paris. He has published translations of Benjamin Fondane and an article on the philosophy of sailing.

Slovak-born **Julia Sherwood** was educated in Germany and England and settled in London where she worked for Amnesty International and Save the Children. Since moving to the US in 2008 she has worked as a freelance translator. She has translated *Samko Tále's Cemetery Book* by Daniela Kapitáňová (Garnett Press, London, 2011) from the Slovak and is currently translating the novel *Freshta* by Petra Procházková from the Czech.

Stefan Tobler is a literary translator from Portuguese and German. His most recent translations are *Água Viva* by Clarice Lispector (for Penguin Classics UK and New Directions) and the contemporary Brazilian poet Antônio Moura (for Arc). He founded the new literary publisher And Other Stories (www.andotherstories.org) in 2011, which is supported and guided by circles of readers, writers, and translators.

Tôn Thất Quỳnh Du was born in 1954 in Quang Tri, Vietnam, and grew up in the old imperial city of Hue, just south of the 17th parallel that divided Vietnam into North Vietnam and South Vietnam. In 1972 he received a Colombo Plan scholarship and came to study in Australia. He has worked as a literary translator, court interpreter and taught at Deakin University, Monash University, and the Australian National University.

A widely published poet, critic, and translator, **Justin Vicari** won the *Third Coast* Poetry Award and was a finalist for the Willis Barnstone Award. His books include *The Professional Weepers* (Pavement Saw, 2011), *Male Bisexuality in Current Cinema* (McFarland, 2011), and *Mad Muses and the Early Surrealists* (McFarland, 2011). He translated François Emmanuel's *Invitation to a Voyage* (Dalkey Archive, 2012).

Padma Viswanathan's novel, *The Toss of a Lemon*, has been published in eight countries and was a finalist for several awards, including the PEN Center USA Fiction Prize. Her short fiction has appeared in journals including *New Letters, Subtropics,* and the *Boston Review.* She is also a playwright and journalist.

Index by Language

Index by Author

Index by Title

Acknowledgments

Pp. 42–46 "21 Days of a Neurasthenic" excerpted from *21 Days of a Neurasthenic* by Octave Mirbeau, forthcoming from Dalkey Archive Press. Translation copyright © 2012 by Justin Vicari. Appears courtesy of Dalkey Archive Press. All rights reserved.

Pp. 104–107 "The Collier's Faith of my Mother" by Tomas Lieske; translation supported by the Dutch Literature Foundation.

Pp. 118–125 "Want zijn vrouw", "Boodschap", and "Zes woorden" by A. L. Snijders; Dutch texts used by permission of A. L. Snijders/AFdH Publishers. All rights reserved.

Pp. 140–149 "Saturday" excerpted from *A Thousand Morons* by Quim Monzó, forthcoming from Open Letter Books. Copyright © 2007 by Joaquim Monzó. Translation copyright © 2012 by Peter Bush. Used by permission of Open Letter Books. All rights reserved.

Pp. 228–235 "The Move" excerpted from *Dry Lives* by Graciliano Ramos. Used courtesy of the University of Texas Press. All Rights Reserved.

A NOTE ON THE TRANSLATIONS

Original texts appear across from their translations. Where feasible, the entire original text is provided for each of the translations; however, space concerns have prevented the inclusion of more than the first page of prose pieces. Excerpts are marked by spaced ellipses. Copyright permission remains the responsibility of the contributors.

In order to express regional differences in language usage, we make every attempt to locate the authors within the literary tradition of a particular country or geographical region. The region is indicated in parentheses following the language on each title page.

About the TWO LINES: World Writing in Translation series

Since 1994, the TWO LINES: World Writing in Translation series has published translations of essential international voices unavailable anywhere else. Every edition showcases diverse new writing alongside the world's most celebrated authors, and presents exclusive insight from the translators into the creative art of translation.

Passageways is a publication of Two Lines Press, a program of the Center for the Art of Translation, a non-profit organization that promotes cultural dialogue, international literature, and translation through publishing, teaching, and public events. In addition to the Two Lines Press publications, the Center makes global voices and great literature accessible to individuals and communities through the Poetry Inside Out educational program and Two Voices, a reading series that presents translators and international writers.

JOIN US

As a non-profit publisher, Two Lines Press relies on readers and writers like you to help support our efforts to share the importance of translation as a vital bridge between languages and people. Please consider making a donation to the Center. Find out more or make a pledge at www.catranslation.org